SUMMER IN SEATTLE

a novel

IVY DANIELS

SUMMER IN SEATTLE

ISBN-13: 978-1-944431-35-8

Email: authorivydaniels@gmail.com

Published in the United States of America.

Cover art @ Estella Vukovic

Other Books by Ivy Daniels

Singles in Seattle:

SUMMER IN SEATTLE

REARRANGED

For Bill. I can't wait to see what comes next.

Chapter 1

I placed baby Clara back in her crib, her like a stick of dynamite that could go off in my hands. I'd just finished mumble-humming *Smells Like Teen Spirit* by Nirvana in her ear while bouncing her in circles. So many circles. Thank goodness it'd finally done the trick.

Once in her crib, she made a few slurping noises but ultimately stayed asleep.

My best friend's child had morphed from the weeks-old angel baby who hardly stirred, into a full-on teething madwoman who had nothing but angry tears and tiny fists of rage for the world around her.

I tiptoed to the glider, sitting quietly, waiting for the possibility of round four. My tired eyelids drooped closed, and thankfully my fantasy about the super-attractive guy who'd run into me in the hallway popped back into my brain, right where it belonged. Mystery guy had been locking his apartment, his back to me. I'd been intent on making an on-time arrival for emergency babysitting duty for my friend and her husband, who were both residents at the hospital downtown. I'd only caught slight movement up ahead.

Then, out of nowhere, a burly shoulder jacked me backward. I'd spun like a drunken ballerina, almost landing on my backside like an idiot. At the last moment, before I could take an embarrassing face-plant, he'd reached around like a modern-day hero and grabbed hold of my elbow, expertly stabilizing me. Well, the wall had helped, since my other shoulder had thudded against it, but that wasn't factoring into this epic two a.m. fantasy replay. It was all him and his super-grippy fingers.

I idly massaged my elbow. Muscly fingers were the epitome of masculinity, right? In my current sleep-deprived state, fighting anyone who disagreed seemed appropriate.

He'd apologized profusely, of course. He'd been at least a head taller than me and felt exactly like a brick wall, if you've ever had the chance to chest-bump into one, which is exactly what I'd done after he'd stabilized me. I'd tripped forward, nose first, hand splayed, right into warm, steel-backed leather.

There'd been no give at all. None. Nada.

Making excuses about being a klutz, I'd hightailed it to Jenny's door, which happened to be right across from the one he'd just exited. I'd made it, thankfully, without falling, stumbling, or otherwise embarrassing myself. Once there, I'd ventured a quick look over my shoulder. His green eyes had been intense. There might've been some twinkling in their depths. One lip was definitely quirked. He'd been amused. Good for him. At least one tattoo had peeked out of his shirt collar like a tantalizing bad-boy secret, but he'd been pretty bundled up, so I might've been mistaken.

The possibility of a tattoo gave my groggy mind the license to wander. My tongue skated along my bottom lip while my brain conjured several tattooed-chest scenarios that worked for me. Maybe one artful pec that led seamlessly into a poetic arm sleeve? Or maybe they were scattered all over his rock-hard abs like graffiti? Or maybe there were just a few here and there that held special meaning, like a beloved nana from the old country. Honestly, every one of those scenarios sounded excellent.

His hair had been a soft, honey brown, sheared shorter on the sides, longer on top. His five-o'clock shadow had been a couple shades darker than that, providing a nice contrast. He'd been dressed in a black leather jacket and some comfy worn-in jeans.

From the small glimpse I'd gotten, the man had been good-looking beyond reason. The most beautiful guy I'd seen up close in a long time, but in a totally not-my-type-of-guy way.

He was a *man.*

I sighed.

My taste in the opposite sex ran toward the goofy, less overtly confident characters. Guys who were nice, but predictable. Sidekicks, not heroes. Leading men like the Adonis with the grippy fingers and the seven-o'clock shadow made me sweat—hands dripping, pits soaked. I'd never been into those types. Except once or twice.

But like with a hot stove, I'd learned to keep my hands away.

Luke Masterson was to blame, honestly. He'd set the stage for my dislike of the strong, swashbuckling types during my transformative years. When the most popular boy in the seventh grade picks the shy, bookish girl, it turns her life, and the lives of all others in close proximity, completely upside down. Then, when he dumps her a month later for the most popular girl in class, the way everyone *thinks* it should be, it sucks.

My shredded prepubescent dignity taught me the basic rules of the dating road for sensitive girls like myself.

Pick the supporting actor.

The best friend.

The foil.

If you lived and died by that rule, your life would be infinitely easier. You never had to worry if he was *really into you*, because if you picked a nice guy, you knew.

For the most part, after limping out of seventh grade, it'd worked for me. There'd been a hiccup or two along the way, but nothing I hadn't been able to handle. But that didn't mean I couldn't fantasize about the leading-man types, with all their scrumptious stubble, muscular bodies, and naughty tats.

My eyelids drifted downward.

They could swashbuckle all over my dreams if they wanted to. *Get those giant man hands around a sword. Make the beard a little longer and dot it with a bit of Scottish red. The helm of a ship seems like a good idea. A ripped tunic would be nice. Dance those pec muscles around, big guy. They're not going to do it themselves.*

Ahhh. Perfect.

Baby Clara sputtered. A half coo, half snort.

It was loud enough to wake me out of my very short, but extremely powerful pirate reverie. How did Hall Guy become a pirate? Who cared? It totally worked.

My body instantly went into self-preservation mode, suppressing any intake of air while I prayed the baby Bengal tiger would stay asleep.

After a few more seconds, and several loud slurps, she quieted.

I sighed. If I wanted to get any real shut-eye, I had to get out of her room. The couch was waiting, complete with a pillow and a soft blanket provided by her thoughtful parents. I made a move to vacate the glider, easing my legs off the ottoman and scooching forward. Not as easy as it sounded. As I tried to stabilize the base, the seat whipped forward quickly, then zapped back like an amusement park ride. These chairs were hydro-boosted and soundless—a technical sophistication that was a blessing for parents everywhere.

After pretzeling my way off, one limb at a time, I cleared the footrest and took a step toward the door. Without warning, the baby monitor in my pocket—the one Jenny had stuffed in there, making me promise I'd take it everywhere, because their high-tech camera one had stopped working this morning—started to wheeze.

Surprisingly, a male voice cracked out.

It would've been completely heart-stopping if I weren't actually *looking* at the sleeping baby, resting as peacefully as a child could with pitifully aching gums. No one else was in the room. Well, except me, but I didn't count.

The speaker was muffled by my sweatpants, which I'd worn for the ease and comfort of overnight Clara-sitting, so I couldn't hear his words.

Then, clear as the air on an icy, cold day, he said, "Yes, I'm hard."

I fumbled the thing out of my pocket so fast it went flying, taking two area rug bounces before spinning like an Olympic snowboarder, landing on the bare ground like a firecracker exploding in a soup pot, finally coming to a clattering stop under sweet Clara's fancy mahogany crib that had been a gift from Jenny's aunt.

From under the baby's cradle, the rusty voice continued, "I'm not taking it out. I'm too tired. I'm rubbing it through my jeans."

A wounded-wildebeest gurgle emerged from my throat as I dropped to my knees, tearing toward the crib like a dog hunting a delicious bone. Clara did some boisterous lip-smacking, and I cursed myself for fumbling the thing in the first place.

"Do you have the red one on?"

Red one, what?

Head in the game, Summer. You are not weighing in on what appears to be a one-sided sex conversation picked up by an ancient baby monitor. Just get it the hell out of there before the baby fist-puncher wakes up.

Flat on my belly, reaching as far as I humanly could, I finally closed the tips of my fingers around the cold, molded plastic. It vibrated as the voice purred out of the holes drilled in the front. "Yes, it's on," the mystery man sighed.

I wondered for a moment if the person on the other end had heard the sigh or not. I had no idea, since I was getting only one end of this naughty interplay.

Grasping the eavesdropping device harder than need be, I began to flop backward like a beached seal, my stomach and hips bobbing up and down. Once clear of the low-hanging crib rails, I began to crawl toward the door, praying the guy didn't start shouting, or worse—*better?*—groaning.

Man, Summer. Hard up much?

Crawling was taking a long time, so I stood, monitor clutched in my hand. As I took the first step, my arm swung next to the base sitting on top of Clara's dresser, and the thing in my hand gave off a horrendous shriek, like a knight dying in battle, a lance pierced straight through his heart.

Having no real choice, and with the incessant need to get it away from the feedback station as fast as possible, I chucked it.

Like a champ, it bounced off the arm of the glider I'd just vacated, spinning like it was trained to do, but this time, instead of clattering to the floor, it landed solidly in the seat with a quiet thud.

Not a second later, Clara gave a frustrated, angry wail.

Dang. I'd been so close.

I walked back to her crib. "What's wrong, baby girl?" I cooed as I scooped her up, knowing full well what was bugging her. "Are those teeth hurting?" I brought her up to my face to nuzzle her, making a raspberry sound near her ear. She calmed for a minute, likely startled.

I'd take it.

As I headed for the door, trying to think of what to do next to get this little angel back to sleep, a moan came from the monitor.

"Stacy, don't. It's too much."

My eyebrows zipped to my hairline. It took me less than a second to hustle back over and snatch up the smut receiver.

What's too much, Stacy? I'm literally dying to know.

Right as the mystery man began to reply, Clara emitted a sharp screech and tried to make a complicated twist out of my arms, fists flying.

"I'm sorry, babe," I murmured, tucking the monitor in my pocket as I rearranged the squirming infant on my shoulder. "But I have to find out what's going to happen next, because apparently I have no shame. I mean, is it really eavesdropping when you didn't go searching for it in the first place?" The baby bellowed her reply in my eardrum. "Okay, okay, it can wait until after we get you some more of that yummy breast milk your mommy left for us." I turned down the hall, murmuring in a singsong voice, "*Here we are now, entertain us. May the milk make you fuss less. I'm a babysitter, who's outrageous…*"

CHAPTER 2

"Summer. Summer, wake up." Jenny's voice landed softly in my ear, accompanied by a gentle shoulder shake.

Blinking a few times, I forced my tired eyes to open all the way. The lids felt like two tiny window shades that had lost their springs. "What time is it?" I mumbled groggily, struggling to sit, removing the blanket.

I was immediately embarrassed to find I'd fallen asleep clutching the baby monitor to my chest. I set it on the glass coffee table as I cleared my throat.

"It's a little after five," Jenny answered with a yawn. "We called you a ride. It should be here in a few minutes. Info's on your phone."

Daniel moved around the kitchen, making breakfast. Their apartment was located by the waterfront. Huge floor-to-ceiling windows gave them gorgeous views of Elliott Bay. The living room and kitchen were basically one space separated by a granite-topped island. "You're welcome to join us for breakfast," he offered. "I can't guarantee Clara won't be waking soon. So, if you're interested in more sleep, this won't be the place." His glasses were slightly askew, his eyes shadowed. Daniel was practicing to become a heart surgeon. Jenny, one of my best friends since college, was going to be an awesome orthopedic surgeon. They were both almost done with their perspective residencies, then on to fellowships.

"I wish we had a spare room," Jenny lamented. "Someday."

That someday would come soon enough. They'd probably have three. "No, it's okay." I rubbed my face. "I'll head home. Sleep is definitely on the agenda." My loft in Capitol Hill was my sanctuary. It was nestled in the eaves of a four-story mansion that had been converted into condos a few years ago. It'd been built sometime in the early 1900s and had a nice view of Elliott Bay. You didn't need to live by the waterfront for a view, you just needed a house on a hill.

In an effort not to seem overly eager to escape, I made a show of grabbing my shoes and coming back to the couch to lace them up.

"So, how was she?" Jenny sat across from me in a leather chair that crackled as she eased her weight into it. My friend looked as tired as I felt. "And don't lie. Clara's been teething the last few days, and she's been a handful." Jenny's long dark hair, which had been clipped back, fell in wisps around her face. "But, honestly, she's not a great sleeper anyway. I'm pretty sure that's why the nanny quit. Thank you so much for helping us out at the last minute. We really appreciate it."

I yawned, covering my mouth with the back of my hand as I continued lacing up my shoes. "She got up a few times, but it was totally doable. I used the gel on her gums like you said and gave her the rest of the breast milk. She went back to sleep no problem. She's an angel." No need to tattle on the poor kid. Finishing my shoes, I picked up the baby monitor and grinned. "But guess what? This thing picked up one of your neighbor's phone calls in the wee hours of the morning. It was quite entertaining. I mean, Clara didn't think it was as funny as I did, but it was still pretty hilarious."

Jenny reached out, and I handed it to her. She examined it. Honestly, after all the tossing around, it was remarkably in one piece. "You're kidding." She turned it over. "That's so strange. My mom brought this over after our fancy one with the video monitor broke." She set it down. "I'm pretty sure she dug it out from when I was a baby. She never throws anything away." She glanced over her shoulder. "Danny, remind me to order a new video monitor today."

"Will do." Daniel directed his spatula, dripping with a bit of barely congealed egg, toward the monitor. "Who was on the other end? Male or female?"

"Definitely male. And it wasn't a typical phone conversation either. It was phone sex. I only heard his side and just bits and pieces. The last thing he talked about was putting on a Mickey Mouse T-shirt. Then I fell asleep. It was super weird."

"Sounds weird," Jenny said. "When I think sex, I certainly don't think about Mickey Mouse, or any Disney character, for that matter. That's some serious kink right there."

Daniel chuckled as he scooped fully cooked eggs onto their breakfast plates. "Animation is a big turn-on for some, but I agree. Imagining Mickey Mouse with any genitalia is extremely unsettling."

I stood, walking to get my coat that was hanging on a hook near the door. Spring in Seattle was breezy and cool, but summer was fast approaching. My favorite season. I'd been aptly named. "It is. Maybe the two of them banged in some dark corner of Disneyland and wanted to relive it?"

Sort of plausible?

Jenny followed me. "Maybe it was the new guy across the hall who *banged* into you?" She waggled her eyebrows. "He's new. We hardly ever see him. I don't even know his full name. His mailbox says 'A.A. Scott.' I actually thought Scott was his first name, but I figured it out before I misspoke. Saved me some serious neighbor shame. I think he introduced himself as Xander or something. We've never really had a full, formal introduction."

"Yeah, it might've been him," I agreed. In my fitful couch dreams, it had *definitely* been him. He'd switched from wielding a sword on the high seas to Hulk-ripping a Mickey Mouse T-shirt off his sweaty, muscular body while levitating in a boxing ring. I loved my brain. "Not enough to go by from the scratchy monitor."

"Jenny thinks our neighbor is *gas-station hot*," Daniel said. "I'd never heard that term before, but she says it's a thing."

It was a thing. But Jenny was mistaken. "Gas station?" I questioned as I shrugged my coat on. "No way. His jaw could easily chisel ice into art, and his chest goes on for miles. He's definitely luxury hot. Expensive champagne with a bowl of strawberries."

Jenny tried to shove money into my hand for the ride. I refused by crumpling my hand into a fist ala baby Clara. "I'm right, you're wrong," she said, finally giving up. "Stubble, tattoos, leather jacket, biker boots, slightly unkempt. That's *dirty* hot."

"He looked pampered to me," I countered. "And he can afford a place like this." I glanced around at all the shiny finishes. This high-rise had been built in the last few years. "Still going with luxury. Oh, and he smelled amazing." I made exaggerated sniffing sounds while letting my eyes flutter a couple of times.

"We can compromise with supermarket hot. But a nice one, like the Seattle Caviar Company."

"You can't just make up categories," I accused, opening my hand and tapped my thumb. "Extinguisher hot—he's so sexy he's on fire. That's always been our number one." I tapped the next finger. "Luxury hot—pull back the duvet and order up some caviar." Middle finger. "Athlete hot—can I please run my tongue over your abs." Ring finger, currently empty. "Farmer hot—you can plow my fields any day." And pinkie. "And last but not least, gas-station hot—lube up your rod and let's go to town."

"Okay. *Fine.* You win," Jenny said, laughing. "I haven't had the chance to smell him yet. But I'm putting in a vote to add supermarket hot." She rubbed the side of her face tiredly. "Lately, the men I've seen roaming the aisles have been over-the-top good-looking. As far as my neighbor goes, whatever category he fits into, he's definitely hot. Too bad he's not your type, or I'd try to set you up."

"He seems like a nice guy from my handful of interactions with him," Daniel added. "Jenny told me you broke it off with Ethan. We're sorry to hear that."

Ah, Ethan.

Very nice. Serious video game addiction. Much too close with his parents. Had trouble meeting my eyes during sex. Had three cats. The litter box was an issue—rarely cleaned. His redeeming qualities were his resemblance to Jake Gyllenhaal's younger brother, if he had one, a cute smile, and an overall happy disposition.

It hadn't proved to be enough.

I'd actually broken up with Ethan a while ago, after dating him for nearly a year. But I'd told Jenny only last week. She'd been busy with Clara and her residency, and we hadn't had much girl time lately. "Ethan and I had run our course. It was an amicable split." I yawned, deliberately ignoring the *not your type* comment. Jenny knew my reasons. No need to rehash. "Same time tonight for Clara, right?"

"Yes." Jenny gave me a quick hug, making a last-ditch effort to shove money into my pocket. I side-stepped. "We're interviewing new nannies later this week. My mom offered to help, but you know how she gets. Once she's asleep, it's like trying to wake the dead."

"It's no problem." I headed for the door, successfully evading payment. I was doing them a favor. Taking their money would be weird. "I love spending time with Clara." The Tooth Terror and I would get to face off again in fifteen hours.

Jenny gave up, giving me a saucy wink. "I'll take my time replacing the monitor. At least then, your long nights can be full of some scintillating entertainment."

"A win-win."

My eyes focused on my phone for a full ten seconds before reality set in. It was noon. *Crap.* I hustled out of bed, which meant I untangled myself from my sheets and scooted to the edge of my mattress.

Next came the ladder.

Not exactly a ladder. More like a short staircase, but steeper than normal. My dad had made it for me when I'd first moved in, since my sleeping area was built over my tiny kitchen.

Even though my cooking area was small, I adored it. A concrete slab I'd poured myself bookended a blue retro fridge and a cute, serviceable stove. A homemade butcher block top sat on top of a small dresser I'd painted a bright, cheery tangerine. The drawers were perfect for storage. My entire place was full of repurposed items, mismatched on purpose. It was around seven hundred square feet, not including the sleeping area, but the open plan made it feel larger.

On the way to the bathroom, I glanced out my big window. It was overcast, but not raining yet. It was Seattle after all. Rain was expected. But even though it was dreary, it was still beautiful. The view had been the ultimate selling point for me. Glass occupied the entire peak and gave me a gorgeous bay view right above the tree line. It was fantastic. I adored my loft.

It didn't take me long to complete my morning routine in my periwinkle and white-trimmed powder room. Though it was pushing afternoon now.

After toweling off, I donned my favorite work clothes—roomy pants and a comfy cotton shirt—made tea and toast, and settled into my perfect, sun-dappled workspace. My desk was situated in a small alcove next to my window. If I turned my head to the left, I could see the bay.

The overcast weather had turned to drizzle. No surprises there.

Being a freelance graphic artist allowed me to work from home, and I had two deadlines to meet next week. My big project was a logo for a startup. The other was for a friend of my mother's who was looking for a simple graphic to brand her homemade scarf business, called Tina's Warm Wraps.

I decided to tackle the scarf design first.

A little over an hour later, I'd come up with three different directions Tina could go, my favorite a knitted scarf intertwining both of the Ws. I emailed them to her and stood, stretching. The toast had whetted my appetite, and now I was ready for lunch.

It was almost two, which was late for me.

Wandering across the room to my kitchen, floorboards squeaking, as they did, I lifted my cell phone off the counter. If it was next to me, I'd never get any work done.

My friend Poppy had sent me a text not even ten minutes ago.

HEY, WANNA MEET FOR A LATE LUNCH?

Poppy, Eve, and I usually met up for coffee or lunch a few days a week. We all lived in the Capitol Hill neighborhood and were self-employed. We'd become fast friends, along with Jenny, our freshman year at the University of Washington. After graduation, we'd all decided to move to Seattle. It was a great city to live and work in, and having regular meetups kept us sane.

I texted her back.

SURE. GREEN FIG?

She replied immediately.

K. SEE U IN TEN.

I opened my closet, conveniently located next to the stove,

and tugged off my work clothes in exchange for comfortable jeans and a black pullover. I'd let my long, slightly wavy brown hair air-dry and now pulled it up into a messy ponytail. Good enough.

Poppy knew I'd helped Jenny with Clara last night. She was going to love hearing about the raunchy baby monitor. She was all about the drama. I chuckled, anticipating her reaction as I plucked my raincoat off the hook by the door and grabbed an umbrella out of my dedicated umbrella holder. Every house in Seattle should have one.

Then I headed out to meet my pal for lunch.

CHAPTER 3

W*hat?"* Poppy slapped the top of the table so hard the water glasses shook, and the silverware rattled on the plates. It was loud enough to summon our waiter. I shook my head, trying to will him to get sidetracked before Poppy caught her next breath. Too late. "The kinky phone sex guy *has* to be the same guy you ran into. Who else could it *be*?"

Our server came to a stop in front of us, obviously overhearing, but not knowing what to do. "We're fine," I told him, barely able to meet his gaze. I'm sure he heard juicier tidbits all the time, but it was still embarrassing. "Just bring the check when you're ready." After he left, I leaned forward, whispering, "Lowering your voice a few decibels while discussing phone sex in an open venue would be a great idea."

She swished her hand dismissively. "For who? Phone sex is fun for everyone. It had to be Mr. Luxury Hot himself. He fits the bill to a T." She giggled. "A Mickey Mouse *tee*, to be exact."

I almost snorted the water I'd just gulped through my nose. I set the glass down. "There's no way to know if it was him or not. It could've literally been *anyone* in the building. It's a huge place. Like, thirty floors."

"Summer," Poppy hissed, watching her voice this time, "you have to be relatively close for wavelengths or whatever to intermingle." She linked her fingers together and wiggled them at me. Then she cocked her head to the side, her blonde, shoulder-length hair sliding across the top of her arm. "I'm getting the distinct feeling that you're protecting this guy for some reason. Do I sense a crush forming?" A second later, she gasped, her chin almost hitting the foam of the latte she'd been in the process of lifting to her mouth. "Oh my *God.* You *are* crushing. Your face is an open book. You're in the mood for some luscious caviar and some razzle-dazzle under a comfy down comforter. I love it! Good for you."

I laughed, reclining back in my chair. "Razzle-dazzle? That's a new one. And, no, I'm definitely not crushing." I glanced around for the waiter, but he wasn't nearby. I chose to whisper anyway. "But he did swashbuckle through my dreams. He makes for a *very* sexy pirate. But that's as far as it's going. I'm totally not interested." I fiddled with my hands, suddenly not knowing what to do with them.

Poppy set her latte down dramatically, letting it clatter into the saucer. "You're definitely interested. Don't lie to me," she scolded. "You haven't talked in this much detail about anyone since Mitch. You collided with this guy in the hallway for what, seven seconds? And yet, you remember every single little detail about him, down to the fact that he has a freckle that looks like a slice of pizza on his neck, and the buttonhole of his jeans was worn from use. I mean, his button*hole*? Not even the button itself? That's porn if I've ever heard it. You're most definitely crushing, if not out-and-out lusting."

"It's not *porn.* Jeez," I muttered. "His jeans were"—I struggled for a description that wouldn't make me sound like a creepy stalker who'd been eyeballing the size of his bulge—"broken in. That's all. You know when you buy a new pair of pants how the buttonhole is stiff?" I set my index fingers up against each other. "Then, when you wear them for a few years, that same hole looks more like a diamond, because it gapes?" I demonstrated the gap by bending my two fingers outward, hoping no one thought I was miming a vagina, least of all our server. Then I dropped my hands into my lap. "Well...his hole was gaping." *Damn.* I closed my eyes.

So porny.

Embarrassed, I picked up my water glass, trying not to blush.

Poppy sat back, looking satisfied. "Gaping holes, huh? Vagina fingers. I'm right. You can't even help yourself. You like him. This is just like Mitch all over again." She leaned forward quickly. Poppy equaled drama. One was never without the other. "But not all men are Mitch-holes. You fell head over heels for that freshman trash, and he treated you like dog-doo. This guy could be wonderful. He could be crazy-attractive *and* be a nice, normal, sweet person. Those are all things that can coexist together in one human man. Happens all the time."

Mitch Bainbridge.

My freshman boyfriend.

My second, and last, relationship misstep.

Once I'd landed in Seattle, newly relocated from Spokane, I'd been ready for college and all the good stuff that came with it, momentarily forgetting all the critical life lessons Luke Masterson had bestowed on me at such a tender age. Like most freshmen liberated from their parents' home for the first time, I'd felt invincible. Due to all the giddy freedom, I happened to have misplaced my brain and all the helpful stuff in it.

Not only had Mitch been beautiful, he'd been a baseball recruit with a body that wouldn't stop. He'd been beyond athlete hot. He'd been extinguisher hot with a side of athlete. Jet-black hair. Bronze skin. A smile bracketed by a pair of deeply inset dimples. Dimples were my kryptonite. They still were. A man could pop a dimple on me right this minute, and my knees would knock together, and things below the belt would tingle.

Mitch's interest in me had shaken me to my core. Literally. My core was in constant vibration. He'd pursued me like a line drive. I'd been in over my head from the very beginning. The problem was, even though I'd known I was probably going to drown, I'd jumped into the deep end willingly. I hadn't even *tried* to swim out of the undertow. I'd just flopped around while he'd sucked me farther out to sea. Then, while I was bobbing around in the middle of the ocean, attempting to dog-paddle back to shore, he'd left me for a beautiful, majestic dolphin with boobs for miles.

If it hadn't been for Poppy, Jenny, and Eve talking sense of self back into me and feeding me gooey sweets and pizza, I might've taken the semester off and moved home to Spokane. Heartbreak and I didn't pair well together. It took the zip right out of me. But my best friends had been there. They'd been my rocks when Mitch had quickly moved on with a Phi Beta Kappa beauty.

I'd recently heard they'd gotten engaged. There was a

ninety-seven percent chance those two were going to live a storybook life.

It still stung.

I rubbed my chest.

Not because Mitch had dumped me, or that I'd wished we'd worked out, but because I'd been stupid enough to let myself fall for a man like him in the first place. I'd known what kind of guy he was. He was slick. He was smooth. He was beautiful. I'd allowed myself to be taken in rather than trust my own instinct, which looking back, had been giving me frantic SOS signals from the very beginning.

I took a breath, centering myself. "This is not Mitch all over again," I stated evenly. Not even a teensy tremor. I was proud of myself. "I hate that Mitch gets attention after all this time. He and I had a *fling*. A short-lived romance. It lasted five months." Eight days, three hours, and forty-seven minutes. "I've dated some really great guys over the past seven years. You're forgetting about Brian, Jared, Seth, and Ryan." I ticked them off on my fingers, staying clear of labia land. "All perfectly nice boyfriends." I'd left Ethan out. He'd been more like an extra than a supporting player. I'd also left out Tim, for the same reason. And Kyle. But that was it. All the rest of them had been perfectly fine.

Poppy's expression softened.

I knew that look.

"Do not," I grumbled, picking my fork up and fiddling with the dregs of my delicious salad, "go there."

"I'm going there. I have to."

I raised my utensil like I was wielding a weapon, a piece of lettuce dangling off the end. "No, you don't. I'm not a baby.

I'm a grown woman who happens to have a lot of relationships under her belt. There's nothing wrong with that. I noticed that Hall Guy has a freckle on his neck because I literally slammed right into his chest, and it's an unusual shape." And I'd instantly wanted to take a bite out of it. "And that his buttonhole was well-worn, because when he almost knocked me over, my head swung near it." And other things. "I haven't formulated any other opinions about him. I don't have a crush. He's not Mitch." He was *way* better-looking—the Mitch that Mitch *wished* he could be. "He'll occupy my dreams for a bit because I'm bored, but he'll move on, and so will I." I stabbed at more salad and brought the bite up to my mouth. The dressing here was phenomenal.

Poppy straightened.

She had the strongest personality among our friend group and was the most confident. When she wasn't placating me, she was usually launching truth bombs, as she knew I preferred it that way. "Okay, so here's the deal. Yes, you've had a ton of boyfriends, and they've all been very nice. And safe. But they don't satisfy you. Or challenge you the way your heart desires. They kowtow to you. Most of them can't believe they netted a girl like you. You eventually get bored and dump them. And that's okay." She shook her head, preempting my rebuttal. I *wasn't* bored. I was...particular. I just hadn't found the right pairing for me yet. The right personality. The right...anything. "It's not a problem that you dump them. They wouldn't have made you happy in the long run. But Mitch made you feel different than everybody else. He had a spark the others didn't." She reclined in her seat, shutting her eyes, crossing her palms over her chest. She was having a moment. "*Ahh.* Yes. There it is. Your face back then. The way you smiled. Like your home was a field of wildflowers. You were content, exuberant, excited. You giggled. You skipped. You talked in run-on sentences. It was dreamy. Because"—she paused dramatically as she exhaled, her eyes opening, her arms fanning wide—"you were in *love*."

Her word choice startled me.

She ignored the furrow in my brow and barreled on. "Since the day Mitch broke your heart, you've never come remotely close to looking or acting like that with anyone else." She extended her index finger, pressing it into the table. "Until today." She tapped it a few times. "I'm a lot of things, but I'm not wrong about this. This is Mitch all over again. But not Mitch. Better than Mitch. Something different than that dick, but something that's equally exciting and must be investigated immediately."

"Is not."

"Is."

☼ ☼ ☼

Poppy's words pinged around in my brain all day, like an unwanted fly trapped behind glass. *Tap, tap, tap.* The noise reached fever pitch as I stepped into the elevator and pressed the button for the twenty-second floor. Jenny had just buzzed me in.

It was ten to nine.

I'd made a point of being early tonight. Poppy and I had continued our conversation at the Green Fig for a while longer, me denying that I'd ever been in love with Mitch and her shaking her head sadly.

In the end, I'd begrudgingly admitted that I'd held a *fledgling*, more like *lusting*, love for Mitch, but I'd also been in love since. I reminded her that Brian and I had almost gotten engaged.

She'd snorted.

That had been it.

Poppy hadn't even bothered to address the matter further. We'd gotten the check and left. On my trudge home, up a steep hill in the drizzling rain, I had to give it to her. I hadn't been in love with Brian. Having a couple conversations about *possibly* getting engaged didn't count as an actual engagement. Not to mention, I'd dumped him three weeks later, just in case he'd gotten any ideas that I was actually considering marrying him.

As for the other part—the part about being in love with Mitch—I wasn't ready to open that box. Instead, I'd shoved it back in the far recesses of my mind, where I had the habit of keeping stuff. It was an effective way to keep the crazy at bay.

A beep sounded. A second later, the elevator doors opened.

Like Pavlov's dog reacting to the mere prospect of a reward, my heart began to patter quickly, like a hummingbird trapped in my rib cage. The mere prospect that Hall Guy was somewhere near me had made me fluttery. *Damn.* I took a tentative step onto the nicely appointed, sedate-blue carpet, certainly meant to calm tired tenants as they arrived home from a long, hard day of trying to afford this place.

Unfortunately, the color was doing nothing to quell the agitated bird. "Get it together, Summer," I mumbled, moving at a tentative pace.

Each time I arrived to babysit, I couldn't act like Freddy Krueger's face was going to stretch out of the wall.

The elevator doors closed behind me, and I jumped, annoyingly, which prompted me to pick up my pace. Then, to my abject horror, the door across from Jenny's began to rattle.

It was *his* place, and he was coming *out.*

Where was Freddy Krueger when I needed him?

With considerable effort, I tried to act casual and did the only thing I could think of to avoid a direct confrontation. I reached into my pocket and tossed my keys on the floor, then made a big show of walking over to pick them up, taking my sweet time. As my hand closed around them, I exclaimed, "There you are!" Like the biggest dork of all time.

When I finally ventured upright, my eyes landed on a huge, beefy chest.

It was much closer than I'd thought it would be.

I'd hoped, because I'd listened to my feeble brain cells, which were obviously on vacation in this man's presence, that he'd ignore me while I was bent over, passing by like two casual neighbors who didn't feel like striking up a convo.

What I saw next made me suck in air so fast, I began to cough like someone had sucker-punched me.

"Are you okay?" he asked, his voice full of growly concern.

This ridiculously handsome man was dressed in a black leather jacket, like he'd been last night, except tonight it was paired with a faded red T-shirt with the unmistakable face of Mickey Mouse on the front.

Mickey was staring right at me.

I jerked to the side.

The movement had been automatic and out of my control. I shook my head as more hacking wheezes came out. I banged my fist on my chest a couple of times before I could finally speak. "I'm…I'm fine." More coughing. "Sorry. I dropped my keys." He stood less than two feet away. "Then I…swallowed a…cough drop." Seemed logical.

"Hey, aren't you the girl I ran into yesterday?" His voice was incredibly sexy—rough and scratchy around the edges. I couldn't believe I'd even considered for a moment that the voice on the baby monitor *hadn't* been his.

I bobbed my head up and down, unable to form words.

"I'm really sorry about that," he continued. "You left so fast I didn't get a chance to really apologize."

"No worries," I assured him, my palm settled securely on my chest, more for comfort at this point. I tried my best to smile, knowing it was likely coming across as a grimace. "I'm clumsy like that. Thus, dropping my keys and everything." *Small talk is not my forte. I really should take a class.*

"Do you live here?" He angled his head to indicate the hallway behind us. "I just moved in a few months ago and work odd hours. I haven't met everyone on the floor yet."

"No. I mean, no. Um, no." My mind was applesauce. The lumpy, unstrained kind. My eyes were doing me a disservice by homing in on his freckle, then sliding down to his buttonhole. All while I tried my damnedest to avoid the faded face of Mickey Mouse as it peeked out at me between the gape of his leather jacket. "Sorry," I tried again, gathering myself. I stood up straight, remembering that I was actually a human being who could interact with others. I blew out a short breath. "What I meant to say was that no, I don't live here. I'm babysitting to help out some friends. They're doctors. Well, they're residents. They both work the night shift at the hospital. Their baby is teething." Needless information. "She's five months old. And adorable." Small talk sucked.

He stuck out his hand, completely throwing me. "It's nice that you're helping your friends. I'm Xander."

Autopilot kicked in, super late, but I was happy to see it. I extended my hand like a regular person, grasping his. It was warm and grippy, just like I remembered. "I'm Summer."

His face quirked in an expression I was all too familiar with. "Like the season?"

Our hands dropped, and it was kind of sad. "Yep, I was born on August first. My parents both love summer. It's my favorite season, so I guess they picked the right name."

His face shifted as he smiled widely, exposing a set of deep-pocketed dimples.

No.

No, no, no.

Full-on tingles as the hummingbird lodged itself between my legs. Uncooperative beast.

"Maybe I'll see you around?"

"Yeah, sure." I edged toward Jenny's door. "I'm back again tomorrow and the next day." Awkward information he didn't need. "I have to go now." I pointed to Jenny's door and gave him a short wave. "They have to get to the hospital."

He nodded, flashing me another smile. The dimples, filled with honey-colored stubble, were incredible. "I leave around nine every night. I'll look for you."

You will?

"Okay. Yeah, nice." *Gah.*

I rapped on Jenny's door, twisting my head slightly so I could watch Xander walk toward the elevator. His jeans looked even more amazing from the back. There was no gap, only two perfectly shaped—

"Summer," Jenny said, whipping open the door. "You don't have to knock. Just come in."

I grabbed on to her forearms, launching her backward, ignoring her muffled scream. "You're not going to *believe* who had a Mickey Mouse T-shirt on."

CHAPTER 4

Much to my relief, and with appropriately acknowledged disappointment, there had been no phone sex last night. I'd arrived home at five thirty a.m. and promptly hit the sack.

My eyes blinked open in tandem with a stretch-yawn, my gaze landing on the chipped white paint above my head. The first coherent thought to enter my mind, after the sleepiness cleared, was: If there hadn't been any phone sex last night, what if there'd been *actual* sex? As in, Stacy had gone over to Xander's, and they'd had in-person sex not even fifty feet from where I'd tossed and turned on Jenny's couch.

The thought left me cold.

I shivered as I unfurled from the warmth of my covers.

Just like the previous night, my dreams had been occupied by Pirate Xander. There'd been a few unexplainable interludes where the Mickey Mouse T-shirt had spoken to me, mouth moving as Mickey spouted kernels of wisdom like, *Keep at it, kid.*

He'll come around, and the more ominous, *Is this what you really want? You know, it might end in dis-a-ster.* Mickey had uttered the word *disaster* in a high, singsongy voice, like disaster was overall fun and kind of unavoidable.

I rubbed a hand over my face.

Clara had been up only once, which was an improvement over the night before. Her first tooth had finally broken through earlier in the day, and the little exposed nubbin had eased the pain. Lots of Clara-free time had given me ample opportunity to obsess over everything Xander and I had discussed in the hallway and how ridiculous and goofy I'd acted.

What if he'd seen me throw my own keys on the floor? And how was doing that *actually* supposed to help me?

Life was a complete mystery sometimes.

I groaned, making my way down my steps, heading to the bathroom. I hadn't been out of the shower and dressed for more than five minutes when a knock sounded on my door.

Both of my arms whipped out like an eagle about to hop-flap off the ground, which was my standard startled go-to.

My first thought was that Xander had found out where I lived.

Before I had a chance to chastise myself for being overly dramatic and loosen my death grip on the butcher block, Poppy's voice chirped, "Your nice neighbor on the ground floor let us in. We have coffee. Open up!"

I rushed over, unlocking the door with relief.

Poppy held a cup aloft from my favorite local coffee shop. Eve stood behind her, holding a bag full of baked goods, grinning. "Jenny gave us a heads-up about what happened last night," she said as she followed Poppy in. By the smell wafting from the package, I knew it contained the café's famous cranberry scones. My favorite. "We figured you were in need of a pep talk or possibly some kind of resuscitation."

I closed the door behind them.

As they made their way to my love seat, I grabbed a couple of plates and forks from the kitchen. Once everything was piled on my cute, reclaimed-wood coffee table, I took the seat opposite them in one of my two slipcovered chairs, a lemon-yellow rocker. It was my favorite place to sit.

Popping the top off of my coffee, I took a few lusty sips. "Oh, that's good." Nothing like Seattle coffee to start the day. That was, unless it was a tea kind of morning. "Thanks for bringing it by."

Poppy busied herself spreading out the goodies. Eve sat back, crossing her arms, her long red hair tangling in the crooks of her arms, shooting me a goofy grin.

"What?" I folded my bare feet under me. "Did Jenny say something was wrong? You didn't have to rush over. I'm fine and in no danger of turning blue from lack of oxygen. Honestly, nothing of any note happened last night. I ran into the attractive man in the hallway again and found out his name is Xander. I babbled incoherently for a few seconds, like a groupie with a stolen backstage pass, then he was on his way. No phone sex, much to the disappointment of my alter ego Coco, who apparently lives for that kind of thing." I took another sip of coffee. "All in all, a pretty lackluster evening."

Poppy spoke first, chuckling. "Well, maybe Coco is the one we should be directing our comments to, then. *Yoo hoo*, Coco, can you join us?"

Eve leaned forward. "Jenny said you pretty much tackled her

on the way in. She also said it took her a good five to six minutes to calm you down and that they were almost late for their shifts."

"Then," Poppy said, cutting a scone in half, plopping it on a plate, and handing it to me, "when she woke you up to go home this morning, you were pretty convinced you should tie a jacket over your head so the guy wouldn't recognize you in case he came out of his apartment."

I picked up a fork and shoveled a bite of delicious pastry into my mouth. I preferred to use a fork, since these were extra crumbly. After I swallowed the tastiness, I said, "Covering my head with a jacket makes perfect sense. I wasn't interested in having another encounter. My small-talk game is completely lacking." I shrugged. "I mean, it could've worked."

"Okay, yeah, that sounds totally rational," Eve said. "Like this guy wouldn't recognize you by your outfit, your height, your shoes, your everything." She glanced to her left. "Poppy also filled me in on your lunch convo yesterday."

I frowned. We didn't keep a lot of secrets between the four of us, but it still felt a little traitorous.

Poppy shrugged, replying, "This is classic open-book territory."

"By the way, I agree with her about everything," Eve said. "You haven't acted this way about a guy in years."

Brushing errant crumbs off the front of my shirt, I cleared my throat. "It's unfair to say that I was in love with Mitch. There's no way I loved him. We went out for five months. I was infatuated with him. And lusty. And young. And the sex was good." Possibly great. "I blame his dimples. They sucked me in. That's it." A flash of Xander's dimples hit me, and I shoveled in another piece of scone, refusing to let the hummingbird loose.

Poppy set one of the coffeehouse's famous Danishes on her plate and reclined back. "So, you're admitting that you're infatuated with this guy, then?"

"Possibly," I replied, not wanting to lie, but not wanting to be overtly truthful. "Jenny must've told you about the garbage that tumbled out of my mouth. I sounded like somebody was beating my brain with the blunt end of a hammer. But that doesn't mean anything. As far as we know, he has a girlfriend. Her name is Stacy. She's a grown woman who loves Mickey Mouse and likes to imagine his cartoon face on her boyfriend's ample chest during phone sex." That last part came out a little more aggressively than intended.

A mini scenario flashed through my mind: Xander and the mysterious Stacy, who was nothing short of top-model gorgeous, having sex, him with the shirt on, her with Minnie ears on, both of them laughing. *Yuck.*

I shoveled in another bite, getting a soothing cranberry surprise this time. These scones were the best. "What it means is"—moistened crumbles threatened to spew, so I chewed and swallowed before continuing—"the man is taken. So even if I was interested in pursuing this further, which I'm most certainly *not*, he has a girlfriend. Hell, she might even be his fiancée. I'm not getting involved. He's not even my type!" That last part got me a little excitable as Luke Masterson and his evil dimpled grin popped into my brain, taking the place of the Disney Sexiteers.

"Jenny said he said he was interested in seeing you again," Poppy said, expertly arching her eyebrow. Hers made mine look like a lazy caterpillar doing a single push-up.

I shook my head, mouth full again. "He did not." Pieces of scone shot out of my mouth. *Gah.* I set down my plate, reaching for my coffee. Hot liquid was the only thing that could sort things out. "Sorry. Apparently, I belong in the zoo this morning. He didn't say he wanted to see me again. He said something along the lines of, 'Maybe I'll see you around sometime.' He leaves around nine for work every night, which is the same time I get there to watch Clara. It meant absolutely nothing. It's merely a coincidence."

Eve picked up a blueberry muffin, her favorite, and took her time peeling off the wrapper. Where I'd devoured my delicious treat like an animal, she would consume hers slowly and politely. "You haven't gone on a date since you broke up with Ethan, which was months ago. And there's no way you can say that you're still getting over him, because you were never into him to begin with. Your track record for picking guys that make you feel crazy in love is not stellar. I'm not going to lie, this is an intervention. Us style. Jenny would be here if she wasn't sawing logs right now. She sends her best." Eve took a single bite, chewing thoughtfully, then set her muffin on the table, resting her elbows across her thighs. "We think it's a mistake for you to pass up an opportunity with this Xander guy. We want you to do more than just wait to run into him again. We want you to time it right, be there when he comes out of his apartment, and ask him out."

I choked on my next sip of coffee, the back of my hand coming to my lips so nothing leaked out this time. "You must be joking." I coughed. "And if this is an intervention, you guys suck at it. Free coffee and scones? Stop by anytime. But there's no way I'm asking that guy out. Nada. Zilch. Zero. The man has a girlfriend he phone-sexes with. I know next to nothing about him, other than his dimples are covered with stubble, and his jeans are well-worn, and that's the way things are going to stay."

"We are so not joking," Poppy said brightly. "I bet if we quizzed you right now, you'd remember every single detail about him."

"Not true," I countered.

"Were his teeth straight or crooked?" Eve asked.

"Straight." Like two rows of white, enameled perfection.

"Were his fingernails clipped or dirty?" Poppy asked.

"Clipped." And super clean. No smudges. They'd appeared recently buffed.

"What color were his shoes?" Eve asked.

"Faded black biker boots, likely Frye." I'd wondered how long they'd taken to mold to his feet so perfectly.

"There. The proof is in the pudding." Poppy's finger waved in the air.

"The proof is in *nudding*," I countered. "Anyone would remember that stuff."

"What was Ethan's favorite color?" Eve asked.

I stared at both of them blankly. "Blue?"

Poppy pointed at me. "Ha! You have no idea. I bet you don't even know if Ethan had freckles, and you dated that boy for almost a year."

"No freckles," I answered smugly. They weren't getting the best of me.

"Yes, he did!" Eve exclaimed. "Right across the bridge of his nose." She ran a finger over her own nose, which was smattered with its own freckles.

Okay, yeah. He did have a few.

"That doesn't prove anything," I argued. "In a few months, I won't remember anything about this guy either."

"Right, keep telling yourself that. We've discussed it"—Poppy was acting like an authoritarian ruler—"and we think it will be therapeutic for you to ask Xander out. No one knows if Stacy is really in the picture or not. Phone sex could be conducted with anyone." She waved a hand like she was an expert about who phone-sexed whom. "After all, it was the middle of the night, which is prime time for a lonely guy to make the ol' 'you up?' call. Don't get us wrong. We don't think this guy's going to be your forever Prince Charming or anything like that. And if he's in a relationship, that will be the end of it. But if we can get you over the hump of asking someone out you actually *desire*, it'll be a step in the right direction for a healthier, happier Summer. So, then, the next time you fall madly, deeply in lust-at-first-sight, you'll be prepared. Look at Xander as a set of training wheels on your brand-new hot-guy bike. It's a super smooth e-rider that can take you places you've never dreamed of before."

Eve giggled. "Yeah, we traded in your old bike, I Guess He'll Do. It's a hell of an upgrade. I'd suggest you take us up on it."

The image of Xander being anyone's training wheels made me laugh. He was a Harley with an extra-loud exhaust pipe.

When Poppy and Eve didn't join in on my boisterous chuckling, I shook my head. "You can't be serious." They were dead serious. "I'm not asking him out. He has a girlfriend, and even if he doesn't, I don't want to. He's out of my league."

Eve bounced on the couch, pointing. "See, *see*?" She elbowed Poppy like they were a comedy team. "I knew this intervention was a good idea." Her beautiful red mane was mussed because of her excited couch-bouncing, so she swiped it behind her ears. "No one is out of your league, Summer. It's time you fully embraced your allure. You're part sporty, part shy, part awkward, part confident, very girl-next-door, and extremely desirable."

"Yeah, we're kind of tired of you acting like Miss Marple moping around your loft by yourself," Poppy said. "The guys you date always appear stunned—like 'how did this awesome woman pick me?'"

"They do not." Maybe Ryan. "And Miss Marple? Isn't she from the board game Clue or something?"

"Yes, they do," Eve chimed in.

"She's the elderly spinster detective in the Agatha Christie books. I loved reading her mysteries as a kid." Poppy swiped another hand in the air. "Forget Miss Marple, she was just an example"—her exasperation oozed through a prolonged sigh—"of an old lady who acts *just like you.*"

"I'm not asking him out." I set my coffee down and crossed my arms, hugging them to my chest. "He has a lady friend he pulls out his junk with on the phone."

Poppy wore a pained expression. "Fine. You're right. He could be in a relationship. So, how about you agree to flirt with him and see what happens? And to aid in that very endeavor, Jenny has devised the perfect plan for you." I began to sputter. "I'm sorry, you're not allowed to opt out. It's all set. Done and done."

I mocked sticking my fingers in my ears. "I don't want to hear about this plan. I hate it already."

"It's perfect, and you're doing it," Poppy replied knowingly.

"Actually, it's pretty ingenious in its simplicity," Eve added. "Jenny's going to stick a note in Xander's mailbox inviting him over for a drink, kind of a meet and greet for her new neighbor, and voila, you'll be there instead!"

My legs flung out from under me as I frantically shook my head, searching for the appropriate words.

Poppy forged on with their dastardly plan, nonplussed by my near-cardiac-arrest reaction. "It'll just be you with an apology that Jen and Dan were paged in for an emergency at the hospital. It's brilliant and makes it look like you're doing them yet another favor. Summer to the rescue." She clapped like she did when she got a gift she liked.

"Nope." I tried to control my movements so they appeared less desperate, but I wasn't having any luck. "Nope, nope, *nope.* It won't work anyway. He works at nine, so he'll have to politely decline."

"That's why Jenny scheduled it for seven," Poppy said gently. "With the added bonus that she and Daniel can go out for dinner before their shift."

"What do you mean *scheduled*? As in, she already put the note in his mailbox?"

Eve nodded, chirping, "Yep! I got confirmation of Operation Note Drop at ten this morning."

"This isn't an intervention—it's stone-cold sabotage," I groaned. I slid out of my chair and marched toward my glorious window. My happy place. "And here, after all these years, I thought you guys were my friends, only to find out you're actually Cruella de Vil's henchmen in disguise. I can't meet this guy." I turned around, my voice pleading. "I can barely talk when I'm around him. This is insanity. I feel like a Dalmatian puppy that just got kicked in the stomach."

"If you don't go," Poppy said, ignoring my drama like a pro, "Jenny and Daniel will hold down the fort. Our aim is *not* to make you miserable or do dirty deeds to puppies with spiky shoes on no matter what's going on inside that brain of yours. Remember, this is supposed to be a training-wheels session. We're doing what's best for you by giving you a shove in the right direction. You need this, Summer." Her voice held a plea that out-pleaded me.

One I chose to ignore.

"There's a chance the man is busy, and the meet won't go down," Eve said, right as her phone hummed. "Oh, wait. He's not. He agreed to come over."

"Oh. My. God," I gasped. "What have you three done?"

Chapter 5

"Baby Clara, this is an inopportune moment to settle into some peaceful z's," I whispered to the contentedly snoring baby flopped over my shoulder like a bag of baby-sized flour. I'd done my job too well. Clara had zonked out not even five minutes after Jenny handed her to me—more like thrust her into my arms and ran.

Jenny had played her diversion well, forcing me to take the innocent pawn, knowing I'd have to attend to the infant, all while apologizing for making me do this, solidly placing the blame on Poppy and Eve, and dragging her bewildered husband out the door before I could formulate any worthy words of objection.

It'd all gone down in less than three minutes.

That had to be a record.

For what, I had no idea. Forcing a romantic encounter against a woman's will? Setting your best friend up for abject failure? Making your pal look stupid while she tended your beautiful baby?

I bounced Clara softly, half hoping she'd wake, half hoping she'd stay asleep. I didn't know which would be worse, trying to make small talk with a sleeping baby on my shoulder, or trying to make small talk with a crying baby pounding her fists into my cheek. Both sounded equally frightening.

Small and *talk* were the two killer words in that phrase.

As history had shown, I was grossly inadequate.

"What the heck am I doing here?" I glanced out the living room windows. The sun had just set, and lights from the ferry dock and homes across the islands in the distance were beginning to blink like twinkling stars in the dusk.

It was ten to seven. I'd arrived on time, like a fool.

My friends, it seemed, had been masquerading as nice people, but were actually monsters. Years of unyielding support, quirky birthday gifts, fun happy hours, raucous out-of-town girls' trips, hugs, and laughter had dulled my intuition.

A soft rap sounded on the door.

I spun around. The motion agreed with Clara, because Little Sore Gums didn't stir. Panic settled over me like an itchy rash. He was early, and I wasn't ready. I mean, I was never going to be ready, but this was too soon.

Like a robot devoid of any human emotion, I made my way toward the door. The lines Eve and Poppy had coached me on this afternoon pinged around inside a void. No coherent thought patterns emerged. I angled my ear toward the door like an idiot, hoping he might go away if I didn't answer.

A few more soft knocks sounded.

"You can do this, Summer," I whispered. "Get it together." With that, I reached forward one-handed and tugged open the door. After it swung wide, I wrapped my idle hand around the baby, clutching her to my chest like a lifeline.

The man was resplendent.

I gripped the infant tighter.

He held a bottle of wine and was in yet another pair of broken-in jeans—how many did he have?—and a black button-up, sans the jacket, with a black T-shirt poking through. He looked soft, yet rough. *So rough.* Thank goodness, Mickey was nowhere to be seen.

His eyebrows edged upward in a look of surprise.

I began to babble immediately, trying to remember what to say. "Sorry, it's just me." Not the right combination of words. "I mean, I'm here instead of them." *Summer, get it together. Try again.* "There was an emergency at the hospital, and Jenny and Daniel were paged in early. They send their apologies." Clara made a soft cooing noise. *Thank you, darling baby.* I transferred my attention to her, bouncing her as I took a few steps back. "If you'd like to come in, they left food and wine. If not, I totally understand. I'm not actually a resident here, so..." Way to snare the beast.

I was acting like a Dalmatian puppy.

The side of his mouth quirked up.

It was my current favorite expression of his.

"Not a problem. I understand. Doctors have busy schedules." He came through the door.

I backed up a bit more, because his physical presence took up *a lot* of space.

Doctors did have busy schedules. Or they were sneaky and underhanded and out having a date-night dinner. But I'd ultimately chosen to be here. Nobody had perp-walked me through the front door in handcuffs.

It was time to woman up. Xander followed me to the island, which Jenny had arranged beautifully with a plate of meats and cheeses, a pretty bowl of multicolored olives, some spicy nuts, and three wineglasses—so it wouldn't look suspicious.

No, not suspicious at all. Everything going on here was totally normal.

Xander set the bottle down and took a step toward me. It took everything I had not to awkwardly move away. His gaze was focused on Clara, his head angled toward her. "That's one beautiful baby."

I nodded. "She really is. Almost too perfect. Her name is Clara, which suits her well."

"I have two nephews, no nieces. Maybe someday I'll be lucky enough to have a Clara."

It was strange to think of this man having a normal, everyday family, without parents named Zeus and Hera.

"I have an older brother," I babbled without being asked. "He's not married. So, no nieces or nephews for me."

Xander moved back to the island and slid two wineglasses in front of him. Neither wine bottle was uncorked, so he took the opener Jenny had left and proceeded to liberate the bottle he'd brought.

I was mesmerized. I'd had no idea muscles could flex like that while opening a bottle of alcohol. Once the ruby-red liquid splashed into both glasses, he handed one to me. I took it, the other arm still wrapped around Clara. "I guess I should go and lay her down," I said. "She's teething. But she seems pretty content now and likes her crib." Likes her crib? *Ugh.*

I turned and trotted down the hallway to hide my lame

small-talk game, toting my wineglass along. Time to relinquish my baby shield.

Surprisingly, Xander followed. His footsteps were loud and confident. "This is the same layout as my place."

I took a moment to let my mind wander to what his bedroom might look like, certain it was decorated in deep chocolates or blues. Perspiration began to sprout along my hairline. Inconvenient.

The shades in Clara's room were already drawn, the light from the kitchen filtering in through the hallway allowing us to see. I set my wineglass by the monitor base. The other end—the one that communicated sex acts—was perched on the coffee table out in the living room.

That monitor and I shared a dirty secret, one that Xander could never, ever find out about.

I laid the baby on her back and covered her with a lightweight blanket decorated in little elephants. My hand lingered over her body, ready to give her a pat if she needed some comfort, but she was peacefully zonked out.

As I turned from the crib, my eyes landed on Xander's chest.

I was so relieved not to see Mickey I almost wiped my brow. But I kind of missed the leather jacket. It suited him. He had a faraway look on his face, and I worried that I was boring him as I grabbed my wineglass off the dresser.

We made our way back to the living area. I beelined around the island to the kitchen side, not knowing what else to do. I busied myself grabbing a plate and setting a few cheese chunks on it, followed by a couple olives. I mean, we had to eat, right?

He did the same, sliding comfortably onto one of the stools. He popped a piece of salami into his mouth, chewing thoughtfully. Once he was done, he asked, "So, are you from the Seattle area?"

I'd just stuffed not one, but two olives into my mouth. Once things were clear, I replied, "No, I'm actually from the east side of the state. Spokane, to be exact. Moving to Seattle was always the dream. After I graduated from the University of Washington, I decided to stay in the area. Are you from here?"

"No, I'm from California, just south of LA."

Of course you are.

"That's interesting." Dumb. "What brought you up here?"

"A business opportunity. Seattle is a great city for startups. I moved about six months ago. I was happy to find a vacancy in this building."

"What kind of a startup?" I asked, taking a sip of wine. It was really good wine. The smooth kind that didn't attack the glands in your throat. I wasn't super into wine, but I always appreciated it when it didn't try to throat-punch me.

"A microbrewery called Zoe's Lager. Or will be, when we get it up and running."

"The craft-beer industry is really booming," I commented. "I've done logos over the past couple years for a few of them. It's a fun job. There's so much energy and excitement involved."

"You're a graphic designer?" His eyebrows rose, perfectly hooding his green eyes.

I nodded, taking another sip. This seemed to be going better than I'd anticipated. The separation of the island helped immensely. And, of course, the fact I was actively blocking conjecture in my brain of what his tattooed chest looked like naked.

The only thing more perfectly suited to him, other than

running a brewpub, would've been him owning a custom bike shop.

"I've been in business for myself for about three years," I said. "My company is called Summer Day Designs. It probably pigeonholes me a little for those who would consider me seasonal for whatever reason, but I couldn't resist using my full name. Overall, business has been good this year, better than usual."

"Your full name is Summer Day?" He smiled widely. Flashing those dimples should be a felony in all fifty states, Canada, and Mexico. Who was I kidding? A felony in the entire world.

I nodded. "Yes. Not only did my parents love summer, but they had a healthy sense of humor. I usually refrain from introducing myself with my full name on the first meet. My middle name is actually Mary, after my grandmother. That helps a lot when I'm filling out paperwork."

"Your name is adorable." He drank some wine, tossing a heated gaze my way.

Was it heated?

It felt hot.

His eyelids were lowered. His lips were pursed.

My idle perspiration morphed into flop sweat. I blushed and looked away, reaching out to grab the bottle of wine, which at the last minute I decided not to grab. Half a glass of wine was enough for tonight. Baby Clara was my priority after all. I settled on mumbling, "Um, thanks. It's just a name."

Xander stood and strolled over to the windows, being a champ and changing the subject. "This is a nice view. I couldn't afford the bay side." He turned, his lips quirking up at the sides, dimples winking. "Maybe someday."

I stayed right where I was, rooted behind the only thing in this entire building that was keeping me from falling over. Tingles had erupted over every inch of my body. The hummingbird had made herself at home the moment this man had entered the premises. I caressed the cool granite with my fingertips, giving silent thanks to its overall sturdiness.

"You don't have to live here to have a great view of Elliott Bay," I countered. "I live in Capitol Hill, and my loft overlooks the water. It's not really a loft, more like a condoized attic of an old house. But I call it a loft. It's super cozy."

He wandered back to the kitchen, likely realizing I wasn't leaving my perch, and settled his elbows casually on the island. His chest flexed with lots of vibrant movement, and I wished, for a single white-hot second, that his T-shirt didn't cover up what I knew lurked beneath.

I was desperate for a glimpse of a tat.

"A loft in Capitol Hill suits you. I can almost picture it." His voice dropped to an intimate level, and shivers raced up my spine like a horde of butterflies on speed. "Hey, would you consider having dinner with me sometime?"

I tried to form words. "I…um…I…" A girl I'd never met named Stacy flashed before my eyes. She was running slo-mo down the beach in a red one-piece, her feet barely touching the sand, her beautiful black hair blazing out behind her, industrial-fan style. I couldn't let on that I knew he had a girlfriend, or at least a friend with benefits. And now I couldn't ask him casually if he had one, since he'd just asked me out. This was supposed to be my training-wheels session, and I was sucking at it badly. I was supposed to say yes, go with the flow, and have a good time.

Instead, I said nothing.

Xander straightened, appearing a little flustered. "I don't

know where that came from. You probably have a boyfriend." He set his wineglass down. The clink of it hitting the counter sounded like the grand finale of a doomed fairy tale. He drew back his shirtsleeve, glancing at a big, expensive watch. "I'm sorry to cut this short, but I have to get going. We have an after-hours meeting every night at the brewery around nine thirty, but tonight I have to be there at eight because we're going over the books."

No!

No, no, no.

How did I hose things up so quickly?

As he made his way to the door, I trailed after him, making small talk that sounded like incessant bird chirping. "That's okay. Work is understandable," I clucked. "Glad you could stop by. I'm sure Jenny and Daniel would love to have you over soon. They're sorry they missed meeting you."

With his hand on the door, he turned. For a single second, it seemed he might say something, but he changed his mind. "The brewpub doesn't have any branding yet. We actually just leased the space a few weeks ago. We wanted to make sure it was a go before we assumed the next step. I'll talk to the team tonight. If nobody's hired a designer yet, would you be interested?"

"Sure!" My enthusiastic reply belied the remorse I felt that our meetup was officially ending in a mushroom cloud, and it was all my fault. I began to babble. "I work on a small retainer, just enough to cover the time it takes to design three samples. If your company doesn't choose to move forward with anything, it shouldn't set you back too much." It felt like I was giving him the hard sell. "What I mean is, if you decide to work with me initially, and you don't like any of the designs, it's okay if you don't continue. No pressure."

He fished his phone out of his pocket. "What's your number?" I gave it to him and watched his super-grippy fingers punch it into his contacts.

I was in his phone.

It was probably the same cell he used to phone-sex Stacy. That thought helped shake me out of what was quickly becoming a murky dream state. When he was done, he glanced up, all business, giving me a half smile, barely any dimple, along with a three-fingered salute. "It was nice meeting you. I'll get back to you soon."

Then he was gone.

After the door clicked shut, I leaned against it, trying not to slip down to the floor in a physical show of vapid depression.

Only then did I realize that I'd never answered his question about whether I had a boyfriend.

Chapter 6

Poppy was sprawled on my love seat, her torso curved across a pillow, the back of her hand dramatically draped over her eyes. Her impression of a distressed Scarlett O'Hara not able to take one more minute of this nonsense was spot-on.

Eve sat next to her. Back straight, lips puckered like she'd just sampled something sour that was not to her liking, legs crossed.

This time, it wasn't an intervention. It was a lunchtime gossip sesh mixed with palpable disdain for my feeble biking skills. I clearly wasn't meant for a fancy two-wheeler.

"He asked you on a date, and you failed to say yes?" Poppy asked for the third time. With each ask, her voice had risen a full octave. "I can't believe you didn't at least reassure him that you were single!" Even though Poppy had minored in drama at UW, she hadn't pursued her love of acting in the traditional sense. Instead, she worked as an acting coach and play director for an after-school community outreach program. The kids adored her, and together they put on some pretty awesome productions. I was always involved in the set design.

"I told you already," I said, trying not to rake my fingernails down my neck one more time. Instead, I clutched both hands around a warm mug of chamomile tea. Caffeine would not be my friend right now. "He changed the subject so fast I couldn't keep up. He asked me to have dinner with him, and all I could think about was that he had a girlfriend named Stacy. Then he was out the door."

"But we don't even know if he *has* a girlfriend named Stacy." Eve was the dissatisfied church marm to Poppy's Scarlett. "The hottest man—*by your own admission*—you've ever seen in your entire life asks you to dinner, and you don't give him an answer? Have we taught you *nothing*?"

Okay, so Poppy wasn't the only one with dramatic flair.

I set my mug down and unfurled myself from my favorite chair, moving toward my beloved window. Looking out was like uttering a safe word. It was full-on raining today. No view of Elliott Bay, just thick, wet fog. I hadn't even bothered to change out of my pajamas. The girls had arrived ten minutes ago.

At five this morning, I'd managed to spit out the entire story to Jenny, but just barely. I'd made my excuses and left quickly. It was just too embarrassing. "I'm not cut out for this, ladies," I told my friends, turning to face them. "I know Xander was supposed to be my training wheels, but it seems I don't like hot-guy bikes. I'm going to stick with my trike. It's much safer." Not the greatest analogy, but they'd already set it up, so I was riding with it.

Poppy sprang off the couch, morphing from Scarlett to Tom

Hanks in *Big*. "Don't talk like that, Summer!" She bounded over to me. "This is a *minor* setback." She clutched on to both of my forearms and gave them a few shakes. "He asked you out, you froze. It's no big deal. It happens to the best of us. But more importantly, he didn't give up. You rebuffed his date, so he offered you another opportunity to connect. That means he's still interested."

"Interested in branding for his microbrewery. That doesn't mean anything."

"Of course it does," Eve said, coming to join us, walking rather than bouncing. "He wouldn't have asked if he didn't want to see you again. If he can't take you to dinner, he'll settle for working with you. That's one of the oldest tricks in the book."

It is? News to me.

"He hasn't texted me yet," I argued, "and his meeting was last night, and it's"—I glanced into my kitchen at my wall clock—"one thirty-seven."

Eve snorted, which sounded regal. When I snorted I sounded like a braying horse. Eve was a former dancer-turned-accountant. She was a whiz with numbers, but that wasn't her dream job. Accounting was her getting-her-to-the-next-thing job. She hoped to open a flower shop in the next year or so. She always joked that she was going to call it Jazz One Floral, to mix her love of dancing, accounting, and flowers.

"The fact that he hasn't texted you yet doesn't mean anything," Eve countered. "These things take time. Decisions like this have to be voted on by a committee. Who knows how many partners he has?"

I glanced out at the bay, which I couldn't see because of the fog. My throat felt itchy again. "I can't babysit baby Clara tonight," I told them. "One of you has to cover for me."

Like the Bobbsey Twins from hell, they stood shoulder to shoulder, shaking their heads. Poppy came to Eve's chin but looked just as fierce. She had her arms crossed, hip out, and one leg jutted forward. "We are not covering for you," Poppy asserted. "You're going back there with your head held high."

"There's no way," I retorted. "Having him leave like that was mortifying, even more so after I analyzed it over and over again all night long." A full nine hours of obsessing. I hadn't slept a wink. "I'm going to have to tell Jenny." I made a move toward my kitchen to get my phone.

"Hold it right there!" Eve ordered. Her voice was forceful enough for me to stop in my tracks. "Now is not the time to be hasty. You don't have to be at Jenny's until nine o'clock tonight. There's a good chance Xander will text you by then and everything will work out. Give it a few hours, at the very least."

"Canceling on Jenny will put them in a huge lurch," Poppy unhelpfully pointed out.

I flashed her some serious stink-eye. "You could cover for me in two seconds. You work in the late afternoon."

"I hate kids," Poppy said with absolutely no guile.

"You do not! You work with kids every single day." It was my turn to cross my arms. "They're your livelihood. Every time one of them stubs a toe or makes a cute joke, we hear about it."

"I meant babies," she answered stubbornly. "Infants freak me out. They're so tiny and breakable."

"I seriously can't do it," Eve added. "I've arranged a meeting tonight with two interested investors. I'm wining and dining them, hoping they'll give me money to open Jazz One."

I dropped my arms, forgetting about my dumb problems. A

hot guy asked me out. I didn't respond. Not the end of the world.

"That's really fantastic, Eve." I gave her a quick hug. "You've been dreaming about this for as long as I've known you."

"Yeah," she agreed. "It's pretty great. As you both know, my nana had a flower shop, which I basically grew up in. Next to crunching numbers and dancing, flowers are my thing. Seattle's an expensive town. I have most of the seed money, but having two investors would make everything so much easier, giving it a greater chance of success. It feels like now is the time to jump in."

"I'm sure they'll invest," Poppy said, giving Eve a long, Scarlett-inspired embrace up on her tiptoes. "Not only are flowers your thing, but so are numbers. Your business plan is rock-solid. They'll have nothing to worry about."

"I hope so," Eve replied. "We'll see tonight."

We all settled back down—them on the love seat, me on my chair—to talk about something refreshingly not about me.

The elevator ride up to Jenny's felt like a death march toward Lord Vader. Like any minute I was going to tumble to my knees, clutching my Jedi-constricted throat, which had itched all day today. Probably why I was conjuring images of Darth in the first place.

That, and the day had been gloomy. No text from Xander, but I was here anyway. In the end, I couldn't bring myself to disappoint Jenny and Daniel. I'd promised to help them, and I was a woman of my word.

I'd arrived a full twenty minutes early, hoping that would be enough time to avoid another run-in with Xander in the sedate-blue hallway. I was thankful this was the last night Jenny and Daniel would need me until next week. I was certain my trauma would calm down by then. It had to.

The elevator doors opened, and I didn't immediately collapse.

Congratulating myself on my good fortune, I adjusted my shoulder bag and hurried on my way, tiptoeing Grinch-style so I wouldn't make any noise. If anyone spied me, they'd think something was wrong with me, but I didn't care.

This was me getting the job done.

Last night, I'd been dressed appropriately for a date, in jeans and a nice top. Tonight, I'd compromised. I wasn't in full sweats, but I wasn't in party clothes either. I wore black leggings and a floppy shirt, the comfy cotton kind that came to midthigh. Good for sleeping. I'd also brought my laptop so I could get some work done. Sleeping in late had dug into my daylight working hours.

I made it to Jenny's door and let myself in, relief ebbing through me like a gush of water through a spontaneously unstuck drain. I shut it quietly, my fingers lightly caressing the wood in silent thanks.

Jenny peeked at me from the hallway, looking a little alarmed. "Are we good?"

"Yes, we're good," I told her, exhaling. "I made it. No Xander encounters. Now I can relax." Her arms were conspicuously baby-free. "Where's Clara?" I asked, heading into the living room while Jenny walked into the kitchen, grabbing a few snacks to take along with her to the hospital.

"She's asleep." Jenny grinned over her shoulder. "In her crib already. She was up a lot today, so she conked out around seven thirty. I can't guarantee she's going to stay asleep, but there's a good chance."

Daniel came into the room. "Nice to see you, Summer. I'm sorry about what Jenny insisted we do last night. I'd like to say, for the record, I was against it. Even though it was nice to get out."

"I appreciate that, but ultimately I chose to be here," I said. "I was fully aware of the situation and showed up anyway."

Jenny waved a banana in my direction. "Luxury Hot asked you out last night. I'm waiting for a thank-you. I mean, it was a brilliant plan that totally worked."

I snorted.

It sounded like a frog choking on a cricket.

"Brilliant? I wouldn't go that far," I challenged. "It was pretty humiliating when he ran out of here with his hair on fire like an anchor in a relay race. He couldn't exit the premises fast enough." I took a seat on the couch, setting my bag on the coffee table. "What I can't figure out is why I care so much. I've seen this guy a total of three times for a handful of minutes. He should rank as a nobody. I need to move on. If he wants me to design a logo, fine. But I don't have to choose to stay obsessed. He's not my type, and it's clear why. I lose my entire self around guys like him."

"The world is filled with hot guys who aren't dickweeds," Jenny said, coming behind the couch to plant a kiss on top of my head. "You just have to find the right one. He's out there. You don't have to date gas station hot, but your next boyfriend has to turn you on *and* be your equal." Spoken like a woman in cahoots with Poppy and Eve. She gestured toward Daniel, who was donning his raincoat. "Each of us is turned on by very different triggers, thank goodness. My hunk of a man right over there is incredibly smart and expertly gifted with a scalpel. He's intelligent, caring, sexy, and an amazing father. Does it for me every time."

Daniel wiggled his fingers. "Having nimble digits is certainly an asset."

"Did you just make a sex joke?" I laughed.

Jenny went over to him and gave him a big, wet, sloppy kiss. "Yes, he did." She turned back to me, conspiratorially bringing her hand up in an arc around her mouth. "He is literally the best lay I've ever had in my entire life. The man can rock it out in the bedroom. Brain, scalpel, and a penis that just won't quit. Highly recommend."

"Oh my goodness." I covered my mouth, chortling. Jenny had always been pretty quiet about their sex life because Daniel wasn't comfortable with everybody knowing the details, and she respected his decision.

Daniel met my gaze, seemingly unfazed, and winked as he headed toward the door. "You don't need an Adonis, Summer. You just need somebody who makes you happy. That's all we want for you."

"I hope Clara gives you a break tonight." Jenny blew me a kiss as she followed her husband out the door, both of them giggling like teenagers.

What they had was exactly what I was looking for. Love, companionship, contentment, and happiness. Jenny was right. The match for me was out there somewhere.

I blew out a breath and dug my laptop out of my bag. I didn't usually work on such a small screen, but I had the programs I needed to start sketching out a few ideas for the startup that printed affordable T-shirts for nonprofits.

But first, I was going to answer the email from my mom's friend Tina. She'd gone with design number one, which was a solid choice.

Halfway through the email, baby Clara made some cooing sounds. I glanced at the monitor on the table. For the first time, I noticed there was a Post-it Note stuck to it. I smiled as I plucked it off.

It simply read *Enjoy*.

After a minute, Clara quieted, and I got back to work.

A few hours later, I had a design of a cutout shirt with a checkmark popping through it with the company's name in block letters beneath it. I got up off the couch to stretch. I wasn't sold on the design. I needed fresh eyes.

Wandering into the kitchen, I tugged open the fridge. The olives from last night were still in there. I took them out and grabbed a carton of orange juice. Who said olives and orange juice couldn't go together?

The clock on the microwave, mounted over the very fancy stainless-steel stove, read midnight. Twelve fourteen a.m., to be exact. I yawned. When I was immersed in my work, it wasn't uncommon for hours to slip by.

I poured a glass of juice and stuck the carton back in the fridge. As I made my way back to my spot, olive jar in one hand, the OJ in the other, the baby monitor crackled, and Xander's voice came out as clear as day.

"Yes, I miss you."

Chapter 7

For one breathless second, I thought he was speaking to me. I managed to set my food items on the coffee table without dumping them all over my laptop, which was a huge victory.

"Not tonight," he said. "I'm too tired."

He did sound tired.

I took my place on the couch, unsure what to do. Now that I knew him, and he'd asked me to dinner, listening felt intrusive. But I couldn't *not* listen.

Right? *Right?*

"Okay, okay."

Okay, okay, what?

I perched on the edge of the cushion. Did that mean he was giving in?

"It's out."

Oh. My. *God.*

I sprang up like someone had electrocuted me, swiping the

baby monitor off the table like it was a grenade about to go off in my face, fumbling with the volume dial on top, finally managing to click it off. I proceeded to grip it to my chest, nestled between my breasts like a precious heirloom. I gazed up at the ceiling, my breaths coming quickly.

I couldn't do this. I couldn't keep listening.

There were so many reasons not to eavesdrop. His privacy. Her privacy. My privacy. So many privacies.

Moving toward the island, I tried to clear my head. Not satisfied that was doing anything at all to help, I bolted to the front door and sealed my ear against it like I was in a comedy spy movie.

Why was I listening at the door? There was no rational reason, other than it gave me something to do.

There was nothing to hear. Not so much as a squeak. And even if I could magically home in on Xander from this distance, between various closed doors, what was I going to do? I scurried back to the kitchen, settling my hips against the countertop, my hands still death-gripping the monitor like it might explode in my chest.

After a moment, I brought it out in front of me.

Should I turn it back on?

Just for a quick second?

They could be done already. Or maybe he'd decided not to go through with it.

Not knowing was killing me. I rotated the knob slowly.

"…yes, yes."

A strangled sound like a moose crossed with a yelping hyena came out of my chest. I snapped the monitor off, barely refraining from chucking it across the room.

Not so precious now.

They were totally doing it. Xander and Stacy were having phone sex.

Not knowing where else to go, but realizing I had to go somewhere, or I'd lose my mind, I made my way into baby Clara's room. With the monitor off, I wouldn't be able to hear her if she whimpered.

It was dark and quiet. Just what I needed.

I situated myself in the glider, unprepared for how quickly it slid backward on me, grabbing on to the rails. Once I was positioned with my feet up on the moving ottoman, I allowed my head to rest against the cushion and closed my eyes.

Get a hold of yourself, Summer. He isn't your boyfriend. You knew about Stacy. He's not your type anyway. If you ever went out with him, you'd freak the hell out. You'd be miserable, always second-guessing yourself, and the relationship would be doomed from the start. Guys like him aren't for you. It's better this way.

These were all extremely good, rational reasons for not caring.

Why weren't they helping?

Focus on the key part of this. The man asked you out when he obviously has a girlfriend. That's the number one thing cocky, confident men do. They always want more. They're never satisfied. You hate that.

I did hate that.

It was everything wrong with the Lukes and the Mitches of the world.

You don't want this man. He's gorgeous, that's a fact. But he's not your type. Let it go.

After an extremely long exhale, bordering on the sigh of

all sighs, I felt better. Everything was going to be okay. Maybe this was my training-wheels session after all. It hadn't achieved what Poppy, Eve, and Jenny had hoped, but it had clarified a lot of things for future me and what I wanted in new relationships. While I might not go for the Xander types, I would choose my next boyfriend based on a new set of criteria. He could land somewhere between super-nice, nerdy guy and handsome, confident man.

Those kinds of men existed, right?

My friends insisted they did. I just hadn't found any yet. Probably because I'd never cast my net in that particular direction before.

With a new sense of peace, I let my eyes drift shut.

My phone chimed from its position next to my bed. I rubbed my neck, willing myself to wake up.

Last night, I'd fallen asleep in the glider. Jenny had woken me up apologetically at five.

I was exhausted.

After I massaged out the kink, I reached for my phone, noting the text on the home screen that had woken me up. My eyes landed on the time stamp. It was after two in the afternoon. *Yikes.* Babysitting Clara was taking a lot more out of me than I'd anticipated. I really needed to get back to my regular schedule. These late nights and later afternoons were killing me.

Kicking my legs free, I unlocked my phone and immediately sat up, almost bonking my head on the slant of the ceiling.

The number was unfamiliar, but the sender wasn't. The text

was from Xander.

WOULD LIKE TO SET UP A MEETING ABOUT LOGO DESIGN FOR ZOE'S IF YOU'RE STILL INTERESTED. LET ME KNOW. X

Breath whooshed in and out of my lungs like I'd been gut-punched by a prizefighter.

Get a hold of yourself, Summer. The X is not a kiss, it stands for his name. He wants to set up a business meeting. You need the work. It will be a good opportunity. You're capable of being professional with an attractive man who adores phone sex.

My finger hovered above the keyboard. Then I drew it back. I didn't want to be hasty. Instead, I hustled out of bed, setting my phone on the countertop in the kitchen, and headed into the bathroom.

Once I was in the shower, my inner monologue wasted no time highlighting all the issues as hot water pounded down around my shoulders. *Working with him is different than dating him. His personal choices have nothing to do with you. If he likes kinky-sex stuff, that's his business. As a client, you can keep a professional distance. If you do their branding, and the company is successful, word will get out, and it will increase your business opportunities. You'd be a fool to pass up the opportunity he's offering.*

Once the temperature changed from hot to warm, I shut off the spray, sliding back the curtain and grabbing a towel. Nice, plushy, big bath towels were a must.

Everything I'd gone over in the shower made sense. I felt calm. *Fine, calm-ish.* Implementing the next phase would be tricky. I was tempted to text Poppy and Eve and get their takes before I made a decision one way or another. But honestly, that would defeat any growth I'd made on my own during this entire ordeal.

With one towel wrapped around my hair and another around my midsection, I padded into the kitchen. The rain had cleared from yesterday, and the sky was a crisp, beautiful blue. I plucked my phone off the counter. I had no new texts.

Wandering over to my favorite chair, I sank down, rocking for a bit, contemplating what to write. My tone had to come across as completely professional.

After a couple of tries, I settled on:

WORKING TOGETHER ON A LOGO SOUNDS GOOD. WE COULD DO THE INTERVIEW OVER THE PHONE, BY EMAIL, OR MEET AT A COFFEE SHOP. SUMMER.

I hit send before I could second-guess anything. The message was antiseptic enough and gave him a few outs if he didn't want to meet in person. It hit all the right notes for me. I felt good about it.

Next, I pulled up my thread with Eve and tapped:

EXCITED TO HEAR HOW THINGS WENT LAST NIGHT! LET ME KNOW. [SMILEY EMOJI]

Eve got the smiles.

This morning when I'd talked to Jenny, I'd left out that there'd been more phone sex. I hadn't wanted to get into it. I'd told her to let Poppy and Eve know that it'd been an uneventful night and that I wasn't in need of any more interventions or resuscitations.

Almost immediately, Eve responded.

PITCH WORKED! THEY'RE IN. WE'RE CELEBRATING TONIGHT AT DRIFTWOOD. U FREE?

After a second, she sent another.

HOPE LAST NIGHT WENT OK. JENNY SAID IT WAS BORING. HOPE TO SEE U LATER. MEETING AT 6.

The Driftwood was one of our favorite haunts. A cozy bar with signature cocktails and a great atmosphere. But you had to get there early if you wanted a table.

I responded:

SO EXCITED FOR YOU. I'LL BE THERE!

That meant I had only a few hours to work. I stood, ready to get dressed and finally start this day.

My phone buzzed again.

Assuming Eve was texting back, I was caught off guard. His name wasn't in the heading, since I hadn't added him to my contacts yet, but the number and message were clear.

HOW ABOUT BRUNCH TOMORROW? I'M PARTIAL TO THE SWEET IRON BUT WILL MEET ANYWHERE. LET ME KNOW. X

Brunch? He wanted to do *brunch*?

I sank back down and readjusted the towel on my head. Getting breakfast wasn't coffee, but it wasn't drinks either. It was a compromise.

But it kind of felt like a date.

Or, in his mind, was it just a work meeting?

My rib cage started to feel fluttery again, and I forced myself to find some Zen. After a few quasi-yoga breaths, I got up and headed to my closet, doffing the towels and hanging them on the hooks I'd mounted outside the door. Dressing quickly, I contemplated my choices. I knew what my friends would say. They'd order me to go. But going out to brunch with clients wasn't the norm. When I did meet them face-to-face, it was either at their office or a coffee shop of their choosing. Seattle was bursting with places to swill your caffeine-filled drink of choice. A cup of coffee wasn't a meal.

I could nip whatever this was in the bud and send Xander

a clear message by making my excuses for Sunday and rescheduling for Monday at a coffee shop.

Or I could just go.

Ugh. Why was this so hard?

It's hard because you like him, but you don't want to like him. Face it.

I grabbed my brush off my dresser, which was located inside my closet, going after my hair with a little more gusto than necessary. Once I was done, there wasn't much more to do, so I picked up my phone and tapped the following message:

SURE. BRUNCH SOUNDS GREAT. I'LL MEET YOU AT SWEET IRON AT 11. S

After I was done, I flung my phone onto my love seat, hoping the cushions would swallow it forever. Or at least for the rest of the day.

Chapter 8

"You did the exact right thing," Poppy assured me with her usual confidence as she handed my phone to Eve, who inspected the texts for herself. "He gave you an opening, and you took it. I'm so proud! My baby is officially riding her hot-guy bike."

"Here, let me see," Jenny beckoned. Eve set the phone into her open palm. Daniel was on baby duty tonight. It was nice to spend time with Jenny outside of their apartment.

It was ten after six, and we were all gathered at the Driftwood.

"I totally agree," Eve said. "You came across very businesslike, which doesn't leave you vulnerable if this is nothing more than a breakfast meeting over a delicious plate of scrambled eggs."

"Honestly, I can't believe he's this polite," Jenny said, handing me my phone. I tucked it into my purse. "You guys haven't seen him. He looks like Mad Max but cleaner. Ridiculously hot in a—"

"Don't you dare say in a gas-station way," I told her, giggling.

"He's regular hot. Just because he wears leather and has a few tattoos"—even though I hadn't seen them, there'd been a lot of speculating on my part—"doesn't mean he severs heads in Thunder Dome or works at the quickie mart."

"I hate to cut you off, but they're here." Eve eased out of her seat excitedly. She'd invited her new business partners and wanted to introduce us, which was sweet. One was a thirtysomething female investor named Amy who had family money. Eve had met her through networking of some kind. The other one was a man, Marco, no background given.

Eve waved them over.

My mouth tumbled open. I leaned over to Jenny, who sat next to me. Poppy and Eve sat across from us. "Is that Marco Cruz?"

"Who?"

"You know, from college?"

"I have no idea who Marco Cruz is," Jenny replied, giving the approaching man a once-over.

It was too late to ask any more questions because they were here. "Hi, guys, I'd like you to meet Amy West and Marco Cruz." Bingo. "These two are my brand-new investors of our yet-to-be-named flower enterprise." Her arm made a sweeping gesture toward the table. "And these are my friends Jenny Baldwin, Summer Day, and Poppy Albright."

A chorus of nice-to-meet-yous and handshakes followed. No one commented on my full name, which was always a bonus.

Eve had already ordered a bottle of champagne, which was waiting in an ice canister next to the table. She poured six flutes, passing one to each of us. Before I could think of a good toast, Marco raised his glass. "To Eve. With her at the helm, this is sure to be a success."

Eve blushed.

She never did that. Her mantra was calm, cool, and collected at all times.

"This wouldn't be happening without the two of you," she chirped. "So glad you're both on board. This is going to be amazing!"

Amy added something nice, and we all clinked glasses.

I shot a look at Poppy, arching one of my eyebrows, caterpillar style. She had to remember Eve talking about Marco. But Poppy was too busy imbibing to recognize my arched brow, even though I'd given it some serious effort.

We settled into some animated chatting, listening to all the ideas and plans Eve had to make this flower shop stand out from the rest. She had some great ones, including featuring local artists, possibly music on alternate days of the week, and teaching classes. It sounded totally cool.

After the second bottle of champagne, Amy made her goodbyes and left.

I had to use the bathroom, but I wasn't going on my own. "Eve," I interrupted politely. When she didn't readily tear her eyes away from Marco, I said her name again, a little louder this time. "Eve, do you have to use the bathroom?" It was our universal signal. One that could *not* be ignored. Whenever any one of us asked one of the others if she had to go to the bathroom, the mandatory answer was yes. It meant there was an emergency, or at the very least, we had something important to share in private.

Eve hesitated for a few seconds. "Sure. Now that you mention it, I do have to go. We'll be right back."

We made our way toward the bathrooms. The Driftwood was a tiny establishment, so it didn't take long. There were a few people in line ahead of us, so we waited in the hallway. I leaned my back against the wall. "Marco Cruz? Are you sure you know what you're doing?"

Her eyes widened, then narrowed. "How do you know Marco?"

I spread my arms wide in the universal *come on* gesture. "Are you kidding? I was your freshman roommate, remember? You had it hot and heavy for Marco at the beginning of the year. You may have thought I was in a Mitch-induced coma, but I remember you talking about him—'gushing' is probably a better word. You *gushed* about that man. Too many times to count." Eve and Marco had never dated, and she'd never mentioned him again after that time period. Her infatuation with him had lasted about as long as my romance with Mitch. If she hadn't reintroduced us tonight, I never would've thought of him again.

Unless, of course, I'd run into him. The man was wickedly handsome. He had a dark, rich skin tone, black hair, wide eyes, lashes for miles, and a striking smile, even without dimples.

We shuffled up in line. "Marco and I are friends," she replied casually. "We've always been friends."

"You've stayed in touch with him since college?" I asked skeptically. "I have a hard time believing that. You've never brought him up once in passing. Not once."

"Okay, not exactly since college," she hedged. "I bumped into him about a year ago."

"Why didn't you mention it? It's clear you're crushing."

She looked aghast, complete with a shocked hand placed over her heart. "I am not! He's about to become my business partner."

"Yeah, that's why I'm asking. Do you think it's a smart idea to go into business with someone you want to make out with?" We entered the bathroom together.

It was a teeny space, only two stalls. One was free, so I took it.

"Are we in the seventh grade?" Eve asked. "I don't want to make out with him or date him. I want to be his business partner."

"How many times have you talked to him in the past year?" I called through the door, as one does. "I shouldn't have to add—picture my air quotes here—while sneaking around behind our backs not telling us that you reconnected with an old college crush." Eve didn't answer as she entered the stall next to mine. "You're so busted. And to think you've been sitting on my love seat pontificating about all the things I'm doing wrong in my romantic life, when you're pretty much doing the same thing."

"I'm not doing the same thing," she argued. "He and I have only talked a few times. What's going on with me is unrelated to your situation. I date successful guys all the time."

"Burn," I said, accepting the hit as I exited and washed my hands. None of the last four men I'd dated could've been considered *successful.* "Then why aren't you two an item?" I asked, drying my hands. "Does he have a girlfriend?"

She was quiet for so long, I figured she wasn't going to answer. Once out of her stall, she headed straight for the sink. "A live-in girlfriend." I detected the misery in her voice.

I understood.

"*Aw,*" I said, not wanting to make a huge deal about it. This was exactly why Eve hadn't told us. We, being us, would've wanted her to be happy, so we likely would've guided—nice word for *enthusiastically prodded*—her in a direction she wouldn't have been comfortable or ready to go in. Kind of like what was happening to me with Xander.

We exited. "I'm fine with it," she said. "Honestly. He's made a killing as a hedge-fund manager. Now, as a side business, he provides seed money for startups. He loves being involved with new businesses. The contract will be bulletproof. I have nothing to worry about."

"I trust you. But I also just witnessed the way you two were looking at each other. Mixing business and pleasure is a slippery slope."

She made a funny face. "Was he looking at me weird? I didn't notice."

I held in my snort because we were closing in on the table. "Yeah, like he wanted to devour you whole," I whispered out of the side of my mouth. "He's smitten."

She clutched my forearm. "He is *not.*"

"Summer," a masculine voice called from behind us.

My head jerked around.

Eve's hand was still on my arm, and I crushed it with my newfound superhuman strength.

"Ow, that's too tight," she whispered, trying to release my grip without success. She glanced around, startled. "Who is it?"

"Xander."

He stood at the end of the bar in all his glory.

It appeared he'd just walked in. A few guys stood behind him. He was dressed in black leather, no button-up. As an added bonus, he wore a black tee underneath his jacket with a scooped neck that exposed not one, but two distinct tattoos. My brain started whirring like an out-of-control washing machine on a hyper-spin cycle.

He was just…so damn beautiful.

"That's *Xander*?" Eve's voice was hushed, almost reverent. "Holy *shit*."

"Yeah," I mumbled. "Tell me about it."

He started toward us. I started to sweat immediately. I was about to become a drenched woman severely out of her league.

"Hi there," he said.

"Hi," I mumbled. Eve nudged me, gracefully managing to separate her hand from my arm.

"I'm Eve, one of Summer's best friends." She extended her hand as though meeting a Roman god were a normal, everyday occurrence.

Xander grinned in a way I adored, exposing the two pockets-full-of-joy bookending his extremely full lips, and shook my friend's hand. "I'm Xander. Summer's new client." He glanced behind him. "My business partners are with me." He gestured behind him. They were busy ordering drinks. "We like to stop here after we're done in the shop on Fridays."

"Is your pub nearby?" I asked. The Driftwood was located in Ballard on Market Street. I shouldn't be surprised. Ballard was a trendy area with lots of microbreweries and indie shops. It was one of my favorite areas in Seattle.

"Yep, just around the block, actually." He indicated with his hand, but I had no idea of the actual direction.

Eve cleared her throat, motioning to our table, which was less than ten feet away. Jenny hadn't noticed us, as we stood behind her, and Poppy was busy chatting up Marco. "I'm going to head back to our table," Eve said. "You two can talk business." She flashed a bright smile at Xander. "It was nice to meet you."

"Likewise," he said.

Then, just like that, she left me hanging like the worst wingwoman in the history of wingwomen. My eyes tracked around the bar. It was crowded, like it was on most Fridays. I was pretty sure my subconscious was trying to locate all the possible exits. Really, there was only one. The front door.

"We love this bar," I said by way of casual conversation. "We come here often."

"Can I buy you a drink?" Xander asked, turning toward the bartender, who was busy. Xander's business partners came over. "Chris and Leo, this is the graphic designer I was telling you about, Summer Day. We're meeting tomorrow to discuss the branding for Zoe's."

They each shook my hand. This little scenario was trucking along like everything was totally *un*extraordinary. And maybe it was. After all, I'd just run into a client at a bar. No big deal. One with two extremely nice-looking, and super-virile, business partners. Leo and Chris were formidable. Both tall, good-looking, and self-assured.

"Nice to meet you," Chris said. "Sounds good about the logo. Xander can fill you in. I'm going to step out and give Molly a call." He thumb-gestured toward the door, which I was eyeing like a getaway portal to freedom. "She didn't pick up before."

Chris took off, and Leo wandered away.

That left Xander and me standing behind a couple who had actual seats at the bar. "What are you drinking?" Xander asked.

"Um, champagne?" It came out like a question instead of a statement. The Driftwood was known for its original cocktails. "We're celebrating Eve's new business venture. How about a Frenchie? Then I can stick with the champagne theme."

"Got it." He lifted his arm, and almost instantly, one of the bartenders hurried over. Xander ordered a Frenchie for me, which was like a flirtini but much better, and a whiskey-something for him.

Of course he drank whiskey.

Xander turned back, and I realized that while we waited for our alcohol, we'd have to fill the void with more small talk. My favorite. "I assume you spend long hours at work," I started. Not a super-strong opener. "I bet it's nice to kick back and have a drink when you're done."

He quirked a smile, flashing one out of two dimples. I'd take it. "A place like this is an inspiration. We don't want our business to be yet another brewpub. It has to have its own original flavor. We hired a designer specializing in restaurant interiors, but it didn't work out. Just more of the same." The bartender signaled that our drinks were ready. Xander paid and reached over someone's shoulder to grab them. He handed me mine.

I took a quick sip. "Maybe my friend Poppy can help," I offered. "Her main job at the moment is fundraising for a nonprofit, but she actually graduated from the University of Washington with a degree in interior design. She's super quirky and fun and has an extremely good eye. At the very least, she could give you a few pointers or recommend somebody here in Seattle who's different."

Xander took a swig of his whiskey drink, which was decidedly amber with no hint of fizz. "That would be great. After we meet for brunch tomorrow, maybe you and Poppy can drop by the brewery. That way, you can get an idea of the space and what we're looking for."

I nodded, grinning. Maybe this business arrangement could

work after all. A business-client relationship with a beautiful man who I definitely wanted to kiss.

"That's certainly a possibility," I said, taking another gulp of my drink. I'd only sipped the champagne at the table and didn't have any kind of reliable buzz, because I hadn't had any prewarning that I should've been fortifying for an encounter with *People's* Sexiest Man of All Time. I was going to need more alcohol to get through this evening.

He looked bemused. One side of his mouth quirked, becoming my second-favorite expression of his. "You're extremely easy to talk to."

"I am?" Nothing could've been more stunning.

"You are," he confirmed, swirling his drink, the amber liquid jumping up to the rim, leaving a streak as it sloshed back to the bottom. "You seem very comfortable with yourself."

It took everything I had not to burst out laughing.

Instead, I brought my long-stemmed glass up to hide a manic giggle. I couldn't say anything like, *Well, dude, I usually am around people unlike yourself.* But overall, I was happy I was appearing normal and didn't want to ruin it. So I took another mouthful of fortifying champagne mixed with something peachy and said, "You are, too."

Damn. Small talk never got any easier.

Chapter 9

I held Poppy's hair back as she emptied her stomach contents into my toilet. My bathroom was small for two, but we made it work. She knelt on the floor, hands gripping either side of the bowl, as I straddled the space above her, thankful I'd cleaned today.

"What are you still doing in here?" she asked on the end of a gasp. "I told you, you don't have to do this. It's vile."

"Throw up doesn't scare me," I told her for the fourth time, giving her shoulders another rub. Luckily, it didn't seem like she had much left in the tank. Exactly ten minutes after I'd introduced her to Xander and five minutes after she'd met Leo, she'd gotten sick. She'd booked out the front door of the Driftwood like she'd been running from Michael Myers, me in close pursuit. "I have an iron stomach," I said. "My parents used to call me unbreakable. They'd be hit with a horrible flu, and I would never get it."

"This is no bug. It's food poisoning," she moaned as I handed her a wet washcloth for her face. "If you'd eaten my lunch today, I guarantee you'd be doubled over. Clam chowder. I'll never be able to eat it again. No one is *that* unbreakable."

"Maybe," I said, scooting back so she had space to maneuver. "I've never had food poisoning."

"I have." She stood and shuffled to the sink, setting the cloth down and splashing water on her face. "It's the absolute worst." She cupped her fist, gathered some water, and took a gulp, swishing it around in her mouth before spitting it out. When she was done, she made her way out of the confined space to my love seat, which doubled as my one and only guest bed. I'd opened it up for her already. It had a mattress—if you could call it that—that was more like a cardboard box with a dip in the middle, accented with some lonely tufts of cotton on top. Poppy crawled onto it on all fours, like she didn't trust herself, grabbing the blanket, flinging it over her shoulders like a cape before curling onto her side. "Thanks for taking care of me."

"Anytime."

She bunched a pillow under her head, the moonlight filtering in through my windows casting shadows, illuminating the space enough to see without any lights on. I took my position on the chair, shifting the quilt I'd been using so I could sit.

"Go back to bed," she insisted. "I'll be fine. There can't be anything left in my gullet. I've lost count of how many times I've puked. The tank is finally empty."

"Five times. If you count behind the bar by the dumpster."

Her hands slid up to her face, covering it as she started to giggle. Then she flung her head back, chortling. "Oh lords, did you see their faces?" She held on to her poor stomach with one hand as she laughed. "Oh, Summer, I'm so sorry! I tore you away from Xander. That has to be a cardinal offense of the greatest order. I've failed you as a friend. Worst diva mama sidekick *ever*."

"You didn't tear me from anything." I giggled along with her. "Things were awkward anyway. Running into someone you're not prepared to see is always weird. And we haven't been each other's diva mama in years." Our inside joke dating back to the time we'd all turned twenty-one within a few months of each other. Jenny had done all our makeup, and we'd all decided for some nonsensical reason that we looked like hot diva mamas. The name had stuck. "But you did shock the hell out of them when you zipped out of there. I'd been eyeing the door all night, thinking about doing the same thing. You beat me to it."

"Don't make me laugh too hard," she cried. "It hurts. I'm not going to have to do any crunches for a week."

"You do crunches?"

"Hell no!" She was rocking back and forth now, both hands gripping her tummy. "And, good grief, you didn't give us adequate warning about Xander. That wasn't fair. The man is…"

"Hot?" I added helpfully.

"No. More than that. He's, like, rustic and…earthy."

"Rustic and earthy?" I chuckled. "I think you might have a temp. You just made him sound like a root vegetable or a wild mushroom. Are you saying he smells like dirt?"

She lifted her hand in a surrender gesture. After a minute, her laughter ebbed enough for her to speak. "Whew. That felt awful and wonderful at the same time." She rolled over, bringing the blanket up to her neck, staring at my ceiling. "No, he doesn't smell like dirt. At least, I didn't get a good whiff. He's just really sexy, but in a rough and tumble way. Salt-of-the-earth type, yet sculpted for normal consumption. Not my vibe at all. But did you see Leo? He was absolute *perfection.* Dressed immaculately in that cute blazer and those flat-front khakis, and oh, that clipped beard. I'm a sucker for nicely groomed facial hair." She sounded wistful. "I'm sad we only had five minutes together."

"Well, I might've done you a solid on that end." I hesitated for a moment, not sure I should spring it on her in her sickened state. I decided to go for it. "I kind of told Xander you're a fabulous interior designer and that he should contact you about decorating their microbrewery." I bit my lip.

"You did what?" She sat up quickly, then groaned and fell backward, straight into a Scarlett pose. "Have you lost your mind?"

I shrugged. "Nope, my brain is functioning at full capacity. I did it because you designing their bar would be a perfect fit. If flowers are Eve's thing, interior design is yours. And before you get all argumentative, I will acknowledge that acting is one of your great loves, too. But design is your passion. All you talked about during college was how you were going to redecorate the world in geometrics or floral patterns, depending on the day. You have to admit, you're crazy-good at it. Your house is *ah-maz-ing.* It's magazine-photo-worthy." I tried really hard not to be jealous every time I went over there, but I always was. The space wasn't much larger than mine, but her modern, chromatic design choices made it seem huge and airy. White walls, perfectly placed art pieces. It was a dream. "Xander and his group already hired a fancy restaurant designer, but they don't want more of the same, so they fired them. I mentioned you, and he seemed interested."

"Ugh," she moaned. "I love design work, and luckily for you, I've kept up my certifications just in case. But I also enjoy what I do now just as much. Fundraising and volunteering feeds a part of me that doesn't get nourished anywhere else."

"True," I said. "And I adore that about you. But you clock in at less than thirty hours a week doing that. Taking an odd interior design job here or there shouldn't interfere too much. I think Xander's launch deadline for the pub is a ways out. It might fulfill you even more to add another thing you love to your life. You never know." Poppy had previously worked at a major design firm downtown, a job she'd landed right out of college. She'd never said as much, but I had a hunch that no discernable recognition and not getting a promotion she'd wanted wore her out. She wasn't meant to be a cog in anyone's factory.

"It might add something," she hedged. "But it probably won't work out. Not after what happened with me bailing so quickly. I ran out of there like murder hornets were chasing me."

"They didn't actually *witness* you vomiting. I made sure to cover our tracks and shuttled you out of there quickly. I had the Uber guy pick us up a block away. We can lie and say you ran into an ex or something."

She started giggling again, running a hand over her face. "Well, I appreciate you being a great friend, as always. If they reach out, I'll figure out what to do. I'm pretty good about listening to my gut—when it's not upending itself. Now let's get some sleep. Don't you have your brunch thing tomorrow morning with the Marlboro Man?"

"I do," I said. "At least, I think I do. We didn't get a chance to confirm in person, but I'm assuming he won't change his mind." I shrugged. "If he does, I'm fine with that. If he's upset I ran after my friend, he's not worth it."

"You're being very grown-up about this," she murmured in a sleepy voice.

"Am I?" I said, rising out of the chair, heading to my own bed. "Whenever I think about him, my insides get fluttery and turn to jelly. I must be a convincing liar."

"No," she mumbled. "You're just a nice, sweet girl caught up in the game of love."

❊ ❊ ❊

My phone chimed, and I reached for it, wiping sleep from my eyes.

It was Xander.

HOPE YOUR FRIEND IS FEELING BETTER. STILL ON FOR THIS MORNING? IF NOT, NO WORRIES. I'M FREE ALL WEEK. X

Apparently, we hadn't fooled anyone last night. *Damn.* I wondered how much he'd actually seen. He and Leo had followed us out, but I'd thought we'd had a good lead on them.

It was eight thirty now.

We weren't set to meet until eleven.

I laid my phone down, massaging my tired face, leaning up on an elbow to confirm that Poppy was still snoozing on my rickety pullout. I hadn't heard her take another trip to the bathroom last night, but I might have slept through it. I'd never had food poisoning before and didn't want to wake her. It might take more than a night to recover.

After a moment, I picked up my phone and typed:

POPPY'S GOOD. STILL ASLEEP. DO YOU MIND MEETING EARLIER? THERE'S A DINER IN CAPTIOL HILL CALLED GLO'S. I DON'T WANT TO

WAKE HER, AND I NEED COFFEE SOON. LET ME KNOW IF THAT WORKS. S

It didn't take him long to reply.

PERFECT. MEET YOU AT 9:30.

I shot back:

GREAT. SEE YOU THEN.

"Now's not the time for flop sweat, body," I whispered to my uncooperative armpits and general crease joints as I crept out of bed as quietly as I could, trying to keep noise to a minimum.

My plan would be to hightail it to Glo's now because the lines were always long, especially on a Saturday. That way, I could grab a cup of coffee and center myself before Xander arrived.

At the end of my loft steps, the floorboards creaked. Poppy made some smacking sounds, ones that sounded remarkably close to baby Clara's, only louder and more adultlike.

She groaned as she turned over, her eyes fluttering open.

I stopped in front of my closet door.

"Are you going to brunch?" she asked groggily. "What time is it?"

"I was trying not to wake you," I whispered. "Yes, I'm going. But we're meeting earlier. I'm going to leave any minute. Sleep as long as you need."

"Okay, thanks," she said, turning on her side, bringing the blanket with her. "I'll take you up on it. I'm not sure my body is ready for anything more than lying here. It feels like a wet noodle."

I threw on a shirt and jeans. "I'll make you some tea and put it and a glass of water on the table."

"I'll take the water, no tea," she mumbled. "Anything with a smell is not welcome in my general vicinity."

I chuckled. "Got it."

Glo's was a ten-minute walk from my place. I pulled my hair back in a ponytail. It was clean enough. I brushed my teeth and washed my face. I didn't ever wear a ton of makeup, but I picked up my tube of mascara and brushed it on. Why not?

Heading for my fridge, I took out my cold-water pitcher and grabbed a fresh glass for Poppy. "Make sure you stare into his eyes," Poppy said, cracking an eyelid as I set the scentless refreshment next to her. "They say a lot about a person. I didn't get a good look at his last night before I had to heave-ho, *literally*. But eyes are the windows into the soul. Don't ever forget it. You can tell if someone's a creep or a liar if they have mean eyes."

"I'll be sure to check." I didn't want to open up an in-depth discussion about the fact I'd already analyzed everything about him, including his eyes. He had wonderfully intense eyes. In fact, I'd never seen anyone look at anything the way Xander seemed to gaze at the world. It was mesmerizing. I grabbed a light coat off the hook by my door. Skies were overcast, but it wasn't raining. This jacket had a hood, which would be good enough if it decided to drizzle. "Wish me luck."

"You don't need luck," Poppy said, her tone completely certain. "He'd be a fool not to be into you."

CHAPTER 10

Glo's was crowded, but not crushingly so. It took twelve minutes to be seated, and much to my relief, the server led me to a two-person table in a quiet spot. I'd just ordered coffee and was arranging my napkin on my lap when I glanced up.

My breath caught in my throat.

Xander stood in front of me, peeling off his leather coat, smiling. "Is this seat taken?" he asked charmingly.

"What are you doing here?" Was the first thing that tumbled out of my mouth. Then I almost slapped my forehead. "Sorry, let me start over. I wasn't expecting you until nine thirty. Please, sit." I gestured toward the vacant seat he was already getting ready to sit in. I didn't need my phone to tell me it was only ten after nine.

He chuckled as he sat. "I came early to snag a table. You beat me to it."

"I guess I did," I said, trying not to be overwhelmed as he

scooted closer with his tree trunk arms. He rested his elbows on the table, completely relaxed. "I thought the same thing. That, and I wanted to get out of the house so I wouldn't bother Poppy."

His eyes became hooded. "Is your friend okay? She didn't look so good last night."

"She is," I said, adjusting the napkin in my lap. "Just a nasty bout of food poisoning. It hit her quickly, so she ran. Needless to say, she's completely embarrassed. I hope you'll still consider contacting her. She's an excellent designer."

"Of course," he replied. "I wouldn't hold something like food poisoning against anyone. It's awful." He scratched the side of his head, and I couldn't look away. The man was utterly mesmerizing on every level. "I wish you would've told us. Leo had his car at the pub. We could've easily taken you home."

I shook my head, my nose crinkling. "Public retching is more for people who've known each other for longer than, you know, ten minutes." I raised my left eyebrow in a fairly good arch. Not as archy as last night's effort, but effective enough. "The Uber guy had to pull over twice, and it's a wonderful thing we'll never have to lay eyes on him again."

"Understood." Xander chuckled. "But it would've been all right with us. Leo was pretty concerned."

"We definitely appreciate the concern." I smiled. "I'll pass that on to Poppy. She'll be thrilled to hear Leo was interested in her well-being." I stopped myself midblab. I had to be careful. Poppy would be disappointed with me for sharing too much, but Xander was proving to be very easy to talk to.

Luckily, the waitress came over to top off my coffee. She glanced at Xander. "Would you like a cup?"

"Yes, thanks," Xander answered.

As she turned over the mug on a saucer in front of him, I watched her fully register him. Her eyes widened perceptibly as she cleared her throat, the pot jerking a bit to the left, a few dribbles plopping in the saucer. "I'll be back in a few minutes to take your order." She hurried off.

It was a small relief knowing he had that effect on other people, not just me.

"I apologize. I didn't bring along my sketchbook or anything like that," I began, trying to kick off this business meeting. "I was trying to get out of Poppy's way. But we can have a general conversation about what you're looking for, and I'll follow up in an email later today to sum up what we discuss."

"That's fine," he said, glancing at the menus the hostess had left behind when she'd seated me. "What's good here? I've only been a few times."

I picked up a menu, but I already knew what I wanted. "I'm a sucker for their Benedicts, but today I'm in the mood for the Eggs Californian."

"The Nicholas has been my go-to, but the Californian sounds good." He set the menu aside, flashing a dimple.

I swallowed, idly stroking my neck. "I live nearby, so I come here often. I'm surprised we haven't seen each other before."

"Maybe we have?" He sat back, stretching his long legs, thick arms crossed and resting against his ample chest. "You never know."

Oh, I'd know. "Yeah, maybe."

"Before, you mentioned you're from Spokane. So, what's your story? How did you end up here?"

"My story?" I chuckled, surprised where this conversation

seemed to be heading. "That's kind of a broad, all-encompassing question, don't you think?"

He shrugged, looking completely confident and totally at ease with himself. "I'm always interested in people's stories. The University of Washington brought you to this area, but does your family still live in Spokane? You mentioned you have a brother. Just wondering."

Huh.

Nowhere in my brain had I thought we'd get into all this. I was prepared to talk branding, but Xander wanted personal tidbits.

My story was complicated.

I poured a little cream into my coffee and took my time stirring, deciding on how much to tell this guy. A man I would likely see from now on in only a limited, business capacity. "Well, my parents are divorced," I started. "That happened around the time I was in junior high. They took their time and did it as nicely as they could. I don't feel scarred by it. They both stayed in Spokane. I do have a brother. He's two years older than me. His name is Gus, short for Gustav, which was my grandfather's name. My dad's dad." I brought the cup to my lips and took a sip, hoping the caffeine would fortify me as I told him the rest. It was always hard to talk about Gus. I adored my brother, but the story was deeply personal. "When I told you before that Gus wasn't married and I don't have any nieces or nephews, it's unlikely I ever will. Gus had a bad snowboarding accident when he was twelve and suffered a traumatic brain injury. My dad took us to the slopes almost every weekend. Gus had a real talent for the sport." I drank more coffee. "He was coming down a run of moguls, ones he'd been down a million times before, and spun out of control. His helmet flew off right before his head hit a patch of ice. It was just one of those freak accidents that you analyze and reanalyze a thousand times. I was only ten, but I remember every single detail. How his body looked broken. How he wouldn't wake up. My father's anguish. The concerned looks on everyone's faces. The blood. The ambulance ride to the hospital. Everything."

Xander sat forward in his seat, dropping his arms, his expression full of sympathy. "I'm so sorry. I didn't mean to dredge up painful memories. You don't have to share more if you don't want to."

"No, it's okay," I said, setting my cup down. It clinked against the saucer, which was somehow comforting. "He's actually doing great now. It's been fifteen years, and each year he surprises us by how much he can accomplish. He lives on his own now, with an aide. His goal is to live alone at some point. He's even talking about hitting the slopes again." I chuckled, remembering how excited Gus had been last week when we'd talked about it. "I really hope he does. Snowboarding is a true passion of his. He's desperately missed it all these years. We're all amazed by his progress. He keeps defying all the doctors' expectations. If he keeps it up at this rate, he could live independently in a year or two. And who knows, he might get married one day, and I could be an aunt. We always say the sky's the limit for Gus. There's no keeping him bound by our boring rules."

"Wow, he sounds amazing," Xander said, respect in his tone. "You must miss him."

"I do," I said. "It's hard to be away for such long periods at a time. The first few years after the accident, things were incredibly hard, as you can imagine. Then my parents split up. It turned out to be impossible for them to stay married. The stress of caring for Gus was too intense. We found that tragedy either pushes you closer together or rips you apart. But after that, Gus kept getting better and better. It made us extremely close as a family, but in a new way. Because my parents weren't trying to live together, they found a new way to deal with each other, built on their shared love of helping Gus. He's actually been written up in a few medical journals over the years, touted as a walking miracle." I exhaled, giving Xander a small smile. "Gus and I talk a lot. I try to get back every few months. He's been to visit me a few times, but he gets anxious traveling." I cleared my throat, polishing off the last few drops of coffee. "Okay, enough about me. How about you? What's your story? You said you were from Southern California and that you came up here for a business opportunity. What else?"

Before he could answer, the waitress came to refill our cups. We gave her our respective orders, and she left.

Xander sat back, his position back to relaxed. "First, thanks for sharing your past with me. I'd love to meet your brother someday. He sounds like a fighter." He grinned. "It must run in the family." I refrained from arching another eyebrow at him, because redundant as it did run in the family. "I grew up in San Clemente, but my parents moved us there when I was six. I was born in South Carolina, along with my older sister, Margaret, who goes by Mags. She's the one with the two boys, my nephews, Dylan and Isaac. And I totally agree with you about a tragedy either bringing people together or tearing them apart." He brought his black coffee, no cream, to his lips, pausing thoughtfully before continuing. Once again, I was mesmerized by his actions. He could literally perform any mundane action in the world, and I wouldn't look away. "I told you the name of our brewpub is Zoe's Lager. But I didn't tell you it's named after my baby sister, Zoe, who was born a year after we moved to California. She died of a degenerative bone disease four years ago. She was fifteen. I promised her that someday I'd do something big for her. At the time, a bar wasn't in my sights, but she'd get a kick out of it nonetheless."

"Oh no." My voice projected the sadness and shock I felt by his admission. "I'm so sorry. As devastating as Gus's accident was, we've always been grateful he survived it. I can't imagine that kind of loss. My heart goes out to you, your parents, and your sister. Fifteen is so young."

"It was hard." He nodded. "But not a surprise." He set his coffee down. "She was born with the disease, and it'd been eating away at her for years. In the end, she was in so much pain it was a blessing it ended. In all honesty, I've never met a kinder, more gracious person in my entire life than Zoe. She brought something to the world that was incredibly special. She never complained and faced each morning like your brother, as a fighter. I miss her each and every day."

"I'm sure you do." Tears gathered at the corners of my eyes. I dabbed them quickly with my napkin. "What are the chances we both had family tragedies?" I wasn't sure what it meant, but my heart began to explore Xander in a new way, which was both frightening and exhilarating.

Yes, he was amazing to look at, but he clearly held greater depth—one born out of pain.

It changed you. I knew that firsthand.

He flashed both dimples. "I didn't know about Gus," he said, "but I sensed something about you from the first moment we met."

I sputtered, flustered, taking time to rearrange my napkin on my lap. "Our meeting started as a collision when you accidentally shouldered me into the wall. Hard to get a true sense of someone from an episode like that." I chuckled nervously, thankful my hands were occupied with a task.

"I'm really sorry about that, by the way," he said, his voice low. "I wasn't expecting anyone to be there. But even though I almost knocked you down, you were gracious, apologetic, and completely nice about the entire thing. If you hadn't disappeared so fast, I would've enjoyed talking with you longer."

"Well, we got a chance to talk the next day, thanks to my interfering friends," I confessed. "Jenny and Daniel kind of arranged that meet and greet. When I told them what happened in the hallway, Jenny took it upon herself to make the introduction official. I should've told you right then and there. I'm really sorry. I was just embarrassed."

"Don't be sorry. I figured it was a setup once I saw you." He grinned. "But I thought it was sweet. And I'm the one who needs to apologize. When you didn't answer my request for dinner, I sort of panicked. Leaving abruptly is one of my signature moves when I'm uncomfortable."

Panicked? Why would he panic?

"Oh," I said. "It's no big deal. You asked me out, and I should've said yes. Instead, I stood there like a dummy. It was awkward for both of us. If I was in your situation, I would've left, too."

He leaned forward. "You would've said yes? You don't have a boyfriend, then? I figured you did—do—which is why you didn't respond."

A mental picture of Stacy formed in my brain, intrusive and unwanted. I had no idea what she looked like, but my brain had conjured a stunning beauty, for no other reason than any woman on Xander's arm would likely be exactly that. I hesitated. "I'm not seeing anyone." I couldn't possibly tell him about the baby monitor. It would be mortifying. "But I figured you might…" I cleared my throat, struggling to find the appropriate way to indicate that I knew there was someone in his life, finally exchanging the coffee cup for a water glass and taking a small sip. "You know, I figured you had a girlfriend." That sounded lame, since he was the one who'd asked me out in the first place.

"I'm not attached to anyone."

Thank goodness the waitress picked now to set down our food.

I busied myself arranging the knife and fork in my hands. Tragedy aside, I knew Xander wasn't telling me everything. He might not be attached to anyone in his mind, but he was certainly keeping himself busy during the wee hours of the morning.

It gave me some fortification to move on. "So," I said, changing the subject as I gathered some eggs on my fork, "we've explored some of our personal backgrounds, now tell me about the microbrewery. I'm really interested in the concept. What makes it unique?"

He smiled. It was a glorious sight. "Other than specializing in craft brew, just about everything."

Chapter 11

You don't know for a fact he's lying," Poppy argued. "You're just assuming he omitted Stacy for convenience's sake. But there could be a perfectly logical explanation why he claims she's not in his life. What if he broke up with her yesterday? Then, technically, he's telling the truth, and he's not attached to her anymore."

I'd arrived home ten minutes ago, happy to see that Poppy was up and feeling better. She'd managed to stuff the rollout away and was curled up on the sofa. She was ready for smells, so I'd made her some tea and toast.

Outside, the sky was already clearing. It was turning into another beautiful Pacific Northwest day. My favorite kind, with deep-blue skies, a cool breeze, and the sun egging on the new spring buds. They couldn't arrive fast enough.

"It doesn't matter," I said, hedging. "There's something I haven't told you." I made my way to the love seat and sat at the other end, facing Poppy. "There was more phone sex. And even if he's no longer with Stacy at this very moment, I can't pretend it didn't happen. It makes me uncomfortable, since he asked me out before he had round two with her."

"What? Why didn't you tell us?" Poppy set her empty plate on the coffee table with a clatter. "More phone sex is pertinent information. How are we supposed to correctly guide you without the needed updates?"

"I didn't tell you because it was sort of horrifying. I didn't listen—well, technically, I listened for a teensy bit." I squeezed my index finger and thumb together, leaving a sliver of space between them. "But ultimately, I was a big girl and switched the monitor off. Then I scurried into Clara's room like a bridge troll and zonked out in the glider."

"Well…" She hesitated. "That's not fantastic news, but innocent until proven guilty and all that, right?" She sighed the exact same sigh I was feeling. "Honestly, I'm still rooting for him. He has nice eyes. He seems totally into you. I want to *believe* that he broke up with Stacy and is a decent human being, and I know you do, too. Maybe she just refuses to let go? You won't know until you ask. Are you going to see him again, like on a date? Or are you going to keep it professional for now?"

"I tried to keep it professional, but he insisted I visit the brewpub building with him tomorrow so I can get a feel for it. It's not necessary, since he told me enough about it, but he wouldn't take no for an answer. I ended up giving in. It feels kind of like a date."

"When are you going?" she asked.

"He's picking me up at noon. I told him I'd find my own ride, but he convinced me I shouldn't waste my money. And since he's the one footing the bill, I agreed."

"*Hmm.* The evidence is mounting he's a master at this," she said. "He knows you're tentative about being with him, but he's not exactly sure why. So, he's picking low-key meetups that won't stress you out. He's taking it slow, which is incredibly sexy. The man definitely has a thing for you."

I reached over and grabbed my water glass off the table. I was beginning to believe it, too. "Aside from him not admitting he has a girlfriend, we talked about Gus." Overall, it'd been a very enjoyable breakfast. After the awkwardness of the girlfriend omission, we'd chatted about his business, his partners Leo and Chris—he'd known them since boyhood—and about his travels. He'd visited quite a few countries.

"That's great," she said. "See, you guys are getting along swimmingly."

"I asked about his family, too." I filled her in about his sister Zoe and where the brewpub's name, Zoe's Lager, came from.

"Oh goodness." She covered her mouth with a gasp. "That's awful. That poor girl. God rest her soul. Tragedy shapes people. As you know too well. If he loved his sister as much as he says and is honoring her memory so sweetly, that just legitimizes my initial thoughts about his character. If you can, go into this meet tomorrow with an open mind. Give him a chance to explain himself." She held up her hand, preempting any pushback on my part. And my part had reasonable pushback to give. "And if you find out he's two-timing Stacy, you never have to see him again. I promise. His name will be worse than mud—it'll be dirty sludgeman. But if there's a reasonable explanation for Stacy, or why he claims he's not with her, at least give him a chance to spell it out." She scooched forward, her expression intent.

"You're not fooling anyone, by the way. We can tell you really, really like this guy. I'm going to be a queen and not dredge up the Mitch stuff again, but you have to admit Xander makes you feel something that no one else has in a long time." She was right. He did. "I know you're scared." She reached out, settling her hand on my bent knee, giving it a shake. So Poppy. "And you have every right to be. Falling for the confident, alpha male has been pummeled out of your comfort zone by dumb, uncaring lugs. In nurturing Gus, you saw firsthand how the world treated him, and you formed a protective shell. It only makes sense. But give Xander a chance. I have a good hunch about this one. If he's a bad egg, I'll go on one of those adventure trips you're always trying to get me to take. You name the place, and I'll scale the mountain or traverse a river, or whatever it is you're trying to ruin my life with."

I chuckled, nodding thoughtfully. The rest of us had been wanting to take a girls' trip with a little action, but Poppy was more of a lie-on-the-beach-and-sip-a-fruity-drink type. "You know, I've never connected my preference in men with what happened to Gus. But you might be on to something. I do feel protective of myself and my family after all we've been through. Arrogant, confident people have always been the toughest on Gus. They have little patience with someone who has to take his time doing things."

"How did Xander react when you told him Gus's story?" Poppy asked, settling back in her seat. "Did you look him in the eye when he responded? Please tell me you looked him in the eye."

"Of course I did," I said, laughing. "He seemed genuinely affected. He responded in all the appropriate ways. He even said he'd like to meet him one day."

"See? That's something, then."

"Oh, and to blissfully change the subject, Leo's going to be getting a hold of you in the next few days. I gave Xander your number." Her expression morphed in an instant, eyes going wide, her Cupid mouth forming a perfect O. "But just so you know, they saw us by the dumpster. They knew you were sick." I continued hurriedly, "But the good news is, they were both very concerned. Xander was miffed because we didn't ask them to drive us home."

Poppy sputtered, "Oh, good *gracious*! Leo saw me retching? *Gah.* That ranks at the bottom of awesome first impressions. They wanted to drive us home? I don't think so." She began to giggle uncontrollably. "Can you imagine? 'Nice to meet you, and oh, could you pull over to the curb while I vomit out your car door?' Thank all the stars in the universe that didn't happen. I'm not sure I'll be able to look him in the eye again, but in case you were wondering, his are *spectacular*. Off-the-charts inspiring." Her gaze drifted somewhere over my shoulder.

I snapped my fingers in front of her, chuckling. "Come back to the here and now, sweet Poppy. I hope you two hit it off. He seems nice and totally your type." I stood. "Now, if you'll excuse me, I need to get to work. I have this vision of a logo floating around in my brain that might be perfect for Zoe's. But stay as long as you like. You can nap here or in my bed." I gestured toward the loft.

"Absolutely not," she said, getting to her feet, albeit a little wobbly, but not too bad. "It's time for me to go home. If these guys are serious about hiring me to do some design work, I'll have to dig out all my magazines. I packed my favorite stacks away a couple years ago." She nibbled at the edge of her lip. "If they want to do something eclectic, I may have just the thing. Of course, I'm going to need to see the space first and understand the concept. I've always wanted to do a restaurant or a bar. They always gave those jobs to Heidi and Joel at the firm. The dream team." She snorted. "Every single time, I knew I could've done a better job."

"Seeing the place first, huh? How about you come with me tomorrow? That way, it won't be awkward between Xander and me, and it definitely won't be a date. You can be our buffer. It's perfect."

"Not a chance," she replied, pinning her eyes on me like someone who knows she's being used for her wingwoman abilities. "You're doing this on your hot-guy bike alone. It'll be a piece of cake. A creamy, dreamy cheesecake with a cherry on top. I won't even know for a few days if they're interested. So much to think about."

"Okay, fine. I'll go alone. But if the wheels fall off, I'm blaming you." I gave her a quick hug on her way out. "I'm excited for you to get this job. This could be the start of something fun. If Zoe's is successful, the word will get out."

"Let's not get ahead of ourselves." She shrugged her coat on, pulling her fabulous-looking hair out of the collar. Poppy had thick, wavy blonde hair that always seemed to know what to do. Even after a night of vomiting. "But yes, it could be totally great. I'm warming up to the idea of adding yet another thing to my life. I thrive on hectic. Thanks for thinking of me."

"Of course."

Once my pal was gone, I settled down to work.

By the time I looked up again, it was edging toward dinnertime. I'd been working for the last six hours nonstop, with only a few breaks here and there. Even though they hadn't paid me a retainer yet, Xander and I had an agreement for me to begin. Everything would get sorted, and I was too restless thinking about it. The drive to get the logo absolutely perfect was intense. I'd designed and redesigned it more than anything else I'd done since I'd started in this field.

In the end, I was happy with the three possible directions. My favorite was a subtle heart hidden inside the foam on a beer stein, with *Zoe's* curving above and *Lager* below, the two words connected by the S in Zoe's and the R in Lager by a loopy line cutting through the foam. You wouldn't know the heart was there unless you were looking for it.

All three designs were rough and unpolished, giving the client space to choose which avenue to pursue. My normal strategy.

I yawned, getting up to stretch as I wandered into the kitchen. I picked up my phone. I fielded a few texts from Eve and Jenny. I'd texted them earlier, filling them in on what had gone down last night with Poppy and breakfast with Xander. They'd both been horrified to learn that we'd left because Poppy had been puking her guts out. We hadn't told them then because we hadn't wanted to ruin their nights.

As I was typing something to Eve, a text came in from Xander.

LOOKING FORWARD TO TOMORROW. I THINK YOU'LL ENJOY THE LOCATION. IT'S AN OLD WAREHOUSE BY THE WATER. PICK YOU UP AT NOON. X

I typed back:

GREAT. SPENT THE DAY WORKING ON DESIGNS. I THINK YOU'LL BE PLEASED. S

I'd given the man my address at the restaurant. A little fluttering came from my rib cage, but with a few easy breaths, I was able to calm it down. After chatting with him about his family and business, I knew I liked him as a person. I wasn't expecting anything more.

My phone beeped again.

I'M SURE THEY'RE GREAT. HEY, WHAT ARE YOU DOING TONIGHT?

I arched my eyebrow at my phone. It had zero effect on the tech. I wandered over to my favorite chair and sat, contemplating what to write.

NOTHING MUCH. GOING TO CALL IT AN EARLY NIGHT AFTER ALL THE EXCITEMENT WE HAD AT THE DRIFTWOOD.

His response was immediate, and a hot rush zipped through my body.

A FRIEND OF MINE'S BAND IS PLAYING DOWN AT PIER 62 TONIGHT. THE WEATHER'S FINALLY COOPERATING. LEO, CHRIS, MOLLY, AND I ARE HEADING DOWN TO WATCH. WANT TO JOIN US?

When I didn't answer quickly enough, he added:

NO PRESSURE. YOU MENTIONED YOU WERE A FAN OF THE SEATTLE MUSIC SCENE, SO I THOUGHT THIS MIGHT BE FUN. FEEL FREE TO INVITE ANY OF YOUR FRIENDS. IT'S CASUAL.

So not really a date?

A low-key group gathering with all of his business partners?

My friends were right, he was kind of a master at this. I did enjoy the Seattle music scene. I don't know many people my age who didn't. It was phenomenal. You could find a band playing almost anywhere, any day of the week. And he was right, the warmer weather had ushered in outdoor concerts, which I adored.

WHAT TIME? POPPY MIGHT BE FREE IF SHE'S FEELING BETTER. I'LL

CHECK WITH HER.

As much as I was willing to go alone, I knew I wouldn't have the guts. If Poppy couldn't go with me, I'd take a rain check.

He responded quickly.

WE'RE MEETING AT THE WHITE HORSE AT EIGHT FOR A DRINK.

The White Horse Tavern was a fun, eclectic bar downtown a short walk away from the pier. I'd been there a few times. I glanced at the clock. That gave me a little more than an hour to get myself ready, both physically and emotionally. If that was even possible. My brain didn't exactly work perfectly when I was around him. Although, I had to admit, our chat over breakfast had been fluid and comfortable once we'd gotten into a rhythm. So, I'd mastered some viable technique, at least. I mean, we hadn't jumped each other across the table in a fit of uncontrollable lust, even though there'd been some serious energy zipping between us, so that had been a positive step in the right direction.

A picture of the resplendent Stacy popped into my brain. *Jeez.* If anything, I could count on flashes of her to ground me around Xander.

WILL TRY TO MAKE IT. I'LL TEXT YOU FOR SURE ONCE I KNOW.

He replied:

LOOKING FORWARD TO SEEING YOU AND POPPY.

He was good. I'd give him that.

Chapter 12

"Summer and Xander sittin' in a tree, K-I-S-S-I-N—" I elbowed Poppy playfully. "*Ow.* That was uncalled for," she responded, giggling. The food poisoning had passed in its entirety, and she was feeling back to her old self and had agreed that a night out would be nice, particularly since Leo was involved. "I'm just calling this what it is," she insisted. "You two are going on a date. Datey, datey, date, date. It's been a while for you, so we're celebrating. It was a big-girl thing to do to say yes. You hopped right on that hot-guy bike without needing a leg up." She patted my leg. "I'm so proud."

"It's not a date." I sat next to her in the back of the Uber. We were three minutes from the White Horse Tavern. "It's a group of people getting together to see an outdoor concert. We've literally done this five thousand times before. It's not a date." I was pretty sure it was a date, but I wasn't ready for it to be a date. So, in my mind, it wasn't. All fixed.

"The man asked you out. You accepted. It's a date."

I turned, giving her a partial squint. A halfhearted stink eye. "If I'm on a date, then you are, too. Leo's going to be there, and you've been hot for him since the moment you feasted your greedy little eyes on him. It's literally the only reason you agreed to come with me tonight. All I hear about is how his facial hair is perfectly trimmed, and you love looking into 'the two dreamy windows to his soul.' If anybody's going to be K-I-S-S-I-N-G, it's going to be the two of you. Plus, Xander's taken." I crossed my arms.

Once the picture of Stacy had formed in my mind, she hadn't left my brain willingly. So, my aim was to enjoy a fun night out with a new group of friends I'd just met and not view this as a date. Poppy wasn't helping.

The fact that Xander and I had both gone through personal trauma in our lives had connected us on a different level. We'd both felt it. When we'd parted ways outside Glo's, it'd felt like we were forming the beginnings of a comfortable friendship, which was probably why he'd asked me to join him and his friends tonight. Was I interested in cultivating that?

Yes, I was.

It would be fun being friends with owners of a craft brewery. I could see lots of friend outings there in our future.

"Man, I hope there's kissing," Poppy lamented. "I haven't had a good kiss in months. Not to mention sex. My lady parts are starting to resemble a dystopian landscape. I wouldn't mind taking a bite out of that perfectly curated beard. But Leo didn't ask me to come tonight, you did. Because this is *your* date. I'm just wingwomaning."

I snorted. Poppy wasn't exactly a reliable wingwoman.

Most of the time, she ended up wandering off to do her own thing. But I loved her anyway. It was hard not to. "Don't lie to me," I warned. "You jumped at this invitation, scrapping plans with your sister in a red-hot minute, just to be near Leo. Don't pretend otherwise."

Poppy swished a hand. "Annabel can deal. She's got friends in the area. She'll find something to do."

I chuckled. "You literally dumped plans with your baby sister, who just arrived from Colorado a few hours ago, so you could be near the guy who rocks a pair of khakis. Did you even consider inviting her to come with us?" I enjoyed Poppy's sister Annabel immensely. I'd known she was coming to town, but I hadn't known it would be today. Poppy might not have even known. Annabel did her own thing, she always had. Where Poppy was particular, Annabel was fluid. She and Poppy were polar opposites in almost everything except humor. There, they were a match made in dramatic heaven. It was fun to see the two of them riff off of each other. It would've been fun if she'd joined us.

"What, and have my sister snatch all the attention away from the hottest guy I've met in a long time? May I remind you, Annabel resembles an Amazon goddess. So, hell no, I didn't invite her!" Poppy hooted, slapping her knee. She was a one-woman show tonight. "Okay, okay, I actually did invite her—tall, annoying goddess genes aside—but she wanted to do her own thing. She even looked relieved I was canceling. The nerve!" Poppy and Annabel had been very close growing up, only a year and a half apart. I knew Annabel missed her big sister. She'd come to visit quite a bit over the years and was contemplating a permanent move to Seattle. "She mentioned something about meeting up with a friend she's been corresponding with online, but she was cagey about it." Poppy waggled her eyebrows. "I think it's a love interest, but I couldn't get her to spill no matter how I tried—and I gave her the fourth degree, believe me." Poppy barreled on, filling our car ride with easy humor, knowing I was nervous for my nondate. "She actually told me not to wait up. Which, I mean, I wouldn't anyway. My place is the size of a cracker box, and even though my couch is a better pullout situation than yours, it's in the living room, and I sleep like the dead." She shrugged. "Plus, I'm not her mother. She's allowed to do what she wants. Speaking of mothers, I'm pretty sure the same woman who birthed Wonder Woman gave birth to her. She resembles no women in our family." Poppy giggled. I rolled my eyes, chuckling along. "I'm kidding, of course. She looks exactly like my father, but more feminine. She got his height and his athletic ability and skin that easily tans. By all means, I should hate her, but I choose to love her anyway. I have such a big heart." Poppy sighed, placing a hand over her heart. "It's a heavy burden, but she's a good egg, so I endure." Poppy absolutely adored her sister. She doted on her and raved about her constantly.

I was laughing as the Uber pulled up in front of the White Horse Tavern. I'd heard all this about Annabel before, of course, but it was still funny. Annabel herself was always completely self-deprecating. But Poppy was right, she was gorgeous.

Abruptly, I stopped laughing, realizing where my decision to say yes to Xander had led me. Jitters took over. I was about to spend the evening with a man who had had a profound emotional effect on me a few scant hours ago, and I would be forced to pretend I wasn't interested because he had a girlfriend.

I was a terrible liar. He'd see right through me. Everyone would.

I was questioning my terrible judgment when Poppy grabbed my hand, marching me forward. "I know this is out of your comfort zone, so we're doing this together. I won't leave your side."

"Please," I scoffed, following along reluctantly. "The minute you see a shiny object—that object being Leo—you're going to be completely absorbed."

"Maybe, but I promise to keep you in my heart."

"Very touching."

* * *

"I think Poppy and Leo are really into each other," Xander confided as we walked toward Pier 62. We trailed the group. Not exactly on purpose, but kind of?

Up ahead, Chris and Molly led the way, followed by Poppy and Leo, who were laughing easily, heads together. They'd been enamored of each other the entire night. As predicted, Poppy had been a terrible wingwoman, but I didn't blame her. It was exciting to have a new love interest. She'd been in two serious relationships since college, and both of them had left her heartbroken.

Leaving both men had been for the best, but especially Michael, her last serious boyfriend. He'd been on the controlling side, and it'd gotten incrementally worse leading up to the split. It'd been a tough break, because she'd loved him and had tried for a long time to make it work. He'd refused to let go, causing them to get back together and break up several times. He'd finally moved out of state, and she'd been able to breathe again and start mending the hurt. She'd needed time to recoup.

But now she was ready, and Leo seemed like a great guy to start something new with.

"I'm so excited for her," I told Xander. "She deserves to be happy."

He cocked a goofy grin in my direction. *Good gods.* He had to stop doing that. So distracting. "Don't we all?"

"Yes, we do." I chuckled. "I just mean she's just getting over a rough patch, so it's nice to see her ready to jump into dating again."

"Leo just got out of a long-term relationship, too. They were together six years."

I whistled. That was basically six times the length of time I'd been with someone.

"It's been hard for him," Xander went on. "He thought they were going to get married, but she ended things abruptly after meeting someone else. So, seeing him interested in your friend is great. I hope they decide to take it to the next level."

"Me, too," I said, crossing my arms in front of my chest, trying not to let my teeth chatter. I'd worn layers underneath a light coat, but as we moved closer to the bay, it was getting decidedly chillier. I adored the waterfront. There was so much to do. But I should've dressed warmer. Outdoors in the spring in Seattle could be unpredictable.

Poppy would blame my unconscious mind for giving me a reason to cut out early. She was probably right. Sometimes my brain took care of me that way.

"Are you cold?" Xander asked, concerned.

I shook my head. "No, I'm fine." Lying was the easiest way to go.

"Like I told you tonight, I run hot, so you're welcome to use my jacket anytime." He chuckled.

When he'd told me that, I'd almost fallen off my stool.

The man didn't realize how sexy he was. Saying things like that, as if they weren't a big deal, had sent the hummingbird fluttering down south without taking a moment to consult my wishes. It'd pretty much roosted there all evening.

I had to admit, when Xander was around, there was no keeping that bird caged. He had the ability to pick the lock. Or maybe the door just flew open the minute he spoke? No, the minute I looked at him?

Hard to know, but I couldn't tame that busy flapper no matter how I tried.

It was kind of a bummer, considering.

Thank goodness Chris's girlfriend, Molly, had been there. She'd been my conversation savior. She'd recently graduated from college and had moved up from Oregon. She'd met Chris shortly after that. She'd been a dream to talk to, cheerful and upbeat, curious about how I'd met Xander. She'd laughed at the stories about the hallway collision and the setup gone wrong, appreciating the humor, because they were funny. How many couples meet by crashing into each other in a friend's hallway?

I'd ended up spending a lot of time chatting with her because it'd been much easier than turning my full attention on Xander. He was just too…all-encompassing.

Poppy could learn a thing or two about wingwoman duties from Molly. Although, to Poppy's credit, Molly had had no idea she'd been assisting me in that job. I'd just been grateful she'd been there.

Now I was on my own.

Xander and I walked in silence for a few minutes. As we got closer to the pier, a crowd was beginning to gather. Xander had mentioned the band name, but I'd never heard of them before. He'd described their songs as an eclectic indie mix, which was certainly a vibe here. Local bands could pack in the crowds. I was looking forward to it.

A few food trucks sat off to the side. Xander gestured at one that served ice cream. "Do you want to get some dessert?"

"Sure, that sounds great," I replied. I had a sweet tooth. I couldn't deny it.

We veered off, walking shoulder to shoulder. It felt nice. I was happy to be outside the confines of the bar. I could breathe easier out here. The food truck was called Sweet + Scoop. We got in the short line. At the counter, I tried to take out my wallet, but Xander shook his head. "It's on me. What would you like?"

"I'll take one scoop of red velvet in a cup."

"That sounds good. I'll have the same." He gave the young girl in the truck our order, and a few minutes later, she handed us cups and told us to have a good night.

"Let's head over by the railing. We still have time before the band starts." He gestured with his head as he ate a bite of ice cream. "This is good."

"It is," I agreed, trying not to smack. "I've had their ice cream one time before, and it was delicious. It was some sort of Cap'n Crunch cereal peanut butter mix that was really good."

"I'll have to try that sometime." He stopped at an open spot. Elliott Bay was set out before us, rippling like a dark, rich blanket. He put his foot on a rail, resting his elbows on top.

The energy zipping between us was unmistakable. I tried to focus on my sweet treat instead. I didn't feel like this was the time or place to discuss Stacy. It was kind of a date, but not really a date. I just wanted to have a nice, uncomplicated night.

"Seattle, as a city, really has its own flavor," he commented. "It's nothing like where I grew up. I really like it."

I nodded. "I haven't visited many other cities, but I think it's wonderful. It feels like home. There always are great nature treks nearby. Getting to a beach town on the coast is easy. The weather's temperate. I could do without some of the rain, but it rains way less than people think. It's a good way to keep the riffraff out." I took another bite of ice cream. So creamy.

"Am I considered riffraff?" he asked good-naturedly.

"Oh, totally," I deadpanned. "Californians are the worst, too. They think they're going to catch waves right out in the bay." I aimed my spoon off into the dark distance. "They have no idea what they're in for. And they're always complaining it's too cold."

He tossed his head back, laughing. "I did not bring my surfboard." Of course he had a surfboard. "And, as this has already been covered a few times this evening, I never get cold."

I shivered. It was involuntary. "I guess you can stay." I shrugged.

"Here, let me give you my coat." He balanced his cup of ice cream on the railing and began to shrug off his leather jacket.

"No, *no*. Really. I'm fine." I shook my head adamantly. "Once we get in the crowd and out of the breeze, I'll warm up."

"Are you sure?"

"Yes. Very."

"Okay." He put it back on. "I guess getting ice cream was a little off the mark for what's turning out to be a breezy, cool night."

I'd just shoveled the last of the sweet deliciousness into my mouth. "Not at all," I said. "I love dessert. It's my favorite meal."

He grinned. "I have to keep that in mind. I guess we should make our way over to the venue so we can get you out of the cold."

We began to walk. "I'm surprised Poppy hasn't already texted me, wondering where I went."

"You guys seem to have a really close friendship."

We wove in between people heading toward the stage. Concerts were free on the pier. They'd just brought them back fairly recently. There were lots of couples laughing and holding hands. Groups of college kids. Seattle was so much fun. "We are." I tossed my cup and spoon into a garbage can as we passed. Xander did the same. "Eve, the redhead you met last night, and I were roommates freshmen year. Poppy and Jenny lived next door. It was a fairly instantaneous friendship between the four of us. Everything just clicked. We studied together, went to parties together, went on vacations together. It was a lot of fun. It probably helped that we didn't continue living in close quarters after sophomore year, which can easily sour a friendship. We all had different roommates, but it seems our bond couldn't be broken." I was so glad and thankful to have them in my life. "It helped that we all stayed in Seattle. Poppy, Eve, and I all live in Capitol Hill and work mostly from home, so we see each other regularly. Though, that might change now that Eve has the flower shop business starting, as she'll be in Ballard a lot. Jenny has a full schedule, which has always been her norm. She's married now with a new baby, so that has definitely changed the dynamic. Even though she isn't with us as much as she used to be, we keep her in the loop as much as we can."

"When she needed you for emergency babysitting, you were there for her."

Poppy waved up ahead. I waved back. "Of course." Xander was getting a lot of looks from the women around us. I was trying not to feel unnerved. "We'd do anything for each other. Jenny couldn't decide who to make Clara's godmother, so we all are." I giggled. "That baby is going to be getting a mountain of gifts every year."

"There you guys are." Poppy was literally bouncing on her feet as she came to meet us. The music hadn't started yet, but several people had personal speakers going. "The band's about start. Come on, we're over here."

We trailed behind as she made her way through the crowd to where the group was situated fairly close to the stage. Once the music came on, Xander and I wouldn't be able to talk. I was disappointed, but relieved at the same time.

Xander began chatting with Leo. Poppy leaned in. "Are you okay? Do you want to stay? Do you want to go? What's the deal?"

"I'm fine," I told her. "It's been nice." I didn't tell her that I'd spent most of the evening chatting with Molly. One thing at a time.

"Great!" she replied jubilantly. "Leo is *ahhhh*-mazing. We've been having the best time." She whispered directly in my ear, "I'm pretty sure he's going to ask me out."

"If he doesn't, I'll lose my wager," I snarked back quietly.

"You bet on us?"

"Only in my mind." I laughed. "Of course he's going to ask you out. He's clearly smitten."

"He is? I can never tell these things. When I'm talking to

people, they always seem happy, but that doesn't mean they're going to ask me out."

"That's because it's hard not to be happy around you," I told her, slinging my arm around her shoulders right as the band came onstage. "You're just naturally magnetic and bring out the best in people."

"*Aw*, thanks, Summy. You are, too."

I snorted. It sounded like a wild boar pawing at the ground. "Not even close."

* * *

Poppy yawned. "That was a fun night. The band was really good. I'd never heard of them before, but I'd go see them again."

My head reclined against the back of the Uber seat. We were on our way home. "It was fun."

"Leo didn't ask me out, which is kind of a bummer, but he asked for my number, even though you said Xander already had it, so that's something."

"Xander told me Leo just got out of a six-year relationship. He probably wants to take it slow, but he was totally into you. He never left your side."

"Six years? Wowza, that's a long time. I bet they were pretty serious." She bit her lip.

I patted her leg. "You have nothing to worry about. She ended it with him, so he's probably a little bruised. He'll come around soon enough."

"Speaking of people who didn't leave each other's sides." She hugged my arm, yawning as she rested her head on my shoulder. "That earthy hunk of a man stood so close to you that everybody in that place thought you were a couple. I saw a few women eyeing him, but they didn't dare come over to investigate."

"He was just being a gentleman, trying to keep me warm. I didn't dress for the weather."

"Yeah, keep telling yourself that." She snorted. It sounded like a cute baby gurgle. "You're such a dork about this stuff." She shook me lightly. "Honestly, the sparks you were giving off were so charged, a mini fireworks display was popping off above your heads."

I chuckled. "How would you know? You were too busy shooting off your own fireworks," I teased.

"Touché." She sighed. "Two best friends about to date two best friends. How weird is that?"

"No," I corrected, "you're about to date Leo. I'm in a business relationship with a guy who has a girlfriend. There's a huge difference."

"No guy who acted like Xander did tonight has a girlfriend. He was completely focused on you, your happiness, your well-being, and your warmth. Everybody there thought you were couple. Whatever is going on with this Stacy girl is nothing serious. Anyway, you two can work it all out tomorrow when you see him. There's no way those sparks are going to die down anytime soon. You guys will probably set the brewery on fire. Mark my words. It's going to be epic!"

"We will not be setting anything on fire."

"Will too."

Chapter 13

Xander pulled up to the curb the next day at noon, as promised, on a motorcycle. A freaking *mo-tor-cy-cle.* I'd been leaning against the small retaining wall in front of the house and spotted the bike a block away. I'd known it was him.

Of course he had a motorcycle. The leather jacket and boots were dead giveaways.

He parked and pulled off his helmet, grinning like nothing was amiss and that he hadn't told me what mode of transportation we'd be using, even though he'd had ample time to do so. No wonder his hair had been tousled yesterday at breakfast. He hadn't come in with a helmet and hadn't mentioned a motorcycle, so I hadn't thought much about it.

He took in my semistunned expression, and his smile faded. "Is this okay? I'm sorry I didn't tell you about the bike. I thought I'd leave it as a surprise. We're lucky it's not raining today. I was going to borrow Leo's car if necessary." He situated his helmet under his arm. "We don't have to ride. We can call an Uber. If you're not comfortable, that's no problem at all."

I swallowed and took a tentative step forward. "It's fine… I've just never ridden on a motorcycle before." Having a brother with a traumatic brain injury meant riding motorized two-wheeled transportation was not on my to-do list. Honestly, though, I had no idea what the accident rates were. I just knew they were high, and if I got hurt, it would break my parents.

He read my emotions correctly and started to dismount. "Let's take an Uber. I'm totally fine with that. I'm sorry I didn't let you know first. That's on me. I should've told you last night."

"No. It's okay. Ballard isn't far. I'll be fine if you don't take the highway."

He paused, studying me. "Are you sure? If it's any help, I'm an excellent driver. Very cautious. I got this the year after Zoe died. It was me giving the middle finger to the world. The plan was to keep it for a short time, but I fell in love with riding it. And in Seattle, it's a lifesaver. It's so much easier to park around town. I promise to go slow and remain vigilant."

I smiled. "It's not you I'm worried about." His eyes were solidly on me. His gaze was intense and flecked with emotion.

We stared at each other for a beat too long.

I looked away, flustered and blushing. Gooseflesh broke out along my skin. I'd never been more turned on in my entire life. His gaze was potent. It'd held intent. And it'd been directed at me. I struggled to pretend it hadn't affected me. Being alone with him was much different than being in a restaurant full of people or in a group of people enjoying music.

This was just him and me.

Good luck ignoring that, Summer.

He handed me his extra helmet, which I put on.

When I was done, he patted the seat behind him. "Use that foot peg." He gestured at the small, cylindrical pedal. "Then just swing your leg over." I wasn't coordinated enough and had to grab on to his shoulder to steady myself.

Once I was settled behind him, there wasn't much room left over. I was pressed tightly against his back and would be for the entirety of the ride.

"You can hold on to me, or there is a grip bar behind you," he instructed as he revved the motor and the bike purred.

All the sensations were completely overwhelming. I felt a little light-headed.

As he pulled away from the curb, I wrapped my arms around his midsection, holding on right above his belly button. He was hard all over. Every square inch of him. Not an ounce of fat.

The ride itself was exhilarating.

As we wound out of Capitol Hill, the views of the bay and the islands were extraordinary. The wind rushed around us, tousling the ends of my hair, flipping them every which way. It was freeing. Gus had tried to explain years ago what it was like when he was in the air in midtrick on a snowboard. The pure exhilaration was like nothing else he'd ever come close to feeling in his life. I was a decent skier, but I'd never had the heart to learn to snowboard after Gus's accident. This might be similar, in a lower-key kind of way.

"How are you doing back there?" Xander called, turning his head to the side so he could hear my retort.

I yelled back, "Great! I'm actually having fun."

"Good to hear. We'll be there soon."

The longer the ride went on, the more comfortable I became,

my front naturally molding to Xander's back, my hands splayed against his chest. I had to stop myself at one point when I realized I'd been on the verge of kneading him.

Xander pulled into an alley behind a squat two-story building. It was gray and peeling with age. It was pretty much what I'd imagined.

He shut off the bike. Xander dismounted first, then helped me off, setting both helmets casually on the seat. I followed him to the back door. He unlocked it and ushered me inside. The look of pride on his face was endearing. This was a big deal to him, as it should be.

A short hallway led to a small cubby-type office space on the left and storage on the right. The kitchen came next. It was almost completely bare except for some old metal countertops and leftover shelves lining the walls. No progress had been made in any stage of remodel.

"This will be the main bar area," Xander indicated as we entered a large, open expanse with high ceilings. It was larger than I'd expected. It was well lit with a number of windows lining the front, continuing almost to the ceiling. He'd already told me they were going to add more.

The space was wide open. An empty canvas.

As we moved toward the middle, he guided me around gently by the shoulders, motioning upward. A small balcony overlooked the room, a few small offices were set behind. "We haven't decided what to do up there yet," he said. "But those two rooms are large enough to host small groups. Either that, or we'll make them into our offices. There's a great view of the bay from up there, especially if we add more windows like we're talking about. We really want this place to have a natural feel.

I guess it all depends on what kind of a plan Poppy comes up with."

"You're going to hire her for sure?"

He nodded, casually grabbing my hand and leading me toward a small, open staircase against one wall. His touch felt electric. Wings began to flutter and bop against my rib cage. He'd blown up the entire birdcage. There was no stopping it now.

At the top, he dropped my hand as he showed me around the space. He was right, the rooms were fairly large. You could get a couple of groups in there, no problem. I glanced up at the ceiling. "It would be great to enhance the natural light in these rooms with a skylight or two."

"Yeah, we tossed that idea around." He gestured toward the outside wall. "For sure we'll add glass there, so we get a view of the bay from up here." As he turned, talking about more plans, his massive bicep dragged against my shoulder. He stood so close, and I was beginning to sweat. Scratch that, I'd *been* sweating. But it was getting decidedly worse. His proximity was also impeding my listening skills. I'd hardly heard a word he was saying. He was just so damn comfortable with himself. It was like we were old friends catching up, except we were new friends with kinetic energy sizzling between us.

And of course, the handholding. Old friends did *not* hold hands.

Microscopic atoms had to be bouncing off his body, then hurtling against mine at breakneck speeds. If human skin could give off sparks, we'd be starting a fire. Poppy's prediction had been right. We were in the process of igniting this place with nothing more than our hands touching. *Dang it.*

I abruptly turned and made my way out the door, heading along the balcony, taking in a few slow breaths to steady myself.

Xander followed, coming to stand next to me, like everything was still completely normal, resting his elbows on top of the railing, both of us looking down on what would become the pub below. "So, what do you think?" he asked, turning, his dimples on full display. His excitement was tangible. This was a labor of love. His dream was coming to fruition.

I made the mistake of staring.

Our eyes locked again.

Nothing in the world could tear me away. An earthquake could raze the city, and I wouldn't stop looking. He was an enigma. A big, hunky, manly, rough, earthy enigma. He was impossible to resist. Watching him straighten from the railing was an out-of-body experience. He moved toward me in slow motion.

This was a dream. It couldn't be real. I knew what was coming and had no intention of stopping it.

We met in the middle, my head falling to the side on its own. When our lips finally touched, flames engulfed me. No, a grenade. An explosion detonated inside my skull, releasing big, bright, noisy currents of energy. They cycled through me like shockwaves.

My back was suddenly up against the wall. I barely noticed. My feet arched up higher. My mouth was open, his tongue intertwining with mine, deep and thorough. His lips were hot. My eyes were shut. All the sensations from our melding bombarded me, making my legs quake.

I moaned.

He moaned.

Mine was more like a mewl. His was more like a growl.

My hands grasped his shoulders, my fingers flexing, inching toward his neck. His mouth fit perfectly over mine. His lips were like nothing I'd ever experienced before. Full and firm, burning me like two hot coals.

It felt like the best sunshine on the warmest day.

Our heads and bodies moved together like they'd been crafted at the same time for this very reason. One of his hands slid toward my neck, stopping at the base, cupping it gently, while the other pressed urgently into my lower back, like I was a skittish colt who might bolt.

He was right to hold on, but I wouldn't be running quite yet.

The kiss, if it could be called a single kiss, went on and on. It would be unthinkable to stop and take a breath.

Life had not prepared me for this level of passion.

As the pace intensified, we began to shift our heads, changing positions every few seconds, hands gripping each other, trying in vain to get closer and closer. His lips dragged against mine, invading, tugging, nibbling, pulling.

I groaned, unable to keep it in, giving as much as I took. He moaned, his body molded to mine. I shifted my thigh, pressing it into him, idly rocking it back and forth.

He was so sexy.

This was so raw.

When my leg came in contact with his arousal, he hissed into my mouth, his hand on my back grasping with more pressure. He ground his body against mine, his lips frantic. I could do this forever. I could live happily in this place. He was an excellent kisser.

Probably because he'd had lots of practice.

No. Don't.

No, no, no.

You're going to ruin it, Summer.

Enjoy this! You deserve it. It's a kiss. No, it's a firebrand. But that's okay! It's something you're going to remember forever. It will nourish you in the darker times, when Xander's light doesn't shine your way. It's going to be okay. Your clothes are on. It's not cheating.

Cheating.

Cheating.

Cheating.

I struggled to come up for air, dazed, licking my lips, my eyes unfocused. I tilted my head slightly away. Xander opened his eyes. They were glassy. We stood close, holding each other. My hands were clasped around his shoulders. His firm, stable, earthy, Conan the Barbarian shoulders. I couldn't move because I was up against the wall. He had to step back to break the embrace.

"Summer," Xander breathed, his head dipping low. "You...that was incredible. I don't think I've ever had a kiss like that." His lips lightly brushed against mine, lingering on my bottom lip, tugging slightly.

I moved to the side ever so slightly, clearing my throat, suddenly embarrassed by our shared passion. It'd sprung out of nowhere and everywhere at the same time. It'd been on simmer since yesterday at breakfast, fostered by our easy interaction last night, but how quickly it'd come to a boil had surprised both of us. It'd manifested in a toe-curling frenzy that had taken the breath literally right out of me. I couldn't find the words to speak.

After a moment, I whispered, "I'm... I haven't either." I would've remembered.

He wasn't backing up on his own, so I gently pressed him

to move. He reluctantly let go, his fingers lingering against my sides. I wanted nothing more than to start up again. To take this to the next level. To kiss him with reckless abandon. But I couldn't. Now that the spell had been broken, life began to filter back in.

I'd honestly never hated the real world more.

Shame for listening in on his intimate conversation with Stacy crept up my neck. Shame for allowing myself to get into this position made my cheeks flame. I pressed the backs of my hands against them, not knowing what else to do.

What did I say to this man now? That kiss—*that firebrand*—would be between us forever.

"Summer." Xander reached for my waist.

I sidestepped him. "It's okay. Really. It was a great kiss—*fantastic.* But I think we should get back to work." I began to slide along the wall toward the steps, but he snagged my hand, gently tugging me toward him.

"Please don't run." He'd voiced his request imploringly, his eyes locked on mine.

Poppy was right. Eyes were the windows to the soul, and Xander's was laid bare. My hand reached up on its own to stroke his cheek. The moment my fingertips met his warm skin, sliding over the soft stubble, his eyes fluttered shut, and he leaned into my touch like it was something he'd been waiting for his entire life. I was up on my tiptoes when his eyes opened. He tightened his hold on me, both hands pressed flat against my back, and we were lost again.

His lips were hungry.

I was hungrier.

There was no turning back now.

Chapter 14

"I came as fast as I could." Eve slid into the booth across from me. "What's wrong? You look like you've seen a ghost."

I hadn't had the energy to text her every detail about my mini breakdown. I'd just told her I needed company. Luckily, she'd been in the area scouting places for her new shop. We looked at each other, and I tried to form words, but nothing came out. Instead, my mouth opened and shut like a gaping fish.

"You're freaking me out, Summer," Eve whispered. "Are you going to vomit? Maybe Poppy didn't have food poisoning after all, and it was the flu, which you clearly caught." She crinkled her nose and leaned across the table for a better look. "Is that a bead of sweat rolling down your face?"

"I don't have the flu," I assured her, swatting at the drip as I picked up my water glass and took a sip. "It's perspiration. Panic sweat. I kissed Xander. Like, a lot. And it was really, really good—like, excellent making out. Lots of tongue. And just in case you're wondering, his big, beautiful full lips are firm and silky soft. My insides are quivering. I didn't even know humans could kiss each other like that."

Eve's face transformed from concerned to a knowing look bordering on a saucy wink. "That's fantastic!" she pretty much shrieked. "First kisses are the absolute best. You can't redo them, so having a great one matters. He was *so* into you the other night at the Driftwood." I hadn't had a chance to fill her in much on our breakfast together, and I'd told her nothing about music at the pier. This was the first time I was talking to her in depth since the other night when Poppy had left the party to puke. "I knew it was only a matter of time before the two of you hooked up."

My arms flopped to my sides in defeat, my head angling back. "No. It's not fantastic." I emphasized my contradiction with a rapid headshake and a groan. Not a sexy one, either. "Those kisses are exactly why I'm sitting here hyperventilating. It wasn't just a hookup. There was all this passion, and all this kinetic energy." I made big hand gestures to mimic roiling energy, or something close. "And now I don't have anywhere to put it, because a few kisses inside a future brewpub is all this will ever be." My head sagged forward.

"What are you talking about? Kinetic energy and passion are exactly what everybody dreams for in a relationship! You have it with him, he has it with you. Why wouldn't you want to explore that further? I'm not understanding." She sat back. I said nothing. We looked at each other. "It's Stacy, isn't it? You're worried he has a girlfriend. If that's the reason, why didn't you just ask him? And don't tell me you did, because I know you didn't, or we wouldn't be sitting here right now. After your scorching make-out sesh, it would've been perfectly okay for you to confront him about whether he has a girlfriend. Then you'd know."

"It's not that simple," I insisted. "I've heard a very intimate moment—girlfriend or not. And it happened twice. I didn't tell you about the second time because I was embarrassed. He'd already asked me out. How do I explain that? There's no good way to tell a man you're super attracted to that you heard him having phone sex with someone else *after* he asked you to dinner. And if he's two-timing Stacy, there is a huge chance he'd two-time me later. That's what two-timers do. They should be called dozen-timers." I pushed my menu away. I wasn't here to eat. "The problem was, I couldn't purge these thoughts out of my brain during our extended interlude, no matter how hard I tried. They manifested on their own, and they were quick about it. I kept obsessing about the mysterious Stacy and what loving a guy like Xander could do to me later. I ended up running out of there like a lunatic." I raked a hand through my hair and blew out a breath. "He was already treating me like I was a fragile, skittish kitten. I'm certain I killed any possibility of anything between us, racing out of there like I did, mumbling about having somewhere to be. But I felt like I had no other choice. The passion took me by surprise, and I became overheated and confused, then sad. I couldn't think straight. So, thank you for showing up. I needed someone to talk to. I appreciate it being you."

She reached across the table and grabbed my hand, holding it tightly. "I'm happy to be here. And I'm going to do what I can to help you, because that's what friends are for. I'm sorry there was more phone sex. That does complicate matters. But to be fair, you have a long history of being incredibly hard on yourself when it comes to men." She shook her head. "Before you start berating yourself, the reason you're the way you are is because your dating road has been difficult. But I'm here to tell you, those failed relationships are in the past, and they don't have to factor into your future unless you allow them to. This guy doesn't think you're crazy for leaving. I'd bet my life on it. The only thing going through his mind right now is how to figure out if you're okay. He sees what we all see in you. You're an amazing, talented woman with so much to offer. Common sense is your friend everywhere in life, except for when it comes to men you're *actually* attracted to."

That was true, as it'd been proven a kajillion times in the last few days.

"You're so busy trying to protect your heart from something that *might* happen," Eve continued, "you don't allow yourself the chance to explore." She let go of my hand. "I know you don't want to hear it again, but I'm going to say it anyway because it needs saying. You have to break down the wall you erected to protect yourself from heartbreak if you want to experience a nurturing, loving, grown-up relationship. You have to allow yourself to dive back into the water. You always compare dating to swimming and, ultimately, drowning. I know that's how you felt with Mitch."

My eyes slid closed. I knew what she was going say next. She'd said it many times already.

"Those feelings are valid," she went on. "I'm not here to invalidate your experience. Jumping into the deep end *is* scary, but at the same time, it's utterly and completely amazing. Mitch was a dick. He treated you badly. But not all guys are going to do that, but you won't know unless you trust yourself and know that if you have another heartbreak, you will recover." Her expression was sympathetic. She was smiling, her voice low. "You don't have to marry this guy. You don't even have to go out with him for any length of time. But I can promise, if you don't allow yourself to enjoy the journey, you're going to miss out on so much that life has to offer. I mean, I'd pay good money to have a hot hookup with a guy in the middle of an empty building. It sounds divine."

I sighed, nodding along. "It *was* divine. In the beginning, I was lost to it. It was incredible." Just imagining being with Xander again made me tingle all over again. "Then the doubts came tumbling in. All the therapy I've had over the years was working hard to drown out Pessimistic Summer and all her worries that shouldn't be worries yet. But heartache is not my friend. It's visceral and ugly and scary. I don't cope with it well." I brought my arms up, resting my elbows on the table, settling my chin in my palms. "You've witnessed it firsthand. My method of survival is the equivalent of curling up in a fetal position and swearing to never get up again. Xander is not only a guy who turns me on, but he's a direct trigger to what causes me the most pain. And that trigger might have a girlfriend. It's just a lot." I rubbed my hands over my face and grabbed my water glass. I took a long drink. "When I wasn't in the moment kissing him, I pictured myself bobbing alone in the middle of the ocean, waves breaking over my face as I began to choke on water, him back together with Stacy and living a perfect life. Then his face morphed into Mitch's, which morphed into Luke's, and it was a mess. Then I was a mess."

She grinned. Not the response I expected. "I get all that."

She leaned forward. "But how good was the kiss?"

"I already told you. Toe-curling good. Fireworks-behind-the-eyes good. Spectacular." I-could-still-taste-him-on-my-lips good.

"I get that it was physically great," she said. "But emotionally. How good did it make you *feel*? Did it make you think this man held some sort of key to your soul no one else has access to? Did you feel safe? Did you want to hold on and never let go?"

I hesitated. "Yeah." I drew out the word, like answering in the affirmative would get me into trouble. "All of those things." It'd definitely started last night at the pier, when he'd used his body heat to keep me warm, made sure I was having fun, and being generally attentive—Poppy had been right, we'd seemed like a couple. That feeling had grown exponentially today. I felt safe with him. He made me feel…secure and happy.

"Well, then, in my professional opinion, he's worth the risk." She crossed her arms like her job here was done. "The training wheels are off, Summer. This is real life. My advice is to confront Xander and get some answers. If you don't, I think you'll regret it for a long, long time. The only way you're going to get over being a commitment phobe is to survive a relationship with an extremely attractive man and come out the other side in one piece. If Stacy's in the past, maybe you stay together." She shrugged. "Maybe you don't. He might even break your heart a little. But that doesn't mean the journey can't be a hell of a good time. Going in with the right mind-set, being honest with him, and doing everything you can to maintain clear boundaries can help you tamp down that fear."

I rested my head against the back of the booth. "Your words make perfect sense, but at the same time it feels too big. How do

I know I'm ready? How can I be certain I can get through it in one piece?" The scariest part.

"Because you're a survivor. You've always been a survivor. Taking care of Gus the way you have, enduring your parents' divorce, graduating from the university with top honors. The fact that you're sitting across from me right now, breathing, living your life, being a happy, well-adjusted, wonderful friend. Those are all the indications you need. These men hurt you, but I refuse to believe they've killed all the passion inside of you. Don't let them have that." She arched her brow. It was an elegant slant, like a turtle dove taking flight. "Don't give them the satisfaction. They don't deserve it. It's you who deserves crazy, kinky sex until the wee hours of the morning. It's you who deserves to fall deeply in love with somebody who makes your toes curl."

I fiddled my thumbs together. "When I was kissing Xander, we couldn't get enough of each other—like, we were seconds away from rip-your-clothes-off, stand-up sex. I was milliseconds away from allowing myself to give in to all the feels. To have sex right there on the old, dirty countertop." Eve's eyebrows shot up. Less turtle dove, more raptor. "But then my heart began to hurt. Like a physical ache. It told me all this happiness would be no match for the heaviness and sadness that would surely follow. It shut me down."

Eve reached her hands across the table again, clasping both of mine. "You're not broken, Summer. You're just scared. I truly believe if you can get through a relationship, or even just some casual interludes with Xander, or a guy like Xander, you can begin to heal that fear for good. By doing so, you'll feel empowered, stronger, and hopefully more fulfilled by your future relationships. You have a wonderful life ahead of you. I know it."

"If not… I mean, I have a great vibrator." I grinned. "It really does the trick. Even if it doesn't have muscles, dimples, or tattoos."

Eve laughed, letting go of my hands. "But is that vibrator going to kiss you like Xander just did? Or spoon you at night? Or put its naked chest up against yours? Are you ready for that kind of bliss? I think you are. You look ready to me." She smiled, giving me a knowing wink. "Or maybe you're content to keep crawling into bed with the next Ethan every night. Safe, but passionless for the rest of your life?"

Damn. She was laying it on the line.

There was no contest.

"I pick Xander." I cleared my throat. I meant it, but I had to say it a few times to actually believe it. "Or someone like him," I hedged. "Because, you know, Stacy." In this very moment, more than any other, I wished I'd never heard what had come out of the baby monitor. "She and the phone sex are a very real issue."

"Agreed. But there's only one way to know if Stacy's actually in the picture or not, and that is to ask him. That's it. Just ask the man if he has a girlfriend. And if he lies to you, he's not worth another thought. And you're free to move on to the next guy. The bartender at the Driftwood is pretty cute. Seattle is worth its weight in gold in great men. There are more Xanders out there than we can both count. Passion is ripe for the picking."

The thought of not being intimate with Xander again made my chest hurt. But I had to face facts. "It's probably too late with Xander anyway. I don't think I'll have a chance to ask about Stacy. I probably won't ever talk to him again. I told you, I ran down the alley, hair on fire, past his motorcycle—"

"Wait, wait, *wait*." Eve shook her head. "You never said anything about a motorcycle. Did you got *on* said motorcycle? As in, did you ride on it *willingly*?"

"Um, yes?" I nibbled a fingernail, knowing what was likely to follow.

Her eyes narrowed, and she flipped her hair over her shoulder. "If Ethan pulled up on a Harley, would you have gotten on it?" She held up her hand. "No. Don't answer that. We both know you'd tell him to get lost. Xander excites you. He hits all the right buttons. More importantly, you feel *safe* with him. That's why you got on his bike. He has a key that no one else has. Again, if you don't try to make amends with him, confront him about Stacy, and see where this goes, I believe you'll regret it. You're not going to lose anything by speaking with him at least one more time."

I did feel safe with him. Even though I'd been unsure about the motorcycle, I'd felt exhilarated during the ride. Similar, yet different, to the way I'd felt when we kissed. Eve was right. I owed him enough to at least talk to him one more time. I bit my lip for what felt like the fourth time today. "He might not want to speak to me again."

"Oh, he'll speak to you," Eve said confidently. "He's probably out searching for you right now, worried sick." She made the gimme gesture, curling her fingers. I reached in my pocket and pulled out my phone, handing it to her, feeling a little sheepish. I hadn't been able to look at it since I'd texted her.

"There. Three texts from him, all completely concerned about your well-being." She handed the phone back to me, which I set on the table, still not ready to look. "Making him worry one more second is foolish." She pulled out her phone, her eyebrows lifting. "Oh, look at that. I have to go. I'm so sorry. Marco's at a location right now, and he thinks it might be *the one*." There was joy in her voice, a giddiness I hadn't heard in a long time. I was excited for her. She was living her dream.

I nodded. "Of course. Go. Thanks for coming to my rescue. I'm so proud of you. This flower shop is going to be amazing."

She slid out of the booth. "You know, I'm fairly decent at giving advice, but I don't always take it when it's given to me. There could be a time in the near future when our positions will be swapped."

Before I could address her comment, she swooped down, gave me a quick hug, and hurried out.

The waitress took this as a cue to check in. "Can I get you anything?"

"Yes, I'd love some tea."

"Hot or cold?"

"Hot. And if it's okay with you, I'm just going to sit here for a bit."

"That's fine with me, honey." The middle-aged woman who resembled my aunt Camille patted me on the shoulder. "Take all the time you need."

CHAPTER 15

The city bus deposited me in Lower Queen Anne, and I'd hoofed it the rest of the way home. Spring was emerging, and the evidence was everywhere. Daffodils wafted in the breeze, birds chirped, new leaves were unfurling, but I hardly noticed.

My mind was full, analyzing and reanalyzing everything Eve and I had talked about—and more important—examining every single solitary emotion I'd experienced with Xander since the time he'd knocked into me in the hallway, all the way up to our afternoon escapade. It felt like I was performing emotional surgery on myself, dissecting all my fears, insecurities, and happiness with a heated scalpel. It wasn't fun. But it was necessary and long overdue.

I hadn't had the heart to text Xander back yet. I was still at a loss about what to actually say to him. Texting him a thumbs-up to let him know I was indeed alive seemed grossly inadequate, but it was the only thing I could think of. Turning up my street,

I stopped in my tracks.

A lone figure rested against the retaining wall. The leather-jacketed figure, obviously Xander, straightened.

He'd seen me. He'd been looking.

Waiting.

My pulse skyrocketed. Emotions I'd been trying to tamp down emerged in full force. Euphoria, embarrassment, fear, elation, anxiety. But the one thing that stood out the clearest—louder and stronger than any other emotion—was pure, unadulterated happiness. A kind I was pretty sure I'd never experienced before.

I'd been a child in my past relationships. Now I was a woman.

It seemed I hadn't ruined everything by leaving. Or at least, Xander was giving me a chance to explain myself.

I rushed forward, trying not to run.

His face was inscrutable. When I was within a few feet of him, he reached out, grabbing my hands. "Summer, I'm so sorry. I came on too strong. I apologize. I pushed you into doing something you weren't ready for—"

He was apologizing to *me.*

My lips silenced his protests.

After a moment of confusion, he encircled me with his arms, drawing me in tightly. His movements were soft, tentative. His apology, his lust, his yearning were all wrapped up in that one kiss.

I broke from him, a little unwillingly. "We have a lot to talk about. Let's do it inside." My voice was hoarse, my breath coming fast.

He nodded, agreeing as his lips captured mine again.

We were lost for a few more seconds.

Instead of saying more, I turned and grabbed his hand,

leading him up the steps. He followed without protest. I fumbled with my key, feeling like a child who was late for curfew. Once I'd inserted the key into the lock, I managed to get the door open and led him up three flights of beautifully restored oak.

My key slid a little easier into the lock on my loft door. Once we were inside, his lips were back on mine. He kissed me down the short hallway and into my living room.

He paused, briefly glancing around. "Nice place."

I nodded, murmuring into his mouth, "Thanks."

We had things to say to each other, but we both needed this reconnection. I edged his jacket off and dropped it on my love seat. He was wearing a navy T-shirt. I began to ease it out of his waistband, tugging it up to his pecs.

"Summer." His voice was ragged as he broke the kiss, placing his forehead against mine.

"I'm sorry." I was completely caught up in the moment. "Yes, you're right. We should talk first. But before we do, I need you to know that my leaving the pub was not your fault. I should've explained everything right then and there." I took a small step back, trying to get my thoughts in order inside my scattered, lusty brain. "The passion between us took me by surprise. I couldn't think straight, and I panicked. I apologize for running off like that. It was—"

He gripped my shoulders gently as he stared into my eyes. "Don't be sorry. Please. This is my fault. I knew you were hesitant about me and preferred to take it slow. I've been reading your signals, picking up on your body language. I wanted to respect that. But when you looked at me like that, I just couldn't help myself." He ran a hand over his mouth. "It's just… It's been so long since I've felt anything like that for anyone. It took me by surprise, too. The spark between us is so good. I allowed myself to act without asking your permission, so I'm the one who needs to apologize."

I shook my head, trying to make sense of all of his words while the flapping wings were doing their best distraction job in my chest. I moved a few steps away from him. Distance would help. "Please, no. You don't need to apologize. You read my signals correctly. I was hesitant, until I wasn't. I fully accept what happened in the building. I enjoyed it very much. But, um, it's a little more complicated than that." I walked over and sat in my favorite chair. He stayed where he was. He appeared hopeful, but wary at the same time. "I have a serious question to ask you. It's one that we've already covered, but I need a real answer and a little more detail. Then I have something to admit to you." I glanced down at the floor. I didn't want to tell him about the monitor, but there was no way around it.

"Okay." His voice held hesitancy and conviction at the same time. "Ask me anything." He took a seat on the love seat across from me. "I promise to answer your questions honestly."

"Are you seeing someone?" It tumbled out. Not a blurt, but close. I was going to wait with the monitor part, but I didn't want to catch him in a lie. So I cleared my throat. "Before you answer that, I have proof that, um, you've been intimate"—was that the right word?—"with someone as of a few nights ago. Not physically in the same place, but..." I had nowhere to go with that, so I left it there.

His brows quirked. He appeared genuinely confused. "Proof? I don't understand."

Mortified didn't seem to be a strong enough word for what I was feeling. Red crept from my neck to my face. My palms started to sweat. "I, um, please know it was not on purpose, but I overheard something. At first, I didn't know it was you." I fidgeted for a second but had to face facts. "Intimate things filtered through Clara's old baby monitor." I stood, unable to sit and continue to get this out. "You and a person named Stacy were, um, getting hot and heavy over the phone. The monitor picked it up. The first night, I didn't know it was you, but then I saw your Mickey Mouse shirt and figured it out." I couldn't meet his eyes. "Then a few nights later, the monitor picked up on it again, but that time, I turned it off. I swear." I held a hand in the air. "Okay, so I turned it on once after, just to make sure it was you, but once I knew *for sure* it was you, I tapped out." I wrung my hands, turning to face him. "When you came over to Jenny's and asked me out, I didn't know how to respond, because I knew about you and Stacy. And…and…I've had a rocky road with men breaking my heart." My breath was coming in short bursts, I tried to calm myself down. "I can't be with you until I know the truth. Please don't lie to me." I finally felt strong enough to meet his gaze. "I need to know."

He stood. "Well…" He scratched the back of his head, turning toward my window. "That's a lot to take in."

I nodded. "It is."

He moved behind the sofa, pacing in the small space in front of the steps to my loft. "First of all, Stacy and I were a thing for a short period of time when I first arrived in Seattle, it's true. But we're no longer together and haven't been for a while. The problem is, she hasn't exactly accepted that yet. What you heard over the monitor was me pretending to be turned on. I wasn't actually…pleasuring myself." His expression was pained. "That has to sound so made-up, but it's the truth…um… I'm not sure what else to say."

It could be true.

Everything I'd heard over the monitor had been patchy. I hadn't heard any super-explicit content, just lots of innuendo. I cleared my throat, bowing my head. "I'm so ashamed I listened in. Please know in the beginning I had no idea it was you. Like I told you, once I figured it out, I turned it off."

He gazed out the window, then back at me. "I'm sorry you overheard that. It's not exactly something I can take back, or you can scrub from your memory. I can't really… I don't want to get into the whole context of what's happening with Stacy right now. It's complicated baggage. I'm sorry. It's just a lot." He looked so sad as he reached over and picked up his jacket, shrugging it on. "I should go." He turned and headed toward the door.

The loss I felt as he moved farther and farther away was like the air being sucked out of my lungs with a gigantic bellows. It physically hurt. "Please don't leave." My breath was barely above a whisper.

He stopped, his back to me. After a moment, he said, "I'm not perfect, by any means, but I swear to you I'm not lying about this. It's just…really complicated and painful."

We didn't know each other.

I was demanding a lot from a man I'd just met and had been in the presence of for less than four hours total. Life was messy. Nobody was perfect. "I believe you about Stacy." I moved toward him, thankful he'd waited.

While his back was still to me, I edged off his jacket. He allowed it.

I tossed it onto the love seat.

Very slowly, he turned to face me. He looked tired and defeated.

I pressed the palm of my hand under the soft cotton of his shirt, feeling his skin for the first time.

He shuddered under my touch, his eyes dropping closed. The soft cotton slid up and over his head without effort. He facilitated it by lifting his arms, eyes still closed, and tossed it aside.

He didn't just have one or two tattoos. He had an array. And they were all beautifully drawn. I spent time outlining their contours with my fingertips.

Neither of us spoke.

He sucked in his breath a few times but otherwise remained quiet. Many of them were abstract symbols. I knew each one had meaning. I stared up at him. His eyes were still shut. "Your tattoos are…wonderful."

His hands slowly found their way around my waist. He pulled me closer, his head settling into the crook of my neck, his lips barely brushing the sensitive skin there.

It was my turn to shudder.

"They're a tribute to my life, my family, and the memory of Zoe. I got the first one a few months after she died. They're all based on her drawings. She was a talented artist."

My gaze landed below his navel, which was tattoo-free and starkly gorgeous. I let my hand follow. I stroked the soft skin beneath it back and forth, just above his well-worn buttonhole.

His gaze lifted to mine, our eyes locking again in that special way. Very slowly, he angled his head down.

It was the sweetest kiss yet.

My hands wound around his neck. I wanted to hold on and never let go. We stayed that way for a long time, locked together, exploring, kissing, both of us eager to discover the other.

After what felt like an hour—but could've been more, hard to know—we'd made our way to the bottom of my steps. Without speaking, we'd both decided to take this further. It felt right. I wanted this man more than anybody I'd wanted in my entire life. I believed he had told me the truth, even though he'd chosen not to elaborate. If we stayed together longer, the story would eventually come out.

"I'm pretty sure we can both fit up there." I nodded toward my lofted bed, my breath coming fast. "It'll be a tight squeeze. You're, um, a little bigger than anyone who's been up there before."

He grinned, flashing his dimples, his mouth hovering just above my lips. "I'm up for anything." He answered with another kiss, this one incredibly deep. He was a master. "We can wait, or we can continue. It's up to you." His eyes were hooded, his forehead resting against mine. It was comforting in a way I'd never known before.

"I want you."

It was enough.

We climbed the steps.

Once we reached the platform, Xander had to duck. I knelt on the bed, sliding over to make room. He was naked on top. I was fully clothed.

Very slowly, Xander eased down beside me. He looked happy. "I really like you," he murmured as he reached over to brush a lock of hair behind my ear. "I hope this is one of many moments between us."

"I hope so, too," I replied as I began to edge up my shirt. He helped, causing it to take longer than necessary because our mouths were locked together, his tongue stroking mine in the most tantalizing way.

Pretty soon, our bottoms were liberated. I had on a decent matching bra-and-panty set gifted to me by either Eve or Poppy for Christmas or a birthday.

As we lay back, Xander murmured, “Beautiful.” He leaned over and placed his mouth over a nipple through the silky material, sucking gently.

I groaned, arching my head back, one hand snaking around his neck to pull him closer. Xander wore black boxer briefs that molded to all of his hard edges.

My hand went down, stroking him slowly through the material. He gasped when I touched him for the first time.

“Did you bring any protection with you?” I murmured against his lips, enjoying the feel of him. “If not, I have some here.”

Xander reached around in his discarded jeans while I waited, still stroking him.

He brought the wrapper up to his teeth and, in the sexiest way I’d ever seen, tore it open in one motion. He hesitated for a second, then handed it to me.

I took it, my mouth back on his, loving the feel of his tongue, his full lips fitting perfectly between mine. I dipped my hand inside his briefs, the condom between two fingers, and ran my palm up and down the length of him, losing myself in his moans and pants as he continued kissing me.

Finally, after teasing him for a few moments, I unfurled it, covering him fully.

Once it was on, something broke inside both of us.

We were frantic. I pulled at his briefs as he undid my bra, both of our breathing uneven as we found each other’s necks and chests with our tongues. Our motions were quick and needy.

He captured a nipple between his lips, groaning, as I straddled him, pushing his shoulders down onto my mattress.

I arched up, pressing him against my wetness, my head tumbling back. Thank goodness there was enough ceiling space for me to do this.

As I slid onto him, my muscles gripped him, tremoring. I was so close. He felt so good, and it'd been a long time since I'd been this turned on.

"Summer," Xander groaned.

I had no words.

Once he was deep inside, I ground into him. My hand slid beneath his neck, guiding him to my mouth so I could latch on to his tongue, sucking as I began to rock faster.

I couldn't get enough. My pace quickened until our mouths broke apart. Sliding his hands up my sides, he cupped my breasts, his thumbs teasing my nipples. As I came down, he came up. His neck muscles were corded, his eyes shut.

"Xander," I moaned. "I'm close."

His head rose as he took my lips one last time. I broke, my hips continuing to rock, jerking erratically in my pleasure.

"Summer," Xander managed through gritted teeth as he grabbed on to my waist, stabilizing me as he pumped inside. I pressed into him, enjoying all the wonderful aftershocks.

Once he found his release, I collapsed on his chest. My lips firmly planted themselves against a sweet, firm pec. We were both sweating. "That was really, really good." I could barely get the words out.

His hands ran lightly up and down my back, caressing me, his breath coming fast and uneven. "It was…everything."

Chapter 16

"What time is it?" My voice was groggy, my apartment dark. I was naked. So was Xander. I was a little discombobulated as I blinked awake. We were tangled up in my blanket. After the incredible sex, we'd talked and fallen asleep. "Was that your phone?"

A beep sounded again.

Xander turned, reaching into his jeans pocket for his phone. "Yes, it's my alarm," he answered, lying back down. "It's eight. I'm due at the pub at nine fifteen. We always end our regular workday there, going over all the plans. I can call them and cancel."

I ran a hand over his chest, enjoying the contours, wishing it wasn't so dark. I wanted to see his tattoos again. "That's okay. You should go. They'll be waiting for you."

He turned, smiling, kissing me lightly, his arm curving around my waist. "I'd much rather stay here with you."

"The only thing I have on my agenda tonight is showering," I told him. "But if you want, after your meeting, you're welcome to come back. I mean, we both need to eat at some point." I felt relaxed and happy.

"How about a shower together?" He caught my bottom lip between his teeth, grinning before his tongue slipped inside.

After a lengthy make-out session, I finally answered, "I wish we could shower together, but my stall is barely large enough for one. Both of us would never fit in there. But I love the idea. *Mmm.* Seeing you with water sluicing over your chest is definitely in our future."

He chuckled, covering my hand with his own. "We can do it at my place, then. If I'm going to meet the guys, I should go home and shower and get into some new clothes."

"Okay," I said.

He placed a kiss on my forehead as he sat up, gathering his clothes. Our eyes had adjusted to the darkness, and thanks to my big windows, enough light filtered through so I could watch his back muscles move. There were a few more tattoos on his back, and I reached out to trace them. He shivered.

"They are really beautiful," I murmured.

"Thank you." He smiled as he moved toward the steps.

"Do you have a day job?" I asked, rolling onto my side. "Or is the brewpub your main thing?"

"I'm a tax attorney."

"You are *not* a tax attorney."

He chuckled as he made his way down. "Why can't I be a tax attorney? What did you think I do for a living?" Once on the floor beneath me, he glanced up as he pulled on his shirt.

I decided to get out of bed, hastily donning my clothes. "I

don't know. I was thinking maybe you built custom bikes. Or worked down at Pike's Place, throwing fish."

His laugh was throaty and low. He slid his jacket on. "I guess I can see why you'd think that. But no. I'm a lawyer. Zoe and my parents were hoping for doctor, but that didn't pan out. I chose tax law because I like numbers, and there's a quantifiable busy time of the year. I think I knew I wouldn't be doing it forever. Running this brewpub is where my real passion lies, and being an attorney is a huge asset. I'm looking forward to the bar becoming successful enough for me to quit my day job."

I whistled, coming to stand in front of him. "I'm so impressed."

He leaned over and planted a kiss on my lips. "I'll try to keep this meeting short. I'll text you when I'm done. Decide what you want to eat, and I'll bring it back."

Everything was so matter-of-fact with him, and I adored it.

The smile on my face didn't disappear for the next two hours.

I took a lonely shower for one and answered business emails. Oddly, I hadn't felt like texting my girlfriends until a few minutes ago to tell them what had gone down. Getting together with Xander was *huge* news, but I'd thoroughly enjoyed keeping it to myself.

Like a precious little secret.

I finally decided it was time, and sat in my favorite chair in my comfy sweats, tucking my legs up under myself. I sent a group text with a brief explanation of what had happened, with the promise of more details to come.

Poppy pinged me back immediately:

OH. MY. GOD. SO FANTASTIC!!!! SEE!? I'M ALWAYS RIGHT. CAN'T WAIT TO HEAR ALL THE GORY DETAILS. GIRTH, LENGTH, OR BOTH?

Eve texted:

SO DAMN HAPPY FOR YOU!!! LET'S MEET UP TOMORROW. I NEED THE DEETS ASAP. HOW WERE THE TATS?

Jenny came last:

GAS-STATION HOT HAS A NEW WOMAN! WHAT A LUCKY BASTARD. CAN'T WAIT TO HEAR ALL. ALSO, WE HIRED A NEW NANNY STARTING ON WED. ANY CHANCE YOU CAN DO TOMORROW? LAST TIME, I PROMISE! LEMME KNOW. AGAIN, SO, SO HAPPY FOR U.

I was about to answer that I'd fill them in later, when a text from Xander popped up on my screen.

ALMOST DONE. WHAT WILL IT BE?

If I smiled any harder, my face would crack. My fingers got busy.

ANYTHING IS FINE. BUT IF I CAN LICK IT OFF YOUR CHEST, IT'S A TEN-POINT BONUS!

I pressed send, then felt sheepish. I mean, we'd been intimate, and it'd been mind-blowingly amazing, but we really didn't know each other that well.

I hastily texted more:

JUST KIDDING. WHATEVER WORKS. SURPRISE ME!

He responded:

I'M GOING WITH LICKABLE. I'LL BE THERE IN 30.

The hummingbird began to perform complicated maneuvers in my chest. I knew this feeling wouldn't stick around at this intensity forever, so for the first time in my life, I chose to savor it instead of fear it.

I busied myself for his arrival, responding only to Jenny's

request. I'd talk to the other girls later.

NO PROBLEM. I CAN WATCH CLARA TOMORROW. I'LL BE THERE A LITTLE BEFORE NINE.

She replied:

THANKS A TON! WE'RE SO GRATEFUL FOR YOUR HELP. FEEL FREE TO HAVE THE HOTTIE KEEP U COMPANY. WINK, WINK. [SMILEY FACE EMOJI]

There was no way I was getting busy with Xander at Jenny's, but I'd be happy to have him there, if he was inclined to join me.

I rushed around, straightening up, if anything to keep my nervous energy active, ending in the bathroom to brush my hair and add a little lip gloss. My place had a buzzer, but I had to physically go down and open the door. Unless, of course, my neighbors recognized my pals. But they wouldn't recognize Xander…yet.

Xander didn't end up needing the buzzer. I heard his motorcycle from several blocks away. That wasn't going to endear me to my neighbors. I hurried down the steps and opened the front door as he came strolling up the walk. He held two bags in his arms. One had the logo of a local ice cream shop on it, the other a Thai place down the street.

My insides tingled with anticipation.

He'd surprised me with ice cream.

"Hi," I said, going up on my tiptoes as he came through the doorway.

He kissed me, walking me back into the short hall. We would've stayed there for an hour, but voices came from the first-floor condo, making it quantifiably less sexy.

Once we were in my loft, I gathered plates and silverware. It was ten thirty, not so late in the scheme of things. Xander helped, taking out glasses and unpacking the food. He pulled the ice cream out of the bag. "I had no idea which one you liked better, so I got vanilla and chocolate." He held them up.

"I like them both, especially mixed together." I grinned.

"Me, too." He placed them in my freezer.

It was hard not to want to start with dessert.

"I'm sorry I don't have a kitchen table," I told him. "I usually eat on one of the chairs or the love seat. My place is so tiny, and with my desk, it didn't make sense to put in a table."

"The sofa is fine," he said, carrying both of our plates and setting them on the coffee table. "I really love this place. It was probably the maid's quarters back in the day."

"Probably," I said, sitting next to him on the couch. "When I first laid eyes on it, I fell in love. I've been here for two years. I can't imagine moving. Although, I know at some point I'll have to. It's too small for more than one person."

"I don't know about that," he said, gazing out my window. Downtown Seattle lit up below us, lights twinkling. "It could be cozy and intimate. At least for a while."

I blushed. "How did your meeting go?"

"Great," he said. "I told the guys all about you. They're happy for us."

I'd just taken a bite of food, which chose to travel to my lungs instead. I coughed a few times, then swallowed, asking, "You talked about us?"

"Of course," he answered easily. "Chris and Leo are my best friends. Don't worry, I didn't go into specific details. I told them we met up today, you saw the space and had some great ideas for branding, and we ended up together this afternoon. They weren't surprised after last night." He chuckled. "They were actually kind of expecting it."

It was sweet he'd told his best friends. "Speaking of branding, once we're done eating, I'll show you one of the directions I went in for the logo of Zoe's. I haven't fine-tuned it yet, but I'd love to get your take before I go any further."

"Sounds great," he agreed.

We chatted about our favorite childhood TV shows as kids and restaurants we liked in the area. The getting-to-know-you stage felt good and comfortable. When we were done, I gathered up the plates and took them into the kitchen, setting them in the sink. "I'll wash these later."

Xander went to the freezer and placed both quarts of ice cream on the counter, giving me a wink. "You know, so they get melty." He managed to make the word melty sound growly. Then he grabbed my hand and led me over to the computer.

I sat. He positioned himself over my shoulder. I clicked on the folder labeled *Zoe's designs.*

"She would've adored you," Xander murmured, his chin brushing the top of my head. "She would've said that when you smile, it looks like a ray of sunshine breaking through the clouds. She would've thought your name was a perfect fit for your personality. She had a sense about those things. Maybe it was because she was ill her entire life, but she was incredibly intuitive."

"I wish I could've met her," I replied, meaning it. "I love it when you talk about her. Something inside you brightens and expands. Please mention Zoe as much as you want. I'll never get tired of it. Plus, each time you do, I get a better picture of her and what she was like."

He surprised me by catching my neck in a sweet, tender kiss.

I opened up the design, letting him take it in before I explained it.

"It's amazing," he said. "It's exactly what I was envisioning. The script works perfectly with the beer stein. It has the feel of an old pub sign but with a modern twist."

I pointed to a little area in the foam. "I placed a heart inside the foam for you and Zoe and your love for each other. You can't see it unless you really look for it—"

Surprising me again, he moved to my side, grasping me by the shoulders and drawing me upright. His mouth was hot and hungry.

We kissed so deeply, it felt like we'd become one person.

"You are so incredible," he murmured. "The heart is everything. It's everything I wanted. You're everything I want." He moved us over to my other chair, the one without arms, and tugged me down on top.

I straddled him, my arms loosely wrapped around his neck.

"Your text set me on fire," he whispered next to my earlobe. "I couldn't wait to get back here."

"I'm so glad you came back."

Our kissing was epic. I felt like I could easily devour him if given the chance. I shifted so I could get his shirt off easier. He had mine off in less than three seconds.

"What about the ice cream?" I asked.

"It's up to you," he said. "We can use it or not. I don't necessarily need any outside stimulus at this point. But it could be fun."

Feeling sassy and completely turned on, I slid off his lap and went to get the chocolate ice cream, tugging off the lid as I brought it back. I dipped two fingers into the carton, sliding them along the top, then stuck them in my mouth, sucking slowly.

"Jesus," he breathed.

I decided now was a good time to get out of my sweatpants, so I let them drop. I wore a tiny thong underneath. My breasts were already bare. His eyes were riveted to me as I ran my fingers along the top of the carton again, bringing the treat to one nipple, then the other, smearing it on, trying not to let it drip, which was impossible.

He reached out and snagged my waist so fast, I let out a shriek of laughter. He drew me back down on top of him, his mouth closing over one nipple. He was feverish in his intent. He went from one to the other and back again.

It was incredible. I was all about the nipples.

He feasted on both breasts until I could barely stand it, my hands threaded through his hair, my back arched, my hips grinding into his jeans.

Glossy eyed, I murmured, "How come you're not naked yet? There's more ice cream."

He paused, and with considerable effort, I detached from him, sliding off the chair. His eyes never left me as he stood and unbuttoned his jeans, easing them off. He was naked underneath. My breath hitched.

I hadn't been able to see him in all his glory in my loft. He was magnificent. I didn't go around ranking penis sizes, but his was more than adequate.

Very slowly, with one foot in front of the other, I eased him back into the chair and knelt before him, ice cream container in one hand.

The groan that erupted from his lips sounded like a happy

foghorn. His hands gripped the edges of the seat like he might break it in half. "Are you *serious?*"

"Of course." My eyelids were hooded, my voice no more than a whisper. "It was my idea, remember?" I grinned, enjoying the look on his face—surprise mixed with raw lust and something possibly a little feral.

I took my time.

The coldness of the application was quickly resolved by the warmth of my mouth. Some women disliked this or felt it was a task to be handled, but I enjoyed it. Seeing my partner's pleasure as he grappled for control did it for me. It really did. The way men lost themselves, each and every time, made it spectacular.

In all of our friend chats over the years, we'd decided that oral foreplay was all around the best kind, for *both* parties.

Xander's hands twined in my hair, guiding me gently. After a very short time, he managed, "You have to stop. I'm close."

I glanced at him, my expression radiating the heat I felt.

He guided me up, standing himself. He had a condom in his hand, but this time, he took care of it himself, pumping his cock slowly, meeting my eyes. His gaze was feverish.

Holy shit.

I'd never been in the position where a man could look at me and bring me to the brink of coming. It was new, but not unwelcome.

I wanted him. Before he could take a step in my direction, I pivoted, making my way to the back of the love seat, bending over and settling my elbows on top of the cushions. The only word I could think to utter was, "Please."

"Summer, I think you might be trying to kill me." His words were gruff, but sweet as he made his way to me.

I felt his fingers first. My head dipped down, my forehead touching the cushion. He circled with intent. "That feels wonderful," I said, rotating my hips in a circle. "But like you, I'm too close. I need you. *Please.*"

He entered me from behind, reaching around to cup my breasts, arching me up as he plunged inside, connecting us in one single, long thrust. My back touched his chest, his hands kneaded my nipples.

Three more thrusts, and lights exploded behind my eyes.

I lost my footing as my legs began to shake. He held me up, letting me take all the time I needed. When I was satiated, I bent back over the love seat, giving him permission to do what he needed. He grabbed on to my waist, pumping frantically, calling my name as he came.

He was the best sex I'd ever had.

No contest.

The world was feeling a lot different at the moment.

Chapter 17

I'm not telling you anymore." I placed a finger to my lips. "I've already said too much." I was blushing, trying to disguise it by taking another sip of coffee. I'd confessed to Eve and Poppy general things, as girls did, but nothing specific. At least for now. I wanted to keep the intimate stuff between Xander and myself.

"Come on, those were bottom-of-the-barrel details!" Poppy complained. "Fine. How about I do hand gestures, and you just helpfully nod along?" She placed her hands about a foot apart. "Is he this big? Because it seems like he should be." She moved them a little closer. "Maybe here?" She changed them into half circles and met them together in the middle. "This thick?" Then she scoffed. "Nobody's that thick. I can't get my fingers any smaller." She made a few more gestures, trying to come up with a thickness indicator.

All Eve and I could do was laugh.

"I'm not answering that," I told her. "Just know that I've never had better. Seriously. He woke me up this morning with his mouth, and that's all you two need to know."

Eve sighed as Poppy clapped her hands, bouncing in her seat. "That's serious morning love right there. I'm so happy for you, Summer! There is no better way to start the day."

We were having a late breakfast out. I glanced around sheepishly, hoping no one had overheard that. I was grateful the waitstaff were occupied with other customers.

Xander had stayed the night but had gotten up early to go back to his place to shower and change for work. He'd agreed to come by Jenny's tonight after his meeting with the guys at the brewpub. I was so looking forward to seeing him again, like I'd never been with any other guy I'd ever dated. Times infinity.

The intensity of it all was startling. I couldn't lie—fear still lingered around the edges. When it came to the forefront, I did my best to tamp it down. It was going fairly well.

"I'm *so* impressed with you," Poppy exclaimed. "Seriously. I wasn't sure you were ready. Now he's all up in your grill, satisfying you like Thor with his magic hammer." She smiled. "Summer, you deserve this. It's been a long time since someone made your heart go pitter-patter. I'm excited for you, even if you're being lame not sharing the juiciest parts."

"She's right." Eve jacked her thumb in Poppy's direction. "You totally deserve this. That doesn't mean you're not going to worry, because we all know you will. But try not to worry *too* hard. Enjoy the adventure. You're lucky to be able to have this opportunity to connect with somebody you're so crazy about." I heard the note of sadness in her voice and immediately thought of Marco and his live-in girlfriend.

I really wanted to enjoy the experience.

"You kind of glazed over all the Stacy stuff." Poppy forked a small bite of hashbrowns into her mouth. "Let's go back to that for a sec. They were together, but now they're not, but she still calls him, so he pretends to whip it out?"

"That's not what I heard at all," groused Eve, elbowing Poppy. "What I heard is that he tried, and is continuing to try, to let this girl down easy since she wouldn't take no for an answer. He broke up with her, but she refuses to accept it, so he's trying to be gracious. The most important thing is, they're not together."

I glanced from one friend to the other. "Yeah. The details are a little hazy, but I believed him. He sounded completely genuine." The emotion on his face had been palpable. "He didn't want to go into details then and there. It seemed like an emotional trigger for him, which I can relate to, so I didn't press for more. We'd known each other by that time for, like, a total of three or four hours. There's plenty of time to figure it out. I will absolutely get to the bottom of it in the near future." I had to admit, the lack of Stacy info was bugging me today, especially after I'd laid it out for my friends a few minutes ago. "He assured me there would be absolutely no future phone sex, pretend or not. If he and I"—I shrugged—"you know, continue down the path we're on, it will get solved."

Eve patted my hand. "Give him time. It's literally been *one* day. And it was a super-intense one, with lots of emotions bubbling all over the place. In the scope of everything, it's early. He sounds genuine, like an honest guy who really cares about you and is not in it for the cheap thrill. I'm certain there's a logical explanation for Stacy, and it'll come out soon. All that stuff about his sister is incredibly endearing. He sounds like a family man to me."

"He's a lawyer." I snorted. "Can you believe it? This rugged, salt-of-the-earth guy is a tax attorney." I shook my head.

"That's actually really strange," Poppy quipped, chewing the edge of a piece of bacon. "I wonder what Leo does for a living. He's probably a zoologist or an air traffic controller. These guys aren't playing around."

"No, they're not," I said. "It sounds like Xander's profession is something he enjoys, but it was ultimately sought to fulfill his family's dreams more than his. But he's really excited about the brewpub. I hope it works out for him."

Eve drummed the table with her fingers. "Okay, I've been holding back. I have news to share." Excitement brimmed in her voice. "Summer, you're done, right? I don't want to intrude on your epic new relationship if you have anything more to say. I was waiting for a natural gap to spill this."

"I'm so done, please go," I prodded. "Did you find a place for the shop?"

"We did! And it's in Ballard. Not too far from Zoe's, actually. It's absolutely perfect. The storefront is just big enough to hold all the merchandise, and it has these huge windows. Then the back has all this extra space. It'll be perfect if I want to teach floral-design classes. We have all these ideas. It's going to be totally brilliant!" She clapped twice.

"That's *so* fantastic." Poppy clapped along with her. "This entire thing seems to be moving at the speed of light, but in actuality, you've been working toward it for so long. I couldn't be happier for you. Our little group is changing and growing. It makes me proud to know you both." She brought her index finger up to the corner of her eye.

Eve grabbed her hand, grinning. "Poppy, will you help me with the interior design? I have some ideas, but with your expert knowledge and talent, I know we can get it perfect! I've budgeted a fairly healthy amount for it, so the funds are there."

Poppy placed a hand over her heart. "I'd love to! Wow, two design jobs in as many days. You'd think somebody's trying to tell me something."

"Summer," Eve said, turning to me, "it goes without saying that I want you to do the branding. We haven't settled on a name yet, but as soon as that happens, we can talk."

"You're not calling it Jazz One Floral?" I asked.

"My business partners aren't super excited about that name, and that's fine," she said. "It was just a funny name that kind of hung around. I'm not married to it."

"Sounds good," I said. "I'm here whenever you need me. I'll make it a top priority. I'm completely in awe of you for pursuing your dream. It's so ridiculously exciting."

"It's a total dream come true. None of this would be possible without Marco." Her eyes downright sparkled. "He's been so amazing about all the details. He's the one that found the space, and he even talked the owner down to a sensible rent. Well, nothing's actually sensible in that area, but it's doable."

Poppy and I shared a glance across the table. "That's really great," I said. "Having Marco in your life again has made you incredibly happy."

Eve hesitated, rearranging the silverware in front of her. It was one of her telltale nervous tics. "I already told you guys we're business partners, and the agreement is ironclad. He's providing seed money, managing some of the details, and once he earns back his investment, with interest, he's out. If the business flops, we all walk away with a small loss. I'm protected either way. Nothing can go wrong."

"What about your heart?" Poppy spoke softly, dabbing a napkin at each side of her mouth. "Summer filled me in. I think I remember you saying something about him freshman year, but Jenny and I weren't there at the very beginning. As your neighbors, it took us a couple months to get the friend group going."

Eve was visibly flustered as she stroked her beautiful red hair behind her ears. "I don't know why you guys are making such a big deal out of this. Yes, I had a crush on him way back when. We worked at one of the student bookstores together, before he transferred to a different location across campus. It was a small, *minor* infatuation. He has a serious live-in girlfriend. They seem happy. It's going to be fine. We're just business partners."

I arched an eyebrow but kept my expression light. "Okay. We believe you. But if things change, please keep us in the loop."

She nodded. "I will. And they won't. I'm sure of it."

The elevator doors at Jenny's opened, and a vision of the first time Luke Masterson held my hand popped into my head unbidden. Shortly after that, he'd tugged me behind a huge tire swing in the schoolyard and kissed me with his chapped, flaky, little-boy lips.

That memory was definitely a step up from feeling like I was on a Darth Vader death march, but it made me feel a little weak-kneed. This was the place where it'd begun, where I'd seen

Xander for the first time. The place where I'd acted like that same flustered little girl in the schoolyard, trying to avoid any interaction with this handsome man so he wouldn't emotionally wreck me.

I straightened, shaking off the memory. Pessimistic Summer had no business being here. So far, I had nothing to worry about. Xander wasn't like Luke or Mitch. He and I had been sending cute, cryptic texts to each other all day. He'd told me how much he missed me, and it'd been adorbs.

The last one had simply said:

KNOCK A LITTLE BEFORE 9.

He'd had an attorney-client business dinner after his work and wasn't arriving home until around eight. He wanted to see me first, before I was due to babysit Clara.

I bit my lip to keep from smiling.

Somehow, I was already in front of his door.

I rapped lightly.

It swung open ten seconds later, and he swept me inside, one hand cupped around my waist, the other clamped around my eyes, his lips near my ear.

"What's going on?" I laughed as I allowed him to whisk me into his apartment.

"Just a little surprise for you." He dropped his hands with dramatic flair. The layout of the apartment was identical to Jenny's. On the island were two lighted candles, two flutes, and a bottle of champagne on ice. "Before you get any ideas, this is for later."

"Later?"

"This is what we'll be doing at five a.m., once you're off duty." He grinned.

Glancing down, I noticed rose petals were scattered on the floor, leading from the kitchen down the hallway toward his bedroom.

I chortled as I drew him close, loving the feel of his rock-hard chest under my hands. "Rose petals on the second date? I didn't think anyone still did that," I teased.

"The rose petals are to rev up some quality fantasies in your head for what's coming later. Hint, you are."

"I get the feeling that you're going to enjoy tormenting me for the next eight hours. I had no idea you were a sadist."

"You can't blame me. I'm forced to work with what's given to me, and if we can't have each other until morning, you'll have to suffer along with me." He made a sweeping gesture down the hallway. "By all means, go and see what's waiting for you."

This man was insane and incredibly sexy. And, I was finding, he had a great sense of humor. This was corny, endearing, and actually hilarious.

I dutifully followed the path that wound through his master bedroom, which was exactly how I'd imagined it—including the king-size bed covered in a rich navy-blue spread—and into his master bath.

The man had filled his tub, which was more than big enough for two, with rose petals. They bobbed on water that would not be close to warm in eight hours.

If I hadn't already been, I'd be a goner.

It was so predictably cheesy and completely delightful.

Only two of my past boyfriends had been funny, and neither of them would've been confident enough to try to pull this off.

I glanced at Xander, who'd propped himself in the doorway, looking smug, arms crossed. "Okay," I said. "Goal achieved.

Rampant fantasies are now activated. Though the rose petals are giving me an *American Beauty* vibe, which I'm not sure you were going for."

He dropped his arms and moved forward, gathering me close and pressing his lips against my ear. "You're right, it wasn't. What I really wanted to show you was the shower." He maneuvered us over a few steps to his beautifully tiled, glass-doored, more-than-ample shower for two. "This is the fantasy. To drench you in hot water, lather you up in soap, and press your back up against the cool tile while I rock my—"

My mouth covered his.

We had only a few minutes before I had to be at Jenny's, and he had to work his second job.

Even though I knew he'd done the bathtub thing as a joke-slash-enticement for later, it had worked us both up. That, and all the flirty texting we'd been doing.

With regret, I had to defuse the situation, or we'd end up on the floor in the next three minutes, making us both late.

I nibbled his earlobe. "Showering works for me. But for future reference, baths work, too. I'm a fan of prolonged intimacy. Now, I have to go." I patted his chest. "And so do you." He followed me back down the hallway. I tossed over my shoulder, "I'm mandating a new rule. If you decide to stop by Jenny's later, there will be no kissing. If we swap any saliva, it could whittle down our control."

He looked at me, surprised. "No kissing?"

I nodded. "Baby Clara is my priority number one. Jenny and Daniel are good friends of mine. I'm not having sex on their couch when their infant daughter sleeps in the next room. So, to add to this elaborate scenario"—I indicated behind him—"we don't kiss again until five a.m. Like adults who are fully in control of our senses."

He smiled. "Well, when you put it that way, it's a deal."

I stepped to the door. "Jenny and Daniel have a stash of board games. I'm sure we'll find a way to have fun."

"It's always fun when you're around. And, just a warning, I will beat you hands down at any game we play."

I laughed. "Challenge accepted." I walked out the door, feeling happier than I had in a very long time.

I hope this lasts.

The relationship game was not for the faint of heart.

Chapter 18

I'd just laid a zonked baby Clara in her crib when my phone went off. It was Gus's special ringtone. He was calling to video-chat, which we did a lot. It was always up to him when we chatted, because interrupting his schedule was not ideal.

I tapped the green circle as I made my way out of Clara's room.

Gus's face filled the screen.

I grinned. "Hiya, big brother," I said cheerfully. "It's Monday at nine. Is your favorite show over? Did you call to talk about it?"

My brother was adorable. His sandy-blond hair was due for a cut, his blue eyes twinkled, and his normal sunny disposition was on full display, even though he'd been through so much. He had a thing for all the crime-show dramas, but the one on Monday night was his favorite. "Yeah, it was *so* cool. This dude croaked, and they had to figure out who did it. It wasn't who you thought it was going to be either." He went on for another few minutes, describing the plot. I nodded and asked appropriate questions.

I tried to catch the show myself, just so I could stay up on things, but I didn't always make it. "Sounds like a great episode," I told him. "I'm sorry I missed it."

"That's okay," he said. "You can watch next week."

"How was your weekend?" I asked. "I haven't heard from you in a while. Is Keith keeping you busy?" Keith was his in-home helper. "Doing fun stuff like going to the movies? Or the aquarium?" Gus loved movies and marine life. He also loved swimming and fishing. He said swimming made him feel like a freer version of himself, like how he used to be.

"No movies. But we hit the hill." He was excited, his face animated, his hands moving back and forth like they did when he had something important to say. "I forgot to tell you. Or maybe I did? Did I tell you?"

I shook my head. "No, you didn't tell me. What do you mean 'the hill'?"

"Dad, Keith, and me went to Mount Spokane. I only went on the little-kid slope, but it was still fun."

I sat on the edge of the couch, bringing the phone in close. "You went snowboarding? Is that what you're saying? Are you kidding me?"

"I'm not kidding. I'm really not." His face turned serious. "I can have Keith tell you if you want."

"No, that's not necessary. I believe you. How was it? How did it feel to be on the snow again?"

"I was wobbly and fell down a lot," he explained. "But it was also really great."

"Did Dad ski? Was Mom there?"

My mom would be emotional about this, which was probably why she hadn't called. She worked full time and helped Gus during the weekends.

"Dad didn't put skis on. He waited at the bottom. He told me he was worried, but proud."

"I'm proud, too," I told him. "That's incredible. I don't think you'll ever stop amazing us. Are you going again?"

"Maybe," he said, furrowing his brow. "I'm not sure."

"That's okay. It's late in the season," I hurried to add. "If you don't go again this year, there's always next year and the next year after that." Long-term goals were big for him.

He placed his hands on the sides of his head, which he did when he was trying to remember something important. I waited patiently. He finally looked up, smiling. "How are you? Have you done any new artwork?" That's how he referred to my job as a graphic artist. He wasn't wrong.

I grinned, not bothering to stifle my happiness. Him asking these kinds of questions wasn't something he did often. "I'm working on a really fun project right now. It's for a new microbrewery in town. It's special because the owner is dedicating it to his sister, who died."

"What was her name?"

"Zoe."

"I'm gonna write down her name so I remember it later," he said, stepping out of camera range. He was back ten seconds later. "What are the letters?"

"Z-O-E."

"How did she die?"

"I don't have all the details, but she had a disease that made her bones weak."

"That's sad."

I nodded. "It is. But her brother is keeping her memory alive." I wasn't going to tell Gus about my budding relationship with Xander. I rarely ever told him about my boyfriends. One thing at a time.

"Are you coming home soon?" he asked.

"I'm hoping to get away in the next month or two," I said. "Mom's birthday is coming up. I'll try to make it for that."

"I got a new bike." He grinned. "I'm learning to ride it." *Me, too.*

My eyebrows went up. "A two-wheel bike?" You never knew with Gus. He called everything by simple names. I knew it wouldn't be a motorcycle, but it could be a stationary bike he was riding in therapy.

"Yes," he said excitedly, his hands going up in the air again. "I can ride it outside on the sidewalk. My balance is getting so much better. Dad is helping me."

Keith stepped into the frame behind him, giving me a wave. Keith was a perfect match for Gus. We all adored him.

"Your brother's a pro," Keith called. "We only got the bike a few days ago. Pretty soon, he's going to be ready for longer rides."

"That's fantastic!" I cooed. "Wow, so much is happening lately. I can't wait to see it all for myself."

Gus leaned in, the middle of his face taking up the entire screen. "I miss you, Summer. Come home soon. I have to go now. There's a new show on. It's not about crime. It's about sharks. I love sharks."

"I miss you, too," I said, feeling a little teary. I was so proud of all his achievements. My parents must be over the moon. "I know how much you love sharks. Get back to your show. I'll talk to you soon." I gave him a little wave and blew a kiss, then punched my phone off.

I sat back on the couch.

I'd been consumed about what my life would be like with Xander or without Xander, but it all paled in comparison to what Gus had gone through in his life. I needed that reminder. It grounded me.

My new mantra would be: *If Gus can do it, so can I.*

My phone beeped with an incoming text from Xander.

MISS U. DOES KISSING THE CROOK OF YOUR ELBOW COUNT?

I laughed while typing:

YES. AS DOES THE INSIDE OF MY KNEE. ANKLEBONE MIGHT BE UP FOR GRABS, THO.

He responded:

I'LL TAKE IT. BE THERE IN AN HOUR OR SO. HAVE THE BOARD GAME READY. I'LL NEED ALL THE DISTRACTIONS U HAVE.

* * *

When Xander knocked on the door, I was ready. Baby Clara had stayed asleep since I'd put her down, which had been excellent.

I opened the door and gave him a hearty wave.

He grinned, understanding the game, giving me a wave back. He came in carrying a bag, and my eyebrows went up. The smell was familiar.

"Are those bakery treats from Shane's?"

"Yep," he replied. "I figured I was going to need to cull some favor if I was going to get a hold of those anklebones." He set the bag on the counter. "Plus, you told me last night you love sweets. Dessert is your favorite meal, so I couldn't resist. It's a little pick-me-up to get us through the evening." The man was too sweet for his own good.

I opened the bag and took out a blondie, one of my all-time favorites. "This will get you partial lip right on the bone itself." I took a bite, groaning. "How in the world did you know I love Shane's? Their blondies are the best in the city."

He took out a chocolate cupcake, taking his time undressing it. I was mesmerized. "I ran into Poppy. She told me this is the quickest way to your heart. Although, I'll admit to being disappointed that it wasn't something a bit more…*melty*."

"Melty is also good. Where did you run into Poppy?"

"She came by the brewery." He shrugged off his coat, laying it over a barstool. Then he brought his cupcake up to his mouth and took a bite, licking his lips. I had to look away so I wouldn't lean in and lick the frosting off myself. "Leo invited her to come and see the place this evening. We all like her. We pretty much agreed to hire her."

"That's wonderful," I said. She hadn't had a chance to tell us yet. Maybe that's because she was still with Leo. Fingers crossed. "She'll do a fantastic job."

"Yeah, right away all her ideas were things we'd never thought of before, like placing the bar in the middle of the room instead of along the back wall. I think it's going to be really great." He glanced around, eyeing the games I'd set on the table. "So, what's it going to be? Yahtzee or Boggle?"

I laughed, popping the last bit of blondie into my mouth. *Damn, that was delicious.* Not as delicious as tasting the man who was sitting too far away from me with chocolate all over his lips, but good in its own way. "I love them both. How about we start with Yahtzee?"

"Deal."

We moved to the living room. He sat on the couch, elbows braced on his thighs as he picked up the Yahtzee cup, shaking it idly, making sure it was quiet enough so it wouldn't wake the baby.

He made shaking dice look erotic.

Once again, I had to look away. Needing distance, I chose to take a seat across from him in one of the leather chairs. It creaked as I sat down. Everything in here was pretty new. "You can go first."

He emptied the dice onto the table.

Five sixes.

An extremely dimpled grin shot my way. "Yahtzee," he growled.

I immediately began to perspire. "You cannot turn this game into Sexy Man Yahtzee," I warned.

"I'm doing no such thing," he said innocently as he marked down his score, gathering up the dice and handing me the cup.

"Yes, you are," I groused, shaking it softly. "We need to meet on safe ground. From now on, we talk about family, school, jobs, and nothing else."

"Your wish is my command."

"How was work today?" I started as I upended the Yahtzee cup. Two threes, one five, one two, and one one. I opted to try for a large straight, dumping one of the threes back in.

"Busy. My firm specializes in tax code for international business run by American citizens in countries abroad, as well as foreign nationals who do the same here. The tax season is always messy, because every country has different rules on what to file, as do we. It can get hectic, but that means the days go by a little faster."

"Wow, that sounds intense." I rolled another five. Grumbling under my breath, I tried again and got a one. I marked down the pair of ones. It was not looking good for Team Summer.

Xander grinned ruthlessly. "How about we make this Strip Yahtzee, no touching? If you don't get the full points for whatever you choose, you have to take off an article of clothing."

"Cute," I said, handing him the cup. "The minute I see a tat, I'm licking it, so that's not going to work for me."

He shook the dice, gazing at me through hooded eyes. "We didn't really define if licking was expressly forbidden."

"I know you're joking, but don't tempt me. As it is, it's hard enough staring at you from across this artful glass table and not tackling you. Let's talk about sports. Did you play any in high school or college?" I knew he had a surfboard, and that was about it.

"Baseball was my go-to, from peewee on up. I also played soccer for a few years and, of course, surfed with my friends on the weekends." Such a California thing to do. "But overall, sports took a backseat to Zoe. I had some natural talent, and my coaches encouraged me, but in the end, it seemed silly to throw my whole life at it. They were just games." He gently upended the cup on the table. Three twos and two fives. He waggled his eyebrows. "I'll take the full house."

"I see why you excelled at sports, you're competitive to the bone." I laughed. "But there is no skill in Yahtzee. You're just getting lucky."

He settled the dice back in the cup, then seared me with a look. "This isn't getting lucky, but I'm about to be *very* lucky in"—he glanced at his wrist—"six hours." He licked his lips.

I cleared my throat. He was not going to break my resolve. I was determined to keep my wits about me. "Did you enjoy school?" I asked as he handed me the cup. I rolled four fours and a two. I dumped the two back in and idly rocked the cup. "High school specifically."

"I did for the most part, but I was distracted. Zoe was young and struggling. My mind was on her a lot. It's hard to fully enjoy yourself when someone you love is in physical pain." He rubbed his neck. "My life, as well as yours, would've been extremely different without the experiences we went through. I have trouble imagining what my life would've been like if Zoe had been born without a disease. I guess she would've been just a regular, irritating little sister." He grinned. "Nah, she wouldn't have been irritating. She was perfect. Always upbeat. I've never blamed her, though. I've never felt like it was her fault or that she took anything from me." Some people definitely could have in his situation. "I just knew I had to be present in her life. She took precedence over some of my needs, and that was fine. I missed parties, dances, games. But it didn't really feel like I was missing out when I was with her. It was a willing sacrifice."

My heart clenched more than once. "She must've adored you. You sound like you were a very doting brother." I rolled my single die. It was a four. "Yahtzee! See? You're not the only one who's getting lucky." I handed him the cup. His fingers brushed against mine.

The touch was intentional, and it produced the intended effect. Heat rushed up my arm. "No cheating," I scolded playfully.

He growled back as he shook the cup, which produced shivers. I continued on with our conversation like nothing was amiss. “I understand about being distracted at that age. It was a little different for us because Gus and I had ten years together as typical siblings before everything changed. I never blamed him, though. How could I? It didn’t even enter my mind. Not even when my parents split up. The first few years of his recovery crept by. He had to relearn so much. Him getting to where he is now, from where he started, is nothing short of a miracle. Even though I was distracted and worried about him, school was kind of my refuge. A place where I could let my hair down. Literally. I used to experiment with fashion.” I chuckled. “I wasn’t very good at it. I changed up my hair a lot, went for styles nobody else was wearing.” I shrugged. “I had a group of friends who did the same thing. We imagined ourselves to be unique, even though we were basically doing the same stuff as everyone else.”

“I bet you looked adorable.” He rolled three fives, one two, and a six. He went for the fives. Logical choice.

I refrained from snorting because I didn’t want to ruin the moment. “Absolutely not. The pictures speak for themselves.”

He shook his head as he rolled another five and a three. He put the three back in. “I’ll never believe that. There’s no way you looked anything but adorable. But I understand the need to have an outlet. I played sports as a distraction, but my main hobby was building models. My dad had done it as a boy and introduced me to it, and I fell in love. I worked in our makeshift garage workshop for hours and hours at a time.”

“What kind of models?”

“Everything I could get my hands on. Boats, planes, trains. I haven’t done it in years, but my mom saved everything.”

"I'd love to see your work sometime." Imagining Xander at age sixteen sitting at his dad's workbench and concentrating on building a model was such a sweet image. I hadn't thought my heart could melt any more. I had a feeling this man was going to constantly surprise me.

He rolled another five. "Five fives." He arched a fairly perfect eyebrow at me, grinning ear to ear.

I took the cup from him, and he trailed his index finger over my hand. It was going to be a long night.

If his mouth met my anklebone, we would both be goners.

Chapter 19

Summer? Um, Xander?" Jenny called lightly. "Time to wake up."

I sat, swiping my forearm across my mouth. I'd been slumped against Xander's shoulder, drooling. That was as close as we'd gotten all night. I was proud of us.

Xander opened his eyes like a pro, leaning forward, extending his hand like he hadn't just been asleep on a stranger's couch. "I don't think we've had a proper introduction," he said, his voice sleepy. "I'm Xander Scott. Your neighbor."

Jenny shook his hand, stifling a snort. "It's nice to finally *meet* meet you. Now we can exchange more than 'heys' in the hallway."

Daniel gave a wave from the kitchen. "I'm Dan. Thanks for keeping Summer company while she watched Clara."

"Not a problem," Xander said as we both stood. He placed his hand on the small of my back, guiding us around the couch.

"We'll have to have you over sometime soon for dinner."

From an angle Xander couldn't see, Jenny mouthed the word *we'll* with her eyebrows waggling.

I shrugged, smiling. I guess we were becoming a *we'll*, which was nice.

I'd already assured her that there would be no hanky-panky while we were babysitting. She'd told me that she didn't really care one way or the other, but I'd been adamant. That would just be tacky and weird.

Xander whisked me out of Jenny's apartment in less than two minutes. Jenny and Daniel would be chatting about our speedy exit for weeks to come.

Before we even got to Xander's door, his lips sealed over mine, my fingers raking through his hair, our tongues meeting in the middle.

Waiting had been a powerful aphrodisiac.

True to what we'd agreed upon, we'd talked about life all night long, until we'd both been too tired to talk anymore. He'd had an upbringing full of travel, with plenty of adventures I had yet to experience. Listening to his stories had been entertaining. He'd thoughtfully asked all about my hobbies, the trips I'd taken, memorable college experiences, and the like. It'd been a very enjoyable night. I was fairly certain we could converse forever and not run out of things to talk about.

When the time came, I'd been willing to sleep on the floor, but Xander had assured me that we could certainly fall asleep without attacking each other. And we had.

But now was a different story.

He struggled to pull out his keycard because his hands were too busy.

Once inside, we stopped against the wall, our heads angling from side to side and up and down. I couldn't get enough of him. His lips were soft and pliable and perfectly bitable.

I yanked his shirt out of his waistband as he began to unbutton the top of my jeans. No sweatpants for this girl tonight. The access would've been too easy.

After a few more minutes of blissful mouth play, I began to maneuver us toward his bedroom.

He broke the kiss, breathing hard. "Do you want champagne?"

"Hell no," I whispered. "You'll be more than enough."

"Good," he said, covering my mouth again.

We made it to his bedroom, me edging toward the bed, him diverting us toward the bathroom.

"I might be too tired for a shower," I managed.

"I have to go to work, and this kills two birds with one stone. And by kill, I mean, utterly hot shower sex will be the oxygen I need to keep going today."

"Okay." I chuckled. "I will not be the one to deny you that. Lead the way."

He backed me up into the bathroom, then broke free to turn on the shower.

Once the spray was jutting, we quickly shed our pants and shirts. He didn't immediately go in for a kiss, as expected.

Instead, he held me at arm's length, slowly shaking his head, emotion swirling behind his eyes. I stood in front of him in only a bra and panties, feeling exposed, but safe. When we were around each other, everything just clicked, like two puzzle pieces reunited after an extended stay under the couch.

Okay, not exactly. Maybe a little sexier, like a screw and a nut dropped behind the washing machine that finally got together.

Close enough.

Running my fingertips lightly across his shoulders, I whispered, "I feel the same way, and it scares me, too." He had no idea how much. "But at the same time I like it." Fairly true. "Everything about you excites me. Waiting for the next minute, the next hour, the next day to happen gives me this jittery, amazing feeling. When I look toward the future, I see light and happiness." My hands clasped behind his neck. I went up on tiptoes.

It was a tender offering.

His hands slid behind my back. "I've never had this before," he murmured. "I feel thankful you let me into your life." My bra clasp came undone. I let go of him, allowing it to drop to the floor. I stepped out of my panties. He got rid of his boxers and grabbed my hand, leading me into the shower. Before I could step fully into the spray, he said, "Wait right here. I'll be right back." He darted away and returned with a condom, setting it on the soap tray.

He began caressing me under the deliciously warm and appropriately pulsing stream of water. His showerhead gave mine a run for its money. It felt wonderful. I dipped my head back, letting the water soak my hair, allowing his lips to linger on my neck.

They slid down, facilitated by the sluicing water. They moved farther, along the top of one breast, before firmly clasping a nipple. I moaned.

The sensations together were amazing. I'd attempted shower sex before, but it had been nothing like this.

We traded places. Now the water cascaded over all his contours.

Showers were the *best.*

I reached for him, grasping his hardness, the abundant liquid an excellent lubricator. He did that sexy growling thing, his eyes gliding shut. He captured my mouth, marching me backward like he'd threatened to do earlier.

The tile wasn't cool. It was ice-cold.

It was the perfect elixir for the heat mounting between us like wildfire.

He reached down, clasping one of my thighs and raising it to his hip. I gasped. The possessive movement made everything inside me clench at the same time.

With the other hand, he plucked the condom off the shelf. Water drummed against his back, pouring over his shoulders, sliding down his chest. He ripped it open and rolled it on in one motion. "I can't wait," he ground out, sounding like a caveman. Chills took over.

"Me neither." The words were barely out of my mouth before he was inside. Both my arms flung wide, my fingers scrabbling against the cold, wet tiles.

This was what ecstasy felt like.

Xander's lips locked on my neck as he urged my thigh higher. I arched my hips to meet his thrusts. The water made everything slippery and awesome. His breath was hot next to my ear. "I'm going to wait for you."

"It won't be long," I said, panting. "Too bad you can't get a hold of a nipple."

He did. The man was talented.

I came hard, my legs weakening beneath me, like usual. He kept me upright.

Xander shouted a moment later, his neck cording as he

arched his head back, bouncing me backward and forward. This only enhanced things on my end.

When it was over, and every pleasure had been wrung dry between us, Xander lowered my leg. My insides were humming. My body felt like mush.

"Are you okay?" he whispered in my ear, using his tongue to trace my neck.

"More than." I tightened my grasp around his neck as he brought us both under the spray.

"I'm sorry it wasn't longer," he murmured, taking a little nip. "I lose myself when you're turned on like that."

"The feeling is mutual."

☼ ☼ ☼

I yawned, stretching at the same time. Xander's bed was huge and comfy, with the added bonus of no head-bonking-on-the-ceiling threat. I was sadly alone, which gave me the chance to reflect on everything that had happened over the last few days.

Man, it felt like a lifetime ago. I'd definitely grown up, which shouldn't be alarming, but was. Change didn't come easy to me. I was becoming more accustomed to the thought of being with Xander and that it might work out.

He'd been incredibly sweet this morning as he'd gotten ready for work. I couldn't believe he was going in after literally a few hours of couch sleep. But he'd already taken a day off recently and had work that couldn't wait. He'd told me to stay as long as I liked, and if I was still here when he came home, there'd be something extra in it for me.

His humorous streak was both unexpected and welcome.

I rubbed my arms as shivers erupted. All I had to do was think about last night—or, actually, early this morning—for my body to rocket into hyperdrive.

Addiction to hyperdrive might become an issue. I smiled.

Xander had been so cute while we'd played Yahtzee. He'd been intent on the game and very competitive, even though I'd won in the end with more lucky shakes than him. He'd taken it like a champ. Overall, it'd been a very satisfying date night.

Much to Xander's possible disappointment, I was going to head home. It was almost eleven, and I needed to get some work done.

But first, I required a shower. I hadn't brought a change of clothes, which in hindsight would've been a good idea.

I made my way into the bathroom, humming some Nirvana. The tub was drained, and rose petals stuck to the sides everywhere. The candles had been blown out. Too much work to clean out the bathtub right now. I was already naked, so I walked right into the shower stall.

Hot spray pounded down around my shoulders as I replayed what had gone on here last night, which was the only natural thing to do inside the shower where you'd just had hot shower sex. Not only had the orgasm been amazing and powerful, as all of them had been in a way that they'd never been with anyone else, but after had been even sweeter. Xander had held me for a long time, then he'd tenderly washed me, murmuring endearing words in my ear.

It'd been heaven.

I grinned, still humming to myself, my brain moving on to what Gus and my parents would think of Xander. My dad would be impressed, not only with Xander's personality, but his accomplishments. My mom would be cautious at first but would accept him quickly enough. Xander had that effect on people. Gus would adore him, because my brother was an excellent judge of character. My brother was also a loyal, unfaltering optimist. He would pepper Xander with a million questions, but Xander would handle them with charm and grace.

The thought of the two of them together made me extremely happy.

I'd only ever brought home one boyfriend. Brian. The one who might've asked me to marry him if I'd stuck around. Everyone had been polite, but there'd been no real connection anywhere.

The sound of a door slamming caught my attention.

The shower was loud, but the slam had been unmistakable. Maybe Xander had come back for an early lunch, along with some other fun stuff. I chuckled to myself as I shut off the water, deciding I'd meet him in the bedroom. Wet.

As I walked through the doorway, a high-pitched shriek sounded.

I was momentarily too stunned to move.

"What are you doing in my home, you filthy slut!" the woman yelled from opposite side of the room in an Eastern European accent.

I froze, dripping water right beside Xander's bed. The one where he'd given me light caresses and sweet kisses before he left for work.

She fully entered the room. All six feet of her. Her gorgeous black hair flowed out behind her. She moved quickly. She was dressed in couture, something a normal person would look absurd in, but looked exactly right on her. A high-waisted wrap with flouncy shoulder droops and complicated ties. She came to a stumbling halt much too close to me on five-inch heels. Maybe six.

"I said, who the hell are you? Answer me!" A bag swung wide from one shoulder as she came to a stop. A hundred tiny Mickey Mouse faces greeted me.

I'd had no idea Mickey Mouse came in couture.

A teaching moment. *Yay, me.*

"Are you another one of his whores?" she demanded. "Is that who you are? You must be, because you're naked." A perfectly manicured finger slit the air in front of me with a dismissive flick. Her face was contorted in rage, her perfectly pouty lips pursed. Her eyes narrowed when I didn't answer, which only enhanced her expertly applied lashes, which were at least two inches long.

Honestly, any photographer in the world would hustle to pick up a camera right now. Her raw motion was staggering.

I continued to stay frozen in place, partly out of fear, partly out of devastation. This woman had a key to Xander's apartment. She hadn't broken in. And she was standing here accusing me of being the other woman.

"Answer me, you filthy whore!" she cried.

"I…um…I'm not a whore." It was the only thing that came to my mind.

She stomped closer. I instinctively backed up. Even though her heels were tall, she'd mastered them. A few more steps, and I'd hit the wall with my naked, wet butt.

"Get dressed, you bitch!" she shrieked. "I want you out of my home right this minute." Then she crinkled up her perfectly patrician nose like she'd gotten a whiff of something nasty. "Why would he want you when he has me anyway? You're… you're so *basic.*" She tossed some hair over her shoulder to punctuate her point.

No shreds of dignity existed anywhere around me. I decided to gather my clothes from where they were mostly piled on the bathroom floor. I scuttled backward, which was incredibly awkward and mortifying, trying not to show any more of my nakedness than necessary.

I had absolutely nothing to say to this woman, who I assumed was Stacy. I didn't want to interact with her in any way. I just wanted out of there.

As I stuffed my legs into my pants as quickly as possible, not bothering with my underwear, which I shoved in a pocket, Stacy sashayed into the doorway. Her eyes landed on the rose petals and burned-out candles. Her beautiful face shifted into a look of longing before quickly morphing back to rage.

Her gaze found me, eyes narrowing dangerously as she seethed, "Stay away from him. We're engaged." She thrust her left hand at me, her French manicure putting all other manicures I'd ever seen to shame. A gigantic rock sat on her fourth finger. I didn't know gem sizes very well, but it looked like forty thousand carats.

Xander had lied. She had a key to his place and a ring on her finger.

Shame threatened to engulf me as I wrestled on my shirt. "I'm sorry. This…this was a mistake." The only way out was to scoot by her. I had no desire to get in a physical altercation.

She seemed to gather herself, understanding now that I wasn't planning on fighting back. I wasn't interested in challenging her dominance or her right to be here. Why would I, when the guy I'd decided to take a chance on had neglected to tell me anything about this woman? To prepare me for what might come my way? If he'd dated her, he knew what she was like. What she was capable of. I didn't even care if they were actually engaged or if she'd made that up. I just wanted out.

"He would *never* choose a girl like you over me. You lack everything he desires. All men stray, and I've been gone for too long, but now I'm home to stay. If I ever see you around here again, you will rue the day." She made a fist, which was impressive since it had to hurt with all those pointy nails.

She actually shook it at me.

Frightening.

"You won't see me," I replied, deciding that ducking by her and getting the hell out was my only real option. I ran past, heading for the door, tears threatening to spill.

Xander was engaged to a supermodel. Or had been. Or whatever this was.

He'd lied about everything by not telling me anything.

Chapter 20

Once I was out of the building, I had no idea what to do or where to go. My underwear was stuffed in my pocket, and tears streaked down my face. I wasn't about to bother Jenny and Daniel, who were sleeping, or trying to. Plus, it was too mortifying to talk about at the moment.

I'd thankfully remembered to snag my jacket on my way out, Stacy clacking her stilettos after me as I went. She'd laughed as I'd fumbled with the doorknob. Humiliating me had likely been the highlight of her day.

But she had been wrong about one thing. Not all men strayed. Only ones like Xander.

I'd bought everything he'd told me, hook, line, and sinker, and when he chose not to talk about Stacy, a woman with a key to his residence, a possible ring on her finger, I'd let him off the hook. I had to shoulder some of this blame.

Later, though. Right now, it could all be his.

I hurried down the street, swiping at the water still leaking from my eyes, pissed it was even there at all. My movements were aggressive. I was angry at myself for not demanding more information about his relationship with a supermodel. I was angry that, during all of our long talks, he hadn't even once mentioned that she could show up unannounced with the kind of rage that I hadn't known existed in most people.

In his mind, he might be finished with her, but he'd been placating her with phone sex not even a few days ago. What kind of mixed messages were those? *Of course* she thought they were still engaged, or whatever. Who wouldn't?

More swipes.

I'd stupidly accepted the tiny morsel Xander had offered about her, because I'd wanted him. Because I'd already fallen for him. I'd cannon-balled into the deep end and hadn't even come up for air yet.

I stopped, digging my cell phone out of pocket. Thank goodness I'd left it in there. The first texts on my screen were from Xander, checking in to see how I was doing. He had no idea that Stacy had come home. I stood a few feet from a public trash can and tossed it in. I couldn't stand seeing his name on my screen.

Shit.

That'd been an impulsive thing to do.

I contemplated digging it out, but the can was chained shut with a small hole on top. Honestly, I didn't really want it back. I'd get a new phone. I'd had that one for umpteen years anyway. Everything was saved in the cloud. A new number, a new life, a new everything.

Stumbling toward a park bench near the water, I sat.

I'd never felt so emotionally drained in my entire life. I set my face in my hands, trying to calm myself down. The interaction with Stacy had been so charged and so painful, I was still shaking. My arms were literally quivering. I'd never, in my entire life, had another woman scream at me the way she had. The anguish in her voice had been unmistakable. By seeing me there, I had driven a knife through her heart. Her beautifully couture-clad heart.

Her delight in ridiculing me and making me feel less than had done its magic.

I felt less than.

I felt...broken.

Okay, get a hold on the facts before you spin out of control, Summer. Take a few deep breaths. You're going to be okay. You just need time to process this. You've only known him for a total of four days. The sex was amazing, but now it's tainted. You couldn't have fallen that hard, that quickly. Get a hold of yourself, and for Pete's sake, stop crying! You can get through this. And once you do, you'll be stronger for it.

The problem was, I had. I'd fallen for him fully and completely.

The undertow was fierce. Being with Xander over the past few days ranked among the happiest I'd ever felt in a relationship in my entire life. It put what I'd felt for Luke and Mitch to shame. Xander was the ideal. I was going to have a happy life with him. None of my previous boyfriends had ever come close to giving me that kind of euphoria.

I stood suddenly.

I couldn't stay here. I couldn't breathe.

Taking calm, measured inhales and exhales, with one hand over my chest, I made my way to the nearest bus stop. Thank goodness Seattle had an easy, efficient transit system.

On the bus ride home, I'd figure out my next move.

You already know what to do. Go home, see your family. Have some quality Gus time. Gather your wits about you. You're not broken, you just have a few fingernail stab wounds weighted down by that million-carat rock. It makes sense you're sore.

A calmness washed over me. A few days at home, and I'd be as good as new. I just needed to clear my head.

The bus ride was a blur. I barely noticed we were moving. I hopped off at a stop a little farther away from home, feeling the need to walk and think. I already felt better. Realizing that I'd learned something from my previous relationships and was stronger for it made me happy.

I ventured a small smile. I was going to be okay.

Xander would absolutely try to track me down so he could apologize. Or explain. Or whatever.

I didn't really want to hear it. Certainly, I wouldn't be ready to hear it for a while, if ever. He'd put me at risk. He knew who Stacy was, and he'd chosen not to discuss her. He'd chosen his privacy over making sure I stayed safe.

Plus, I couldn't help feeling that Stacy was right. Guys like him chose women like her. I was the other woman.

I'd leave town as soon as possible.

Hopefully, Xander wouldn't know I'd gone until after he arrived home from work and found his fiancée curled up in my place. The thought of them together made me physically ill. I placed my hand over my mouth just in case something came up.

Okay, so I was going to be okay, but it was going to take more than a day, retching aside. Her beauty had been so striking it'd hurt.

Not the way I was hurting now, feeling the betrayal of a man who could've easily come clean when asked—but a different kind of pain. Like, a why-did-men-always-seem-to-pick-beauty-over-everything-else ache. It was degrading. What had Xander seen in me if Stacy was what he preferred?

I turned down the next block toward home. No one stood in front of my house. I held my head high. I'd have to tell my friends what had happened, of course. That felt weighty, so my shoulders slumped a little. But they were going to be happy I was okay and just needed a little time away to process.

I didn't have a phone, so it would have to be over email.

Once inside, I grabbed a duffel bag out of my closet and threw in some clothes. Enough for a week. I could do laundry if I needed to. Mom was going to be so excited to see me. Gus was, too.

Then I fired up my computer and checked the Busbud website and was relieved to see there were still tickets available for a bus leaving at one fifteen today. If I rushed, I could make it. No way could I catch a flight that quickly.

I purchased a one-way ticket, not knowing at this very moment when I'd want to come back. It would be a five-and-a-half-hour bus ride to Spokane, a little over four in a car.

After that task was completed, I fired off an email to my mom. She checked her in-box regularly because of all of Gus's appointments, so she should get it before I arrived. I was vague on details on why I was coming but told her when and where to pick me up. If she didn't get the email, it wasn't a big deal. I'd figure it out.

Visiting on the spur of the moment wasn't out of the norm for me. I'd done it a few times in the past to surprise them.

Then came the harder part. Emailing my friends. They

would understand and support me, but the humiliation of it all still stung like a thousand bees attacking my face at once. Stacy calling me a whore kept replaying in my mind, much to the detriment of my fragile psyche. I decided a group email was the best way to tackle things.

> Hi guys,
>
> Just wanted you all to know that I'm on my way to Spokane. I had an incredibly awkward (insert humiliating) run-in with Stacy this morning while Xander was at work. Yes, *that* Stacy. Apparently, she might've been his fiancée at one time? Hard to know. She had a gigantic rock on her finger and claimed it was from Xander. She's a supermodel, too, so yay for working stereotypes! She was not happy to see me and hurled quite a few insults my way while I stood there naked and wet. But I'm okay! I swear! There's no need to come to my rescue. I just need to spend some time away to recuperate and clear my head. Oh, and I ditched my phone. It was a spur-of-the-moment decision that I'm kind of regretting now. It's in a garbage can outside Jenny's building. When I get a new phone, I'll reach out. Again, I can't stress this enough—I'm fine. This isn't a crisis! I'm actually feeling pretty strong. I've only known the man for a few days. He chose not to tell me about Stacy, even though I asked. His choice. But the last thing I want to do is talk to him about it right now. Going to hang out with Gus, which is always therapeutic. I'll email you

again once I get settled in Spokane so you won't worry. Again, I'm good. I really am!

Love, Summer

Surprisingly, I did feel okay. I wasn't lying. I felt like a grown-up. I'd jumped in with a guy I was unsure of, I got a little burned, but I was handling it. I brought my hands out in front of me and turned them palm side up. Nothing was on fire, and the shaking had gone away.

I shut off my computer, stuffed my laptop and toiletries into a large bag, slung it over my shoulder, and headed out.

This was one of the things I most enjoyed about being self-employed. I could do my job anywhere, and it was certainly an asset today.

* * *

Five and a half hours went by quickly, considering. I'd read a book and dozed on and off. By the time the bus pulled into the station, my mind was clear. I'd replayed almost everything that had happened over the last few days a couple times, then I'd put it away.

Out the window, I spotted my mom's green Subaru. I stood, gathering my things from the top rack, awaiting my turn to exit. I'd already decided that I wasn't going to mention Xander or Stacy or any of it to my family. I didn't want to worry them unnecessarily. Instead, I was going to use this time to work on myself and spend some quality time with the people I loved.

I rounded the front of the bus, heading toward the car. To

my surprise, the passenger door opened, and Gus emerged. I grinned, calling out, "Gus!"

He ambled toward me, his gait smoother than the last time. He walked right into my embrace. "I came with Mom," he said proudly. "I like running errands now. New places don't scare me as much."

I held him close, then at arm's length, taking him in. He looked great. "That's wonderful news."

My mom stood behind us, waiting for her turn. "It's good to see you, Summer," she said as she pulled me in for one of her signature embraces, patting the back of my head and rocking me. "It's been too long. We're glad you decided to come." She grabbed my duffel and put it in the back of the car.

"Where's Keith?" I asked, bending over to see if Gus's helper was in the backseat.

"Oh, he's at home," Gus told me. "He doesn't have to come with me all the time anymore. I'm practicing doing things by myself or with Mom or Dad. Dr. Lindall thinks it will help me get better."

I arched a brow at my mom, who was grinning. "That's even more fantastic news." Gus got in the passenger side, and I climbed in the back. As my mom turned the car around, I realized I should probably explain myself a little. "I've been so busy the last few months, which is great, but I woke up this morning really missing you guys. After we finished chatting yesterday evening," I said to my brother, "I figured a little time with the fam was in order." My tone was lighthearted. "It was a spontaneous getaway."

Gus chattered back. "If it's okay with you, Mom and I want to pick up burgers from Morrie's and bring them back to my apartment. Is that okay with you?" His voice was anxious, like he thought I might object.

"Of course," I answered. "Burgers sound perfect."

My mom glanced at me in the rearview mirror and winked. "Then you and I can go home and have some girl time. I'm so glad you're here."

I settled back in my seat, glancing out the window at my hometown. "It feels good to be back." I meant it.

"Dad wants to pick you up for breakfast tomorrow," she said. "You can call him later from the home phone."

Gus turned around. "What happened to your phone, huh? People don't usually lose their phones. At least, that's what Keith said. Mom said you might be wanting a social media break. Is that it? Social media is hard for me, but I like looking at pictures with words. The pictures are funny sometimes."

I patted his hand. "I accidentally dropped my phone in the bay, but I'm enjoying a break from social media. I'll get another one soon."

He continued, "I like to look at animals." He described a favorite meme featuring a polar bear.

"That sounds like a funny one," I agreed.

"I'm glad you're home, Summer. I've missed you," he said.

"I've missed you, too."

Chapter 21

I blew out a breath. I was becoming a master at extended sighs. My dad was on his way over to pick me up for breakfast, so I decided now was a good time to open my laptop. I wouldn't have a chance to email everybody back, but I wanted to be a good friend and let them know I was okay. I'd jotted off a quick email last night, as promised, to let them know I'd arrived and had been out with my mom and brother, but I hadn't been emotionally ready to read all their responses.

I flicked the power button on.

My computer efficiently remembered the location from the last time, and I was patched into the Wi-Fi. I fortified myself as I clicked on the email icon.

I had twelve new messages, a few of them from clients. I was relieved to see none was from Xander. My website wasn't hard to find. He could've sent me a comment directly from my site but hadn't.

The emails were listed in order of their arrival time, so I went to the first one, which was from Poppy, and opened it. She had clicked on reply all, which made it easier.

> OH MY GOD, SUMMER!!! I'm so sorry this happened. You were right, and I feel so much shame for the part I played. I can't believe he had you stay at his place when he knew she was around and had a key! My heart is breaking for you. I'm so glad you're with your family. It's the perfect place to hunker down and recover. If you need anything, let us know, and we'll be there lickety-split. I can borrow Annabel's car if you need me. Let me know. What a scumbag!!!! I'm so angry right now I want to punch somebody! Do you want me to cancel my appointment with Leo? We're set to meet in a couple days. Let me know. I'm happy to do it! Anything for you. I know you've got this. No man will get the best of you, not on my watch.
> Sending SO much love! I'm here if you need me!
>
> XOXOXO
> Poppy

Poppy was the sweetest. She was such a good friend. If left to her own devices, she would probably punch Xander if she saw him. It would likely be a slug in the shoulder, but still. She always attributed her spitfire attitude to her maternal grandmother, Carlotta, an Italian who'd married a Swede. Poppy's mother had married an Irishman. The rest was history.

I blew out another breath and opened the next one, which

was from Eve:

> Oh NO!!!!! OMG! How awful. What an Asshole with a capital A! I can't believe he put you in that position. That's the lowest of the low. A snake in the grass. A fiancée?! I never would've guessed in a million years. I feel incredibly guilty for forcing you to be with him. But you just seemed so happy! All we ever want is for you to be happy! If I could take back any influence I had, I would. You have my love and support. I know you're strong, and you have this, but if you need anything, I'm there. Thinking about you and sending hugs!
>
> XOXO
> Eve

I could always count on Eve. She'd been there to help pick up the pieces with Mitch, and she was here now. I appreciated that. The next one was from Jenny.

> That rat bastard!! I'm so sorry, Summer. I feel like this is all my fault. If I hadn't needed a nanny, none of this would've happened. I'm at the hospital on a short break, sneaking some phone time in. I'll send more later when I get home. Anything you need, let me know. I'll even move if you want me to (tho, convincing Dan will take time). Sending you love and hugs and kisses!!!
>
> XO, J

I adored my friends. There were more responses on the email chain, but I didn't have time to read them all now. I hit reply all and wrote:

> Thanks for the support, guys! I appreciate it, as always. Heading out to breakfast now with my dad. Feeling really good and upbeat. I haven't had a chance to read through all the emails, but I will when I get home. Still no phone. More to come.
>
> XOXOXO
>
> Summer

I closed my laptop.

I'd slept fitfully, tossing and turning, thinking about Xander, as well as everything that had happened. But I woke up feeling centered, and I was thankful for it. He was just one guy.

I got up and wandered over to a table full of photos. I focused on one of my favorites, a picture of Gus and me sitting in the snow in snow pants and hats, jackets strewn to the side, abandoned on a warm day, our arms locked around each other's shoulders, heads almost touching.

He was probably eight, as I was around six.

We'd been so innocent then. Not knowing what the world had in store for us. No worries, nothing tragic to deal with. Like I'd told Xander, we'd been two average siblings who'd fought, giggled, conspired, and loved each other. I smiled as a single tear tumbled down my cheek.

A car horn beeped outside and I ran a fingertip from my face to Gus's. I was who I was because of Gus's accident, and I liked me.

I grabbed one of my mother's light coats near the door and went out to greet my father.

"There she is," he said as he came around the back of his SUV to embrace me.

Whenever Gus needed to go anywhere for an extended period of time, my dad was always the one to take him. Gus needed a lot of stuff to feel secure, so a big car was essential.

I walked into his arms gratefully. "Hi, Dad."

"I've missed you." He planted a kiss on my cheek and let it linger.

I quickly knuckled away another tear as we both stepped back, hoping he didn't notice. "It's so good to see you."

He went around the car, and I got in. "You, too."

I pulled open the passenger door, and by way of explaining myself, said, "I know my visit is unexpected," I shut the door and strapped myself in, "but I woke up yesterday after finishing a couple of projects"—a lie—"I realized how much I missed you guys. So I figured now was a good time for me to visit."

My dad put the car in gear. "Well, I'm happy you made that decision. Gus has been asking for you the past few weeks, wondering when he could see you. He's over the moon that you're home. He talked to me for a good half an hour about it this morning, filling me in on everything you did and said last night. Damn if that kid doesn't improve by the hour. I would've brought him this morning, but I wanted to catch up with you first."

I nodded. "I'm glad you did."

"I was thinking about heading to Ralph's Diner for one of their killer omelets."

"Perfect. I need coffee."

"They have the best in Spokane."

We drove in silence for a few blocks. "You took Gus snowboarding," I said. "That had to have been an emotional day."

My father's grip on the steering wheel flexed. "Yes, it was quite a day. I thought it might wreck me, but it ended up having quite the opposite effect, which was a pleasant surprise. To see how far he's come and realize how far he can go and seeing the pure joy on that kid's face—it was an amazing sight. He'll be out there again for sure."

I glanced out the window. "I wish I could've seen it. I definitely would've been emotional."

"He wasn't anywhere near his old aptitude, of course. But I could see the intent lurking there. He hasn't forgotten how. That was the exciting part. Keith couldn't believe his eyes. It was a great day."

"Sounds like it."

"We decided not to take him back this season, not that we can, as the mountain is melting fast. But he made so much progress just being there, we want it to sink in a little bit." He pulled into Ralph's parking lot and shut off the car. "Here we are. Not too far to go for good coffee." I grabbed the handle to open the door, but my father's hand on my arm stopped me. I turned. His face was filled with compassion. "Listen, I can tell you're down about something, but I'm not going to pry. We're going to go in there and catch up on all the mundane things in our lives. You can tell me about work and your friends, and I'll tell you about my new hobby collecting old coins. It's amazing what you can find on the internet. We're going to keep it nice and light." His expression softened. "I love you, Summer. I'm happy to see you, no matter what brought you here. You're hurting, but we don't have to talk about it until you're ready. I'm just looking forward to spending time with you."

A tear trickled down my cheek, and I smiled. "Thank you, Dad. I appreciate that. I am a little sad, but nothing I won't be able to bounce back from."

He patted my hand. "You can talk about it when you're ready. Now let's go get some of that stellar caffeine."

"Deal."

Chapter 22

After a pleasant breakfast with my father, who'd been true to his word and hadn't asked me a single personal question, we sat idling in front of my mom's house. I was going to go visit with Gus later this afternoon.

"Thank you for taking me out." I leaned in and gave him a quick hug. "It was wonderful to catch up. I'll probably be here for at least a week, so we can do it again."

"How about I take you and Gus out for dinner in the next night or two?"

"That sounds good. I'll check with Mom and Gus to see what day works."

I was about to get out, but he stopped me again. "Summer, I just want to let you know that I think you're a wonderful person. You've blossomed into a smart, successful, independent woman, and as your dad, I couldn't be prouder. Your business is thriving and you're a talented artist. You bring a lot of good into this world. Don't let whatever has you down affect your outlook about who you are. Not all men understand how to interact with their more intelligent counterparts. I was pretty crummy at it myself. But given time, most of them come around."

I smiled. I hadn't given anything away, but he had deduced this was about a man. "Thanks, Dad. I appreciate your nuggets of wisdom. They're always helpful. I knew you were too intuitive for your own good. But I'm not letting it affect me other than allowing myself to mourn the loss quickly and move on with my life." I gave my father a quick peck on the cheek. "I'll see you soon." I opened the door and hopped out.

"Chin up. The right one will come along, and when he does, you'll know it."

I made my way into the house, feeling better about everything. Not even in Spokane for twenty-four hours, and this place was already grounding me.

Inside, I grabbed my laptop. After I caught up on emails, I planned to curl up with one of my mom's books—she loved reading and had overflowing bookshelves—and then go see Gus. It was going to be a very low-key, enjoyable afternoon.

There were a few more unread emails since I'd checked before breakfast. My heart began to pound when I saw the address—info@zoeslager.com. I almost slammed my laptop shut.

Instead of being a baby, I took a few breaths.

Ignoring the one from Zoe's Lager, as I was clearly not ready to go there yet, I clicked on the one that had come in after Jenny's yesterday. It was from Poppy:

> Just checking in on you. Your silence is kind of freaking me out, but I understand. I really do. Just

want to know if you're okay. If you need anything, and I mean *anything*, please call. I have your mom's number, but I'm using restraint. This is me restrained. I'm practically sitting on my hands. You'll probably get a few more of these until we hear from you.

I love you oodles. Thinking about you nonstop.
XOXOXO with sugar on top

P

Poppy had sent this not even a half an hour after she sent her first. I'd been on the bus on my way to Spokane. The next one was from Jenny, marked around eleven thirty last night.

OMG!!! Just got home. Dan said there was a bunch of yelling and screaming across the hall while he was home with Clara. He said it happened around dinnertime. The police came. THE POLICE!!!! He's just telling me this right now. I'm furious he didn't try to get a hold of me at work! He only opened the door once because he didn't want to seem like a nosy neighbor. He said he couldn't see anything. He wasn't sure if it was coming from Xander's apartment or not—why, I have no idea. I have to teach him to be more observant and spy-worthy. Not sure what's going on, but I'll keep you posted. I'm planning to drum up an excuse to stop by and talk to the neighbor who lives next to Xander. If she knows, she will spill. More later.
XO, J

The police were at Xander's? What did that mean? My heart slid into my throat, pumping furiously, making it hard to swallow. I quickly clicked on two more emails, one from Poppy and one from Eve, both commenting on Jenny's email, urging her to hurry up and figure out what was going on. The next one was from Jenny, time-stamped early this morning.

> Neighbor wasn't home. I don't have any solid details, but I'm working on it. Every time I hear so much as a squeak in the hallway, my eye is at the peephole. It's possible Xander came and went while I was giving Clara a bath, but I haven't seen him yet. I'll try again soon. Thinking about you and hoping you're well. Hunker down with family. I'm not sure what all this means, but I'm starting to believe there might be more to the story than we know, which could shed some light into this dark abyss.
> Sending lots of love,
> XO, J

The next one was from Poppy, replying to the email I'd sent this morning before I'd had breakfast.

> Happy you're seeing your dad. You haven't said anything about the police at Xander's?? What do you think it means? Waiting for Jenny to get the scoop is driving me crazy! I think it means Xander came home from work and found Crazy Lady there instead of you, and things got heated. It feels like we're missing a few

> facts here. I'm sending as many good vibes as I can in this one. Jenny, what's going on?? We need more answers! We're dying on a vine out here.
>
> Hope breakfast was nice. Email us soon!
> XOXOXO
> P

The only thing left to do was open the email from Zoe's Lager.

The only other email that had come in after his was from margaret@crisisfamily.com. I had no idea who that was. With all the info about the police, I was curious what Xander had to say. In the end, I wanted answers—I *needed* answers. My finger hovered over the button. I clicked it, and the email filled the screen.

> Summer, I'm so sorry...

I closed my eyes. I wasn't sure if I could do this.

You have to read it. You have to get closure. Reading his email doesn't mean you have to reply or say anything to him ever again. You need answers. Get this done. Rip it off like a Band-Aid. I opened my eyes.

> ...you had to find out about Stacy like that. I apologize for not finding your email address sooner. It took me a while to figure out you weren't going to answer my texts. I went to your house and sat out on the stoop all night. I don't think you were home. I didn't see any lights on. I can certainly explain everything in an email, but I feel like this should be a face-to-face

> conversation. I want a chance to explain everything in person, and I'm hoping you'll grant me that. I made a huge mistake by not telling you everything about Stacy. My relationship with her is extremely complicated.

I turned away as tears threatened to fall. Even though I knew I had to make it through, it was tougher than I'd thought it was going to be. He was admitting he'd had a relationship with the beautiful woman who'd called me a whore. The one he'd known could find me naked and vulnerable in his bed.

Wiping my face, I forced myself to continue.

> I've never done anything like this before, but I've asked my sister Margaret, Mags, to email you. She's a therapist. I went to her for advice about Stacy early on. I feel like if you hear the basics of the story from someone other than myself, you'll be more likely to want to hear from me after. I know you're hurting. I'm so sorry. I made a gigantic mistake, the worst of my life, by not telling you everything when you first asked. I wasn't lying when I said I'm not with Stacy. I'm not. It's just a really screwed-up situation. Please read the email. My sister is amazing. Then please reply to this. I'll be waiting to hear from you.
> Xander
>
> PS. Please don't give up on us. You're the best thing that's happened to me in a very long time.

My throat constricted. I stood, setting my computer aside. I would read Mags's email, but I needed a second to process everything Xander had said.

He still claimed he wasn't with Stacy.

I walked to my bedroom window, which looked out onto the backyard, a modest-sized lot with ample trees. My mom's garden occupied the space where we used to have a swing set. A two-car garage was beyond the wooden fence. My mom occasionally rented out the second stall to people with campers to make a little extra money. None of it had changed much since I'd been gone. The trees and shrubs were a little larger and thicker, and there was a bench in the sun near the garden. My mom had more time to spend in the yard, so there were more flowers, early bulbs sprouting. A few shallow piles of hard-packed snow remained beneath the shade of the trees.

My mind turned back to Xander. Why had the police been called? He hadn't addressed that. Maybe Daniel had been mistaken. Maybe there'd been a break-in. Why hadn't Xander mentioned anything? That was pretty big news.

He'd said I was the best thing to happen to him in a long time. Funny, I'd felt the same way up until a few hours ago. Now I only felt numb.

Moving away from the window, I headed back to my bed. I was curious to see what Mags had written. I knew, even without reading it, that her words would have a huge impact on how Xander and I moved forward. Either I could handle what she said, or I couldn't. I also knew that whatever was in that email wasn't going to be an easy read.

Setting my computer back on my lap, I clicked open the email. It was longer than any of the others. I scooted back against the bed frame, propping my pillow behind me, and began to read:

> Hi, Summer,
>
> My name is Margaret, Mags for short. I'm Xander's big sister. I want you to know that I've never done anything like this before—for a family member or a client—so bear with me. I love my brother beyond reason, which is why I agreed to explain to you what I know about this situation, with my brother's permission, of course. A little bit of background about me. I've been a crisis counselor for the past eight years, but in reality, I've always been one. Having a sick sibling, I was the person in the family constantly making sure everyone was okay. I'm sure you know the type—the caretaker. The emotional fixer. The peacekeeper. Now I help other families through similar grief. I think I'm fairly good at my job, but you'd have to ask my clients.
>
> Again, with Xander's permission, I'm going to let you in on some of his backstory first, as I think it'll help in further explaining this complicated situation. He and our sister, Zoe, were extremely close throughout her entire life. It was clear to everyone, even in the beginning, that they had a special bond. As she got older, he willingly became her primary caregiver when he was home, which meant he got up with her in the mornings, made her meals, helped her dress, tended to her throughout the day, administering meds and whatever else she needed. Then he put her to bed. He

did this by choice. Of course, there were others there to help. My parents were heavily involved. She had medical staff in and out. But when Xander was home, he was her everything. Then, when he went away to college, then law school, he came home regularly just to do these things, and Zoe adored that.

There's no question her death hit him the hardest out of all of us. We knew it was coming. We had fair warning, but somehow Xander couldn't make that connection until it happened. Our entire family had been in therapy for as long as I can remember, so we were all familiar with talking about our feelings. But after her death, Xander closed down and needed more intensive help. After about a year, he was able to work through some of the emotional loss of our sister enough to live what I'd call a regular life without bouts of depression that left him bedridden. Experiencing her loss changed something inside him.

He hasn't dated much in the past few years, as connecting with people on an emotional level is scary for him. He's terrified of experiencing another loss like Zoe's, so that makes putting his love and trust in another person extremely difficult. The few women he's dated have tended to be unemotional characters, easy to leave, easy to stay detached. You probably know the type. Stacy was one of those. In his words, she was a casual hookup. He'd just moved up to Seattle, which was a big deal for him to be so far away from the family, taking that step to fulfill his dream of owning his own business. He was lonely. He never had an emotional investment in her, I can promise you that much.

Unfortunately, Stacy had issues of her own. I can't speak for her, nor do I know the particulars of what she's been through, or her current mental health status, but from what my brother's told me, I would characterize her as being a narcissist and having a delusional disorder at the very least. This kind of disorder can be brought about by severe childhood trauma, but since she's not a client of mine, that's just an educated guess.

Right from the start, she rewrote their relationship, making it into something it wasn't—after just two meetings, she claimed they were engaged. Xander was alarmed and tried to back away. As he tried to break contact with her altogether, it triggered something in her. She became suicidal, voicing suicidal thoughts and actions directly to my brother. You'll need to ask him for those specific details.

My brother has one of the tenderest hearts I've ever known. He wouldn't hurt an insect, much less someone in crisis. So he called me, and I agreed to help. We were working through some healthier methods for him to break from her, including connecting with her only over the phone, trying to appease her, but avoiding physical contact. We hoped that eventually she would let go. He tried to get her to visit a therapist in Seattle, but she refused. Her job as a model takes her out of the country often, so he was hopeful slow disassociation would work. He'd been at it for months and believed it was working, but it was wearing on him. He was caught up in an abusive relationship with a woman he barely knew, and he had every right to leave, no matter the consequences, but he stayed because he felt he couldn't risk her life. There was no way for me to evaluate if her actions were intentional or purely to manipulate him. So he continued to appease her as best he could.

When he met you, everything changed. Stacy was out of the country, and he consulted with me, already deciding he was going to let her know it was definitely over, that he couldn't keep up the charade any longer. He called a suicide hotline, and they gave him some valuable information. I gave him some names of a few local psychiatrists and psychotherapists. He had numbers ready if he needed them. She wasn't due back for another week, so he felt like he had time to prepare.

I don't want to give you the impression that he spoke to me about you. He did not. He was extremely reticent about this relationship and insisted on protecting your privacy at all costs, as he should. He's not sure what happened between you and Stacy, but he knows it was bad. When he confronted Stacy, she lost it, threatening suicide, so he was forced to call the police. They have taken her to a local hospital.

There's one more piece of information I want to share before I sign off, and I promise I'm not trying to influence your decision to meet with my brother and let him explain in person, which is, of course, his end goal. That's for you to decide. I'm telling you this as a big sister who knows and loves her brother. Xander didn't have to spell out to me on the phone how important you are to him. I heard the anguish in his voice. He was beside himself, knowing that he'd hurt you. He cares for you deeply. It was surprising to me, because I wasn't certain he'd be able to form those kinds of bonds for a long time. It made my heart soar. You must be a very special woman. I hope that someday I get a chance to meet you. If not, I wish you the very best. May success and happiness follow you along in your life's journey. If you want to get in contact with me, I'll leave my number under my signature. I'm happy to talk about this in person, but there's absolutely no pressure to do so. I appreciate your time.

Thanks for reading,
Margaret Scott Brennan, PhD

With tears streaming down my face, I did the only thing I could do. I clicked on Xander's email and wrote five words:

I will meet with you.

Chapter 23

"I thought you were going to stay longer." Gus was agitated. "My favorite TV show is on tonight, and you said you'd watch it with me." My brother wasn't whining or angry, just confused and a little hurt.

I'd been careful not to let on to Gus that I was leaving until a few minutes ago.

We'd had a nice afternoon together. He'd shown me some of the projects he'd been working on. It seemed he was turning into quite the artist. Art therapy was good for the brain.

Last night, I'd promised him I would stay into the evening so we could watch his favorite crime show together.

But after my back-and-forth with Xander this morning, he had insisted on driving out to Spokane today so we could talk, so I was forced to amend my day. A shift in Gus's game plan was difficult, but I knew he'd be okay.

"I said I would watch the show with you, and I meant it. I'm coming back," I told him, resting my hand on his forearm. "But a friend of mine is surprising me with a visit today, and I didn't find out about it until this morning. I have to meet him because he's driving all the way from Seattle. But I'll be back in time so we can watch together. I promise."

Gus's expression brightened. "You can bring your friend with you. Maybe he likes TV shows, too."

"I'm not sure this particular friend will be staying that long." I wasn't sure about anything. I'd been replaying Mags's email in my mind all afternoon. It'd really hit me hard and resonated for a variety of reasons, including that Xander had tried so hard to help Stacy.

But I needed to hear the entire story from him before I made any decisions about how I felt.

Instead of explaining everything to my girlfriends, I'd edited Mags's email, taking out the personal and private stuff about Xander, keeping the stuff about Stacy, and forwarded it to them. I hadn't stuck around my computer to catch their responses, but I could imagine a flurry of activity had followed. There would be more than a few hallelujahs and a couple of I-told-you-sos.

Xander had responded to my email almost immediately. He'd been waiting. We hadn't gotten into anything other than his insistence about talking to me today and me giving him my mom's address. He'd said he would leave as soon as possible.

That was at noon. It was almost four.

"Okay," Gus replied sullenly. "But if he decides to stay, bring him over. It's been a long time since I've seen any of your friends." During my years in college, all my girlfriends had visited. They all loved spending time with Gus. "I don't have many friends. Except Keith. And Charlie and Bob from therapy.

And Hal from swimming."

Keith was in the other room. When Gus had family over, Keith tried to be as unobtrusive as possible, which we all appreciated. "You're forgetting Larry and Dana from cognitive therapy. They love you," I told him.

"Yeah, but I don't see them much anymore. I'm doing so good I'm not there as much."

"Which is incredible. I'm so proud of you," I said, patting his leg. "You've come such a long way. You're a pretty amazing guy. I hope you know that."

"When do you have to leave to meet your friend?" he asked, ignoring my praise. "I like having you here."

"I like being here. I have to go in a few minutes," I said. "But if things work out, I might bring him back. But don't get your hopes up. I don't want you to be disappointed."

"What's his name?"

"Xander Scott."

"He has two first names?"

I chuckled. "I guess he does."

"Is Xander short for Alexander? Is it a nickname? Like me. I have a nickname. Gus is short for Gustav."

"I assume it's short for Alexander, but I'm not really sure. I've never asked him." Nothing like not knowing the guy's first name to illustrate how short your time had been together. I remember Jenny telling me that his mailbox read A.A. Scott. One of those As had to stand for Alexander. It only made sense. "Dad wants to take us out to dinner sometime this week. How do you feel about that?" I asked, changing the subject.

Gus perked up. "Can we go to Fireside Pies? I like their pizza. They also have root beer. Not many restaurants have it.

Dad said they all had root beer back in his day."

"Of course. Fireside Pies sounds perfect," I said as I stood. "Now I have to get going." Gus's place was within walking distance of our childhood home. I grabbed my coat, another one of my mom's, and made my way toward the front door.

Gus followed me. "You're coming back, right? You're not going to leave Spokane without saying goodbye?" I heard the anxiousness.

"Yes. I'm coming back. I'm just visiting with a friend. I'll be back when I'm done. I'm not sure what time." To assuage his fears, I reached out and hugged him. "I'm staying for a week. Like I promised. You can't get rid of me that easily."

He hugged me back, holding on. "Good. I've missed you, sis."

My heart clenched. Gus hadn't called me sis since we were little. I stroked the back of his hair. "I've missed you, too. I'm happy to be here to see all your progress." We parted. "Now don't be sad. I'll be back later tonight. I'm not sure when. I don't have my phone, so don't try to call it."

"Okay," he said. "I'm going to work on a painting while you're gone."

"Sounds good, bud." I grinned as I opened the front door. I used to call him bud all the time. It felt good to use it again.

Another little piece of my brother was back, and this was like getting a coveted corner piece of the puzzle.

I hurried down the street toward my mom's house. I should have enough time to get ready before Xander arrived. I was beginning to get fluttery inside, knowing I was going to see him. It was going to be awkward, but at least that sorrowful, heartbroken feeling in my chest had eased somewhat.

Once home, I prepped a little, combing my hair and changing

clothes. My actions were more like nervous tics than anything else.

I took my laptop into the living room, where I could see out the front window.

As predicted, my in-box was lit up.

I scanned the messages. Poppy and Eve expressed their relief that there was an explanation for this predicament, but both kept their I-told-you-sos to themselves. Poppy ordered me to get a new phone immediately. Jenny was both relieved and horrified to find out the reason for the police presence in her building. They'd likely taken Stacy to the same hospital where she and Daniel worked, and she wanted to check into it. She knew a few doctors on rotation in the emergency psych ward.

I replied to Jenny to ask her not to do that.

Stacy was entitled to her privacy. It sounded like the model had a lot of emotional baggage to work through, and my heart broke a little for her. The relief that Xander hadn't proposed to her was overwhelming, even though I'd been leaning toward it probably not being true.

There was nothing like having validation.

My friends were all in awe of the eloquence of Mags's email and the thoughtfulness of Xander to ask her to send it, just as I was. It was a prime example of how families took care of each other. But Mags had done it in a way that had been completely professional and nonthreatening. I felt enormously grateful for that. Xander had been right to have someone else lay out clinically what had happened. It had left the messy emotion off the table.

I heard a car but almost didn't look up, expecting a motorcycle. Surprisingly, the car edged to the curb and parked.

Setting the laptop down, I made my way to the front door, opening it as Xander emerged from a dark sedan that must have been Leo's. I wasn't sure what the make or model of it was, as I hardly ever paid attention to cars, but if it was Leo's, he was a good friend to let Xander use it.

Even from this distance, I could tell Xander was weary.

He had on a dark green shirt and a charcoal wool jacket I'd never seen. His hands were shoved in his pockets, his head down. When he was almost to me, he looked up, startled I was waiting. He flashed a small, tentative smile.

I propped open the screen door, which still had its storm window inserted, since it wasn't warm enough for the screen. "Hi," I said. "Welcome to Spokane."

He didn't try to reach for me, and I was glad. And sad. We weren't at that point, but having him this close and not being able to touch him felt harder than I'd thought it'd be. I knew what those lips tasted like and what that body felt like under his clothes. I wanted to caress him. And be comforted by him.

"I drove through downtown. It's bigger than I thought it would be."

"Everyone says that. It's a great city. I enjoyed growing up here."

"Summer," he started once he was inside, turning toward me, anguish at the forefront. "I should've told you about Stacy from the very beginning. All of it. This is all my fault—"

"Yes, you should have," I cut him off. "But instead of doing this right here, inside the foyer, let's head out to the backyard. My mom has a nice garden out there with a bench in the sun. We'll be more comfortable out there."

He nodded.

I led him through the house and out the back door, which was off the kitchen. He murmured nice things about my childhood home, which I appreciated.

Once we were in the garden, I took a seat on the bench. He sat next to me, close enough, but not touching. The sun felt fortifying. He was definitely tired, but he was still absolutely beautiful. The man took my breath away.

"Before you start," I cautioned, turning toward him, "I want you to know that I appreciated Mags's email a lot. Your sister is amazing. She gave the entire situation much-needed clarity. I've been thinking about her words all day." I stared at the ground. "Actually, I'm not sure what I would've done if she hadn't taken the time to explain it all. Thinking about talking to you felt so… painful and awkward. I was mad and hurt, and she changed the way I viewed what happened. I wasn't sure if anyone could do that."

"My sister is the smartest and brightest of us." He smiled. "I knew I could count on her to deliver the whole debacle in a clinical way."

"Did you read the email before she sent it?"

He shook his head, his face projecting the same sorrow I'd felt yesterday after meeting Stacy. He was unsure what the outcome of this meeting would be. "No. I trust her. I wanted it to be between you and her. I came to tell you my side of the story. That was the deal."

I settled a hand on his thigh, my fingertips immediately feeling buzzy, excitement mixed with uncertainty. He met my gaze, showing his surprise that I'd reached out. "The love and trust you have for your family is endearing," I told him. "That, along with everything else, has helped me understand why you chose to do what you did with Stacy. But I'm still struggling with why you didn't just explain it all to me. It hurts that you didn't. Trust is a big thing for me. Huge. I've had some awful relationships with men in the past, and you not being honest will be hard for me to work past. We've only been together for a few days, and we haven't dived into any past relationships, so I realize you didn't know. But honesty, integrity, and respect are absolute must-haves."

"I totally agree. And if me not telling you is what ends this before it has a chance to start, it'll be one of the biggest regrets of my life." He took in a breath before he began. "My main reason for not telling you, which seemed rational at the time, was that I feared that if I gave you all the ugly details that day in the loft, you'd bolt." He threaded his hands together, head down. "You were already wary of starting anything with me, and selfishly, I thought that if I could keep this information from you for a while—my extremely short hookup with a model who turned out to have mental health issues—you'd be emotionally invested and more likely to give us a chance." He paused for a moment. I let him gather his thoughts without interrupting. "Please know that I planned to tell you at some point. All of it. I was just hoping to tell you *after* I'd dealt with Stacy, and it was in the past." He rubbed the side of his face. "You disappeared that day from the pub so fast, and I was crazy-worried that I'd messed it all up. Then you came back. I felt like I'd been given this miraculous second chance. I didn't want to ruin it." He slid a little closer, meeting my eyes. "Then the next day, when we were talking at Jenny's, playing games and having so much fun I couldn't bring myself to bring it up. But I should have. Then, right before we fell asleep on the couch, you made a joke about you and hot guys never working out. I asked what you meant but you didn't go into details."

I remembered that very short conversation. I'd been very sleepy.

"I really wanted you to like me," he said. "I wanted you to respect me. I honestly didn't think I'd get another chance if I messed things up. Stacy, and my handling of the entire thing, was such a huge screw-up. I believe, looking back, I would've done just about anything to keep you at that point, even go against my better judgment, which is exactly what I ended up doing."

When I was ready, I replied, "I understand what you're saying. When you lay it out like that, your thought process makes some sense. We hadn't known each other for very long, and we were caught up in a great deal of excitement and lust. But I asked you about Stacy. I asked for the truth. I can't be in a relationship with someone who I don't trust, who doesn't respect me enough to give me hard news."

He nodded sadly. "I can understand that. All I can say is that my thinking was irrational at the time. I've never omitted the truth to anybody like that before, especially when they asked me something up front. It's not a tendency of mine to lie, but you don't know that because we don't have a history together." He scrubbed a hand over his eyes. "I was just so worn out by Stacy"—his head bobbed down in defeat—"and everything she's put me through and so happy to have met you, it clouded my judgment." He looked up. His eyes were the deepest green with a hint of blue at the center, and they were filled with sorrow. "Honestly, Summer, you're the kind of girl that I've been dreaming about my entire life. You embody everything I want in a serious partner. You're smart, funny, sexy as hell, independent, comfortable in your own skin, happy, close to your family. I could go on and on. We share a similar trauma that has shaped our lives. I didn't know how much that would mean to me, or how much I needed that connection in a partner, until now."

At the mention of *serious partner*, a warm feeling flooded me. I felt the same way about him. The warmth made me feel like a daffodil unfurling in the sunshine for the first time.

"If I'd been more confident in the beginning and not as skittish around you," I asked, "would you have told me the truth then?"

"I hope I would have," he said. "But I can't promise you that for sure. The entire thing with Stacy has been such a burden. It's hard to believe that dealing with her like that had become my life. Leo and Chris don't even know the extent of it. I kept it all close because I was embarrassed and genuinely worried about her. I was also upset I didn't see the signs or had been capable enough to stop it before it spun completely out of control. I was working with my sister, hoping there'd be some disassociation, but each time Stacy called me, and I didn't cooperate fully with her, she threatened self-harm." He angled his face up to the sun and closed his eyes. We both needed to be fortified by its energy right now. "I wasn't sure if she was serious or if she was just trying to manipulate me, but I wasn't willing to risk it." That's exactly what Mags had said. "I figured with enough time, and my complete disinterest in her, she'd give up. Or she would find someone else to latch on to, since I'm pretty sure that's her thing. But that didn't happen."

"How did you two get together in the first place?"

"I met her the first week I was here. I moved up right after the holidays, after accepting a job at a law firm. I was tasked with scouting out the area and talking to other bar owners about the brewpub before Leo and Chris would commit, so I was alone up here. I met Anastasia at a bar."

Anastasia. That fit.

"It was at the Four Seasons," he continued. "I'd just finished a dinner meeting with a client who'd flown in and was staying there. Stacy came into the bar like she owned the place. I knew she'd taken inventory and decided that I was her best bet for the evening. I hadn't been with anyone in a long time, and she told me she was fine with a casual hookup. She talked about her jet-set lifestyle and how she wasn't in the same city very often. We had a few drinks, flirted with each other. When she invited me up to her room, I went." He cleared his throat before continuing, shifting his gaze into the garden. "In the morning, as I got dressed to go, she acted a little possessive, but nothing too crazy. She insisted that we meet for dinner, since she was leaving town soon, and I agreed. I felt it was appropriate since my intention had been pretty much a one-night stand, and I didn't want to hurt her feelings. We had an enjoyable evening, which surprised me. After a few drinks and an entertaining conversation about her life abroad, and more flirting, we went back to my place. I wasn't living where I am now. It was a temporary situation, a penthouse owned by one of my parents' friends who was out of the country at the time. They were gracious enough to allow me use of it until I found a permanent place." He paused. I could see this was hard for him. It was hard to hear. "The morning after, she was a completely different person. She acted like I'd proposed to her, and it freaked me out. I tried to end it right there, telling her I wasn't interested in any sort of committed relationship and—"

I gave his hand a squeeze. "It's okay."

He cleared his throat, obviously emotional. "The penthouse had a deck. She got up on the railing and tossed one leg over. We were really high up. I'll never forget seeing her there, half her body on the other side of those small bars. She said she'd rather die than live without me. So I went on autopilot, telling her all the things she wanted to hear until she climbed down. I was so scared." He glanced up at the sky. "The weird thing was, she immediately believed all the lies I spewed in my panic. Once I coaxed her to leave the apartment, I broke down and called my sister. We worked on a solution together. It wasn't the greatest, but I was able to avoid Stacy, making excuses about working late, until she left a few days later on a shoot. It was a little harder the next time she came into town to make her believe the reasons why we couldn't see each other, but I managed to dodge any physical stuff. She's only been in town twice since then, only staying a few days." Xander looked exhausted.

I felt like stroking his hair or running a hand along his cheek. But I didn't. Instead, I waited for him to finish.

"What I haven't been able to do is stop her from calling me. It's been torture. I feel pressure to pretend like I'm interested. She insists on video-chatting once in a while. I can usually fob her off, but sometimes I can't. Occasionally, she gets worked up, and I worry she'll hurt herself, so I give in." His shoulder settled against mine. "I may have kept details from you, but I never lied to you, Summer. I was with her a total of two times in the very beginning. I never dated her. We were never in a relationship. In hindsight, I should've done something more to break permanently from her. Insisted she see someone if we were going to 'stay an item' or whatever. But I was emotionally spent and didn't have anything going on until I met you."

"If you were never together with her at your current place, how did she have a key?"

"She didn't." He shook his head. "She knew where I lived because she demanded the information once I relocated from the penthouse. She wanted to know all about it, I'm assuming so she could compare it to what she'd seen. She was expecting it to be lavish, I'm sure. She sweet-talked the manager yesterday, saying she forgot her key. She flashed that ridiculous fake ring, claiming she was my fiancée. As soon as I get back, I'm filing a complaint."

Xander hadn't left me that morning knowing Stacy could show up. It made me feel so much better. "I'm sorry, Xander," I whispered. "This entire thing has to be so hard. Thank you for telling me."

He reached for my hand and gripped it tightly.

I rested my head against his shoulder.

Chapter 24

We sat for a long time quietly, hand in hand. I felt at peace with the situation, finally. I stood suddenly, making a quick decision. "Come on." I pulled him with me. "Let's take a walk. There's a park nearby, and I want to show you something."

"Okay." He gave me an easy grin, even though I saw apprehension lingering.

I led him around the house. The park was only a few blocks away and had been one of my refuges when Gus had been hurt. "In the days right after my brother's accident, I spent a lot of time at this park," I told him. "It's not very big. There's a small playground, a few park benches, a drinking fountain, and a patch of beautiful trees that are dense enough to make it seem like there's a mini forest in the middle of the city. My parents used to take us to play there often. As we got a little older, we were allowed to go with a group of kids, but never by ourselves. After the initial trauma and uncertainty of Gus's accident, I would sneak off to visit by myself, even though if they'd known, my parents would've been very angry."

"No parent wants to discover their child missing."

"I was lucky they never noticed. I'd always come up with a reason why they hadn't been able to find me that would satisfy them, so they never found out. I wouldn't be gone for too long, because I didn't want to worry them." My mind drifted back to those beginning days. They'd been so hard. Nothing in life had prepared me for that kind of pain and sadness. Processing it as a child had been even harder. "They were caught up in their own grief, hospital visits, and next steps, so I was left behind a lot. I understood, but it was hard."

"You told me you were ten years old at the time of your brother's accident. That's a little young for sneaking out."

I nodded as we headed down the street. "It was. I was completely oblivious to any harm that could befall me. I was locked in my own little world. No one ever bothered me, which was lucky for a little girl out on her own alone. There were always families around. I could've gone to them if I had any issues. This predated cell phones and the like. I just craved the quiet and peacefulness of that little forest. It became my sanctuary. While I was there, I could pretend the world was anything I wanted it to be, with no triggers of my family or Gus nearby. I was in a land far, far away of my own creation. It was pure bliss." We walked for a while. "I've never fully reflected on what this place meant to me, other than it coming up a few times in therapy. But I'm sure it was essential in helping me cope through those early dark days." I smiled, trying not to let my mind wander back to the darker times. "Now that I'm thinking about it, my little sanctuary could've been why I was so drawn to my loft. It gave me that same feeling of contentment the moment I walked through the door. A sense of safety, tucked away from the rest of the world. With my big window, I can sit and look out, but remain cozy and safe. It's really comforting."

Xander slid his arm around my waist. I let my head fall onto his shoulder. We were both exhausted by the emotions of the past twenty-four hours, and this was the perfect way to start leaving it all behind.

"I can imagine your special place helped you cope," he murmured, lips against my hair. "There were nights when Zoe was having a very bad time, and after she got settled, I would go down to the beach and sit for hours, just staring at the surf. But I was a little older than you were. There's comfort you can get from nature, a peacefulness that doesn't exist anywhere else."

"Agreed." We crossed the street. "I was extremely thankful for it. It allowed my mind to daydream about whatever it needed to see or feel at that very moment in time. I always felt refreshed when I returned home."

We walked for a few minutes in comfortable silence.

As we continued to stroll, Xander said, "The neighborhoods here, and in Seattle, are so beautiful and lush. They're very different from the ones I grew up in. The trees are deciduous, the streets are laid out in a grid, they have curated boulevards. In my neighborhood, everything was on a curve, the sidewalk very close to the street. The houses were more homogeneous and built really close together. All the garages faced out. The trees in my neighborhood were shorter and scrubbier than these beautiful oaks and elms." He gestured at a yard with several tall trees. "We had palms, of course, but those were few and far between because everything was so crowded. Every inch of viable space is used on the southern coast. I like it here much better. There's room to breathe. The air feels clearer. I don't remember South Carolina very well, because I was so young when we moved, but our neighborhood there had a similar vibe to this. I prefer it. Feels much more like home to me."

I smiled. It made me happy that Xander enjoyed it here and that it felt comfortable to him. It was nothing we had to worry about now, but maybe someday, if we were lucky enough to have this work out, we'd have to decide where to live.

We arrived at the park, and I eagerly guided him across the last street, taking his hand. Several children ran around the equipment, which had been updated in the years since I'd been a regular visitor. The day had warmed up beautifully, the sun on its way down, still warm.

I veered us into the trees. It wouldn't look extremely weird for two adults to head here, as it was a cut-through to the neighborhood on the other side. There was a small, well-trodden dirt path, but I took us off it pretty quickly.

The brush was overgrown, even more so than when I was a child, lots of sticks and tree limbs in the way. A thick, yet condensed, cover of brown leaves coated the ground. I tromped over the small barriers, citing words of caution to Xander, even though I was pretty sure he could handle himself.

A soft chuckle erupted behind me. "You weren't kidding about this being a forest."

"It's even denser than I remember," I told him as I stepped over a large branch. I worried for a second that I wouldn't be able to find my special spot. "I wasn't the only one back then to find a sanctuary here. But I think it would be hard for kids nowadays to do the same."

"The world is definitely a different place," he agreed. "Parents aren't just going to let their kids come in here and play freely."

After a little bit of searching, I let out a small shriek. "Here it is!" I made a beeline toward a large oak, like those Xander had noticed in the yards as we'd passed by. This one was split into two huge trunks. At the bottom, where they joined together, was a small, flat area. It was the perfect size for a small child to squeeze in between. "It looks so much tinier than I remember. I haven't been back in years."

He chuckled. "You were much smaller then. Go ahead, see if you still fit."

I cleared debris from the perch, my perfect notch, and turned around and tried to sit. My butt hit the wood with some effort, my thighs squashing together, but it worked. I fit. I laughed. "Back then, I had enough space to cross my legs or stick my knees up and rest them against the more slanted trunk. I was a gangly child." I glanced around wistfully. The canopy overhead wasn't nearly full yet, as the leaves were just beginning to sprout everywhere. It would seem much more secluded by the middle of summer.

Xander casually leaned against the trunk opposite me, bracing his elbow above his head. He was smiling, happy. "I can imagine you sitting here. You look right at home in your little nook."

"Sometimes I'd bring a book, and sometimes I would take loose branches and sticks and prop them all around the opening on both sides so nobody would see me if they were looking. One time, I brought a little pocketknife and carved mine and Gus's names into the seat. I wonder if they're still here." I struggled to get out of the crevice. Xander reached down and offered me his hand.

I grasped it, and he pulled me up easily.

But he didn't let go.

Instead, he brought me close, resting his forehead against mine, his eyes closed.

We stood like that together, the two of us soaking up my little safe space as a child together. It was the first time I'd shown anyone where I'd let my fantasies run wild. The fantasies that Gus was fine, that the accident had never happened, that my parents were at home planning a trip to Disneyland. The place that had helped the little girl in me begin to accept what had happened and start to heal.

Healing that would take a long time.

"I'm so sorry," he murmured on the barest of breaths. "I made a big mistake not thinking you could handle the turmoil in my life. Clearly, you've been a fighter since you were a little girl. You found a way to survive and then thrive. You would have listened to my unfortunate story, and instead of running away, you would've helped me. We would have found a way to solve it together. It won't happen again. I promise. I hope you can forgive me."

"I forgive you."

His lips were soft and giving. His tongue warm and welcome. I wrapped my arms around his neck, kissing him deeply as a single tear rolled down my cheek. He braced his hands tightly against my back, holding me impossibly tighter, the bark of my tree pressing against me, calming me, soothing me.

Then, all the feelings I'd been suppressing when it came to him—to possibly loving a man like him—evaporated into the sky above us. I broke the kiss with an exhale of relief, cupping my hands around his face, my forehead against his. "Thank you for not giving up on us," I murmured.

What that little girl who'd sat in that special place hadn't known all those years ago was she'd been secretly wishing for someone like him to come along. Someone to share her grief, someone to kiss away her tears, someone to comfort her, so she didn't have to do it all by herself.

He was finally here.

"Summer?" my mom called from inside the house. "Are you out there? There's a strange car parked outside."

Xander and I had just come around the house into the backyard. I'd found the faded remnants of the names I'd carved into the notch. It'd been cathartic. There was a newfound energy buzzing between Xander and me, and I was incredibly happy about it.

"I'm out here with company," I called, turning to Xander. "Are you okay with meeting my mom?"

"Of course," he answered easily.

We arrived at the back door right as my mother opened it. "Hi, Mom. I'd like to introduce you to my boyfriend, Xander Scott." I grinned, noting her surprise, then watching her expertly hide it, like this had been the plan all along. "He had some free time today, so he drove out from Seattle." There would be a time in the near future when I would purge the whole story to my mom, but now was not that time. "Xander, this is Helen Day, my mom."

"It's a pleasure to meet you, Ms. Day," Xander said, extending his hand. "You have an amazing daughter, but I'm sure you know that already."

"I do. It's nice to meet you, Xander," she said. "Is that short for Alexander?"

He turned to me, grinning like he had a really good secret. "Actually, Alexander is my middle name. I was named after my grandfather, August Archibald Scott. But instead of Archibald, they went with August Alexander, for which I'm eternally grateful. I'm not sure I could've rocked the name Archie." He totally could've. "I haven't told Summer yet, because I was saving it for a special occasion, but I think this more than qualifies."

"You're kidding me." I laughed. "Your real name is August? August is dating Summer?"

"The first time I heard your name, I thought it was meant to be. I couldn't wait to tell you." He looked absolutely wicked as he slid his hand around my waist. "I was thinking up all these elaborate ways to break it to you, but I think now is completely perfect."

My mother looked between us, smiling wistfully. "Why don't you two come inside?" She gestured toward the kitchen. "We'll have a toast to the season summer, which, with any help, should be here soon enough. Xander, how long are you planning to stay?"

I hadn't asked Xander what his plans were. We hadn't gotten there yet. "Just for the night. I rented a hotel room a few miles away. This was a last-minute trip, and I didn't want to put anyone out. I borrowed a friend's car, and unfortunately, I need to get it back to him by tomorrow. I was missing Summer, so I came to say hello."

His hand caressed my back.

Shivers bopped up my spine.

"How nice. Before you go," my mom told us, "you should definitely meet Gus. He'll be devastated if he misses out on meeting Summer's new friend." She glanced at the clock on the wall. "His program starts in about an hour." She turned to me. "Taking Xander tonight might be a nice idea. Gus would appreciate it so much."

I glanced at Xander. I didn't want him to feel obligated in any way to do the family thing with me, and I hadn't mentioned my plan to head back over to my brother's place. "I'm heading over to Gus's to watch his show with him. I promised. You're welcome to join us. He would love that."

"Sure. That sounds great," he said. "Summer has told me a lot about Gus. I'm looking forward to meeting him."

"Are you sure?" I asked. "He'd be thrilled to meet you, but there's absolutely no pressure."

Xander flashed a grin. "I wouldn't miss it."

My mom busied herself taking out a bottle of wine, arranging wineglasses on the counter, pouring, then handing them to us. "Here's to August and Summer, may they continue to bask in the sunshine of their lives!"

"Mom, you're so corny." I giggled as we clinked glasses and drank. "But you know I love it."

"Not corny," she said. "Just someone who adores seeing two people in love."

Chapter 25

"Do you like to fish?" Gus asked Xander eagerly. It was easily the two hundredth question he'd asked since we'd arrived. Xander had been amazing. Calm and patient as he answered each and every one of my brother's questions. Sometimes they were repetitive, as Gus couldn't always remember the topic we'd just discussed, but Xander didn't seem to mind. "Because I like to fish. Maybe I can come to Seattle, and we can fish."

My eyebrows rose. Gus offering to travel meant he felt comfortable with Xander. That was a great sign.

"I enjoy fishing a lot," Xander replied. "A friend of mine has a boat. The next time you come into town, we'll go." Xander turned to me from his position in the middle of the couch, me on one side, Gus on the other. We'd finished Gus's show about an hour ago and had been chatting. "Do you like to fish, Summer? I've never asked."

"I do love to fish," I answered. "My dad took us a lot when we were little. Then Gus got back into it a few years ago. There are some great lakes nearby and some big, beautiful ones in Idaho. The scenery is gorgeous over there."

Xander slung his arm around my shoulders. "We should plan a weekend trip. That would be fun."

Abruptly, Gus interjected, "Are you two going to get married? Like Mom and Dad used to be?"

I chuckled. "Not quite yet. Like I told you when I introduced Xander, we've only been friends for a little while. People usually get to know each other for years before they decide to take a big step like marriage. They need time to figure out if they work well together."

"But you like each other a lot," Gus said. "I can tell."

"Yes," Xander answered. "Your sister is one of the nicest people I've ever met."

"Summer's nice," Gus agreed. "She's my best friend. She's always been there for me. I can't imagine going through my accident without her."

I sat up quickly, reaching over Xander to clasp Gus's hand. "You're my best friend, too. I want you to know, even though Xander and I are together, my relationship with you is rock-solid and unbreakable. I will keep reminding you."

Gus smiled. "I like Xander, too. He's nice. And he likes to fish. He makes you laugh, and when you do, your forehead crinkles like this." He pointed to his own forehead. "He makes you say silly things. When you smile, you show teeth. I like it."

"I like it, too," I replied a little sheepishly.

"I mean, we could get married," Xander added cagily. "Who knows what the future will hold?"

"I do," Gus said. "Fishing."

We all laughed.

"Definitely fishing," I said. "I'll talk to Mom and Dad about a trip to Idaho this summer. Does that sound good?"

"Yes," Gus said.

I stood. It was time to go. "We had a fun night together, but now we have to get going. Xander has a long drive back first thing in the morning. I'm glad we got to watch the show together. It was a good episode."

"Where is he sleeping tonight?" Gus asked, pointing at Xander as he stood.

"He's staying at a hotel."

"Are you going to stay with him?" Gus asked.

My eyes met Xander's.

We hadn't talked about it. We were taking it one step at a time.

"She probably won't stay overnight." His gaze held some smolder as he glanced at me. "But I hope she decides to stay for a little while."

Flutters started in my neck and whipped down my body, moving quickly. "My curfew is midnight."

He took my hand as we walked toward the door. "I accept."

Gus followed us. "Are you going back to Seattle with Xander tomorrow, Summer?"

I wasn't going to go back on my word to my brother. "No, I'm staying for a week, as promised. I'll see Xander when I get back." I gave my brother a hug and reminded him about the pizza night Dad was taking us on soon. "I'm sure I'll see you during the day tomorrow, too."

Xander reached out for a handshake, but Gus chose to embrace him instead. Xander hugged him back, and I felt those good ol' tears waiting for another release.

I held them back, but just barely.

"It was a pleasure meeting you, Gus," Xander said. "I hope we get to see each other again soon."

As we walked out to Leo's car, I said, "Thank you for being so patient with my brother. I know he can be a lot. He doesn't always track during a conversation, and he gets easily confused."

Xander opened the passenger door for me, and I got in. He walked around to the driver's side. "Are you kidding? Your brother is fantastic. I can't wait to go fishing and snowboarding with him."

"He likes you a lot, too," I said. "Contrary to his cheerful demeanor, he doesn't like everyone. He can usually sense when someone's not being genuine."

As Xander drove us through the streets of Spokane, my anticipation of being alone with him built. After a short drive, he pulled into the parking lot of a modest hotel near downtown and parked before turning to me. "There's absolutely no pressure for you to come up to my room. I'm fine with taking it slow. We can go into the bar and have a drink instead. Anything is good."

I answered by kissing him. Our mouths connected seamlessly, like there'd never been any time apart. "I want to come up," I murmured.

He smiled. "I'm glad."

"I could've invited you to stay at my mom's house, but I knew we wouldn't have the kind of privacy there that I want. I hope that's okay."

"It's perfect."

We got out of the car.

Holding hands, he led me up to his room on the fourth floor.

It was a no-frills place, but nicely appointed. A king bed took up the majority of space. A desk, a dresser with a TV on top, and a plainly tiled bathroom were the only other accoutrements. The shower was big, but not as big as Xander's.

"If it's okay with you, I need a break from bathrooms," I told him. "I was in the shower when Stacy arrived."

He shrugged off his coat and slung it over the desk chair, leading me to the edge of the bed. We both sat. "I meant to ask you about that. Stacy rambled incoherently, so I have no idea what actually happened. I did get her to admit that she hadn't been physical with you, and I was thankful for that. She's never been physical with me, but I worried."

I fiddled with my hands in my lap. I didn't want to really relive it, but he deserved to know the truth. "She pretty much just hurled insults at me. It didn't help that I was completely naked when she arrived. I was thinking you had come home for a quick visit." I flashed him a tentative smile. "I'd just gotten out of the shower, so I walked into the bedroom, dripping wet. I was so shocked by her sudden appearance, and how beautiful she was, I really didn't say much, other than saying I wasn't a whore and that I didn't want any trouble. I dressed as quickly as I could, and ran out of there."

Xander's forehead pressed against mine in that special way that I now loved. He wasn't afraid to be intimate and vulnerable. It was incredible. "Summer, I'm so sorry you had to go through that. From the bottom of my heart, I wish I could take it back. Erase it from ever happening. If I'd known she was even in the country, I would've insisted we stay at your place. But she didn't contact me. Apparently, she wanted to surprise me. I'm extremely happy it didn't escalate more than it did."

"Even in her fury, she was incredibly beautiful," I whispered. We were getting everything out after all.

"She doesn't come remotely close to you," he murmured, his lips lightly settling over mine. "Beauty like that is a full-time job. It's an illusion meant to snare." He pulled away slightly, meeting my eyes. "Even though I went up to her hotel room that first night, I had a hard time…getting worked up. There was absolutely no emotional connection between us. With you, it's effortless. Something inside me springs to life like it's on fire. I feel unstable and off-balance. I love it. No one's ever made me feel like that before."

If my heart could sing actual notes, it would've.

"Me, too. All those things. In the past, it made me scared beyond reason to allow myself to be as free as I've been with you. But I want to embrace that fear so I can give you everything I have." My hand began to explore below his belt buckle.

"You're not the only one who is fearful," he said softly. "If I fall deeply in love with you, and end up losing you, I'll experience extreme loss again. It's terrifying. But we can do this together, especially if we support each other." Very gently, he eased us back on the bed so we faced each other. "Everything about you is perfect to me." He brushed a lock of my hair off my forehead. "I'm looking forward to making you happy."

"Likewise." I slid my hand along his cheek. The stubble was a little longer than usual. "Did you really wait outside my house overnight?"

"Yes. It wasn't an option not to," he answered. "I wanted a chance to explain to you in person what had happened."

"And none of my neighbors were suspicious?"

"One guy came out of his house, but I gave him a wave and

a smile, and he went back in."

"My neighbors are going to hate your motorcycle," I said.

"That's fine. I'm selling it."

I gasped. He quelled it with a sweet kiss. I almost forgot what he'd said as our kisses became more intense. I broke away, nibbling his earlobe. "Please don't get rid of your motorcycle because of me."

"It's not because of you. I'm not really a true motorcycle guy at heart. I've been meaning to sell it for a while. I just put it off because parking it in Seattle is easier than a car. Plus, it rains a lot, which is a drag." He kissed my cheek, sliding his lips down my neck. "I got it during my dark time after Zoe's death. It'll be cathartic to get rid of it. I'm in a much different place in my life, thanks to you."

"As long as you're sure—"

Xander's hand reached my breast and I forgot everything. Possibly even my name.

We undressed quickly, climbing under the covers. A few tears of happiness involuntarily leaked out, and Xander kissed them away. I had a hard time believing that just a few hours ago we'd been unresolved, and now we were here. It was becoming a little more incredible that I hadn't suspected Stacy had issues, knowing Xander as I had over the last few days. I'd been too busy guarding my heart, waiting for the other shoe to drop.

Those days were over. I was all in.

There was no other way I could be. I couldn't be in a healthy relationship with this man if I spent all my time second-guessing myself and our connection. It was either trust him and jump into the deep end, or walk away.

This was me swimming, but for the first time in my life, I

didn't feel like I was in the water alone. I had a partner, and we were going to help each other survive the crashing waves together.

Xander went impossibly slowly, his hands sliding up and down my body, exploring everything. It was incredibly sexy.

I reciprocated, straddling him while tracing the lines of his tattoos with my tongue, pausing to nibble and bite. Every contour of his body was hard and smooth. I've never loved anything more. I placed my mouth over one of his nipples, nipping it with my teeth, flicking my tongue over it again and again.

"Oh…damn," he said, panting. "That feels…"

"Good," I suggested, chuckling.

"I was going to say interesting." He half moaned as I teased the other one. "But I'm going to have to settle with…*ah*…great."

"*Hm.*" One of my hands slid down between his legs. "What if I pair it with something like this?" I began to lave his nipple while stroking his length, my fingers featherlight over his most sensitive parts.

"Is it possible to die from pleasure?"

Driving him crazy was my new most favorite thing to do in the whole wide world. "I don't think so." I chuckled. "But we can try."

Taking me by surprise, he hooked his leg over mine and flipped us. Now he was on top, grinning down at me like he planned to give me full payback for all my evil deeds.

I couldn't wait.

Very gently, he eased both my hands over my head. "Is this okay?" he asked.

He hadn't done more than that, and I was literally quaking.

"When you look at me like that, you can do anything you want. I trust you." I meant it. I was all about maximizing pleasure.

He leaned closer, placing the tip of his tongue on a jutting nipple, the pressure more pronounced because my shoulder blades were flexed, as he kept my arms secure above my head. He lingered on one, then the other.

It was literally the best torture ever. I wiggled, unable to keep still, antsy for more. "If you continue this madness, I might find my release without you."

He brought his head up looking regal and sexy as hell. "Well, we can't have that now, can we?" Instead of letting me go, he captured the entire nipple with his mouth, sucking like his life depended on it.

Oh. My. God.

My head thrashed back and forth as he switched from one to the other, giving them equal attention until my hips were bucking. He transferred both of my hands into a single grip, bringing his other hand down, lightly caressing it over my belly, teasing, finally hitting my wetness, circling.

I cried out, thrashing.

"You reap what you sow," he murmured in my ear, increasing his speed. "We're not stopping for a condom now. Come for me. I want to see you break."

His voice was incredibly sexy, and I was quite certain I'd never been this turned on in my entire life.

As his fingers entered me, he got his wish. I arched into his waiting hand, grinding, calling his name. When it was over, and I was panting like I'd just run a marathon, he gave me the sweetest kiss.

"Summer..." His voice cracked with emotion, his head

resting on my shoulder. I could feel the wetness of his tears. "You're so incredible. I'm so lucky."

He released my arms, and I brought them around his shoulders, hugging him close, stroking his hair. "I'm the one who's lucky."

"I'm sorry, I'm not trying to ruin the moment," he said, propping himself up on an elbow, staring down at me. "I'm just overwhelmed. I've never—" He cleared his throat. "I've never had this kind of connection with anyone before. I've never allowed myself to be this vulnerable. And your passion, your trust in me… It just… It blows my mind." He bowed his head. "I feel like I won the lottery."

I guided him to my lips, kissing him softly. "You never have to apologize for being emotional. I feel the same way. This is who we are. Two people who've been raised with emotional trauma learning how to love each other." I smiled. "And you are most definitely not ruining the moment. That was amazing. You just gave me everything I didn't know I wanted and more. Now let me return the favor."

My hands found his hardness, and I began to stroke, reaching for the condom he'd put on the bedside table. I took my time applying it, teasing and caressing, then I guided him on top of me. He went achingly slow, filling me fully.

His thrusts started slow, our mouths melding together, our bodies finding a sweet rhythm. The pace quickly increased, both of us excited, the anticipation building.

"You feel so good," Xander murmured. It was more like a groan.

My fingers pressed into his back as I wrapped my legs around his torso, pulling him tightly against me. He felt right.

He slid his hands down, grabbing on to my ass with both hands, squeezing while he murmured sexy things in my ear that sent me over the edge for the second time.

His teeth grazed my shoulder as he followed.

Once we both came back to ourselves, he stayed on top of me, his elbows braced on either side of my head, his hands brushing my sweaty hair away from my face. He leaned down, his lips meeting mine.

I would never, ever get sick of his kisses. Not in a million years.

He whispered, “I can’t wait to start my life with you.”

I smiled. “It’s already started.”

Epilogue

Xander nuzzled the side of my head. I playfully swatted him away. "Be good." I giggled. "This is an important night for Eve."

"I know," he murmured an inch away from my ear. "But you're just too sexy. I can't resist."

"I've been back for three weeks," I countered, barely resisting a kiss, but I managed because we were in a very public setting. "You've definitely gotten your fill of my sexy."

"Hardly," he said. "Six days without you was like being marooned on a deserted island. I'm making up for lost time."

"We've barely been apart since I got back." I laughed. He was spoiling me rotten, and I loved every minute of it. The sex continued to be amazing and very frequent. I wasn't under any illusions we would stay in this heightened state forever, but we were certainly going to make the most of it while it lasted. It was not a hardship, trust me. "We haven't left each other's side except for work. Naked Yahtzee was especially entertaining."

Before Xander could reply, Poppy cleared her throat from the middle of the room, champagne flute lofted, interrupting our nuzzling session.

We were all gathered in Eve's new retail space. They'd signed the lease a few weeks ago, and this was the official kickoff celebration. The space was adorable, a roomy interior with a large window and a white, weathered door complete with a bell over the top. It'd been a stationery shop.

"To Eve, Marco, and Amy," Poppy called to an array of guests, mostly family and friends of the three investors. "May the Watering Can be wildly successful and continue to bloom for years to come!"

Cheers erupted, along with a bunch of *hear, hear*s. The crowd was jubilant, as they should be. Eve had created a beautiful event, with catered food and wine, and the drinks were flowing.

After Poppy finished, Xander leaned in for a full-on kiss.

As predicted, my parents had completely understood everything that had happened and appreciated the fact that Xander had driven all that way to explain. They were sympathetic about Stacy and relieved that Xander hadn't intentionally put me in harm's way.

Overall, my visit had been wonderful. My dad had been bummed that he hadn't been able to meet Xander in person, especially after my mom and Gus raved about him, but I promised we'd be back soon.

I'd meant it.

"Ahem." Poppy tapped me on the shoulder. "I understand that being young and in love makes people feel like they're living in an altered reality, I really do, but you're actually here in a soon-to-be flower shop-slash-art house, not a luxury hotel room under a down comforter. So be sweet and come up for air for a second or two. Have either of you seen Eve? Or Marco? They're supposed to be around here somewhere. I swear I saw her not even five minutes ago. That's why I decided to do the toast."

"I haven't seen either of them since we first arrived a half hour ago," I said.

"Me neither," Xander added.

"You guys are no help," Poppy muttered. "The minute I turn my back, you'll be off in your own little world again." She swished a hand. "But you know I love it. Continue on."

Leo came up behind her, looking concerned. "Have you found her yet?"

"No, but keep looking. She has to be here somewhere." They both wandered off.

While I'd been in Spokane, Xander and his business partners had officially hired Poppy to design their brewpub. She'd been spending a great deal of time with Leo. But each time I'd questioned her about what was going on between them, she'd remained coy.

Poppy's younger sister, Annabel, rushed up to us. She'd made her decision to move to Seattle permanently last week, and we'd all gone out to celebrate. It was going to be fun to have her around.

"There's a really angry woman up front who's looking for her fiancé," she whispered, leaning in, her eyes wide, her voice hushed. "Marco someone? I almost told her he ran off with the florist, but I didn't. Because what if he did?"

Annabel didn't know how right she might be.

I'd seen Eve only a handful of times since I'd been home,

because she'd been so busy with the new business. She'd told me that Marco had gotten engaged. She seemed to be handling it well, but I knew she was bummed.

Now she was nowhere to be found, and neither was Marco.

"We have to find her," I said. "Before everything hits the fan."

"Um, are you talking about the fan who has a gigantic ring on her finger?" Annabel said. "If so, I think it's already hit."

"Do you think Eve's with—" I was cut off by the sound of a door shutting behind us.

"Hi, guys," Eve said a little breathlessly as she emerged from around the corner, fixing her hair. "Are you enjoying the evening?"

Annabel gaped at her.

I suppressed a laugh as Xander's lips found my ear. "Did she just come out of the storage closet?"

"I'm pretty sure she did," I murmured. "Now it's our job to capture everyone's attention so they don't notice she was missing." Like a champ, Xander took the job upon himself, making his way through the crowd, grabbing a champagne flute off the table as he went.

"I'd like to propose a toast," he boomed once he reached the front. "I want to personally thank Eve for being friends with my beautiful girlfriend, Summer, and taking her to the Driftwood to celebrate this business venture. Or I might never have met her." He was utterly captivating, not only to me, but everyone else in the room. He went on to praise Eve and predict that her floral business was going to be a giant success.

Hands gripped my forearm. Poppy was back. "You got yourself a keeper there."

"Don't I know it," I replied, trying not to swoon.

We ignored the sound of a door opening and closing somewhere behind us. I didn't want to know. Whatever was going on with Eve and Marco was their business.

Okay, so I wanted to know a little bit.

Obviously, we'd get to the bottom of it soon enough. Helping Eve navigate being deeply in love with a guy who had a fiancée was going to take some time. I'd be there for it, along with Poppy, Jenny, and now Annabel.

But, right in this very moment, all I wanted to do was focus on the beautiful man at the front of the room. I couldn't believe he was mine.

He found my gaze. We shared a look.

I'd finally picked my leading man.

And he was totally worth the wait.

Singles in Seattle: Book 2

RE-ARRANGED

a novel

Ivy Daniels

Chapter 1

I *want you so much, Eve.*

I can't stop thinking about you.

You're the one who got away.

He'd said all those things to me tonight.

My dream man.

The guy I'd been obsessing over for the past eight years. Okay, more like seven and a half, but close enough. And when I said obsessing, I did not take that word lightly. I'd always felt that when it landed in the middle of a sentence—and it's a *really* big deal—it should be punctuated with a capital O. The small o was just too puny for those of us who obsessed frequently.

I was guilty as charged.

My O game was strong.

I couldn't lie. Hearing him say those words rocked my effing world. I'd been waiting for him to say that for so long. *So long!* It was a dream come true—as well as my absolute worst nightmare. Firstly, I didn't love having my world rocked. I was more of a stationary-type gal. Feet solidly planted on terra firma at all times. I liked things in their proper slots. Order was beauty. When life was unbalanced, my entire soul felt off-kilter.

Secondly, he had a fiancée.

He has a fiancée!

"Knock, knock, is anybody home?" Poppy asked, settling a hand on my shoulder. Poppy Albright was one of my best friends in the entire world. I'd met the most amazing three women during my freshman year in college, and trying to get through life without them would be unthinkable.

I snapped out of my daze, practically bounding off my stool, glancing around the empty storefront of my brand-new soon-to-be floral business, surprised to see that everyone else had left our kickoff celebration party. I kind of remember making my goodbyes. At least I think I did.

I'd deal with that embarrassment later.

Brushing an errant strand of red hair behind my ear, I shook my head, more than a little flustered. "Sorry. I was thinking about something else. My mind is going in a million directions these days."

To help cover my befuddlement, I hurried over to one of the tables to start tidying up. The caterers had taken all the food and dishes away, which was a relief. I wasn't up for a full clean at the moment. My brain was too busy whirring like a spin cycle stuck on Extra Panic Attack to tackle anything more than a simple tidy-up.

Poppy eyed me like I was an unsteady toddler. "It was a great party," she began, her tone nice and light. "Everyone had a ton of fun. The Watering Can is going to be completely amazing!

I can't wait for it to open. I'm going to buy all of my flowers here. I swear." She settled one hand over her heart and gave me a three-finger salute, making me smile. I could always count on her for that. "I won't even demand a best-friend discount." She fiddled with a red rose, rubbing a petal between her index finger and thumb. It was one of my favorite things to do. I loved the silky feel and how the scent lingered on my fingers. "Well, maybe sometimes because, you know, flowers are expensive. But most of the time, it'll be 'give me the works!'"

I laughed. "Of course you're getting the best-friend discount. Each and every time. I wouldn't have it any other way."

Realizing my dream of owning my own flower shop—an innocent wish as I'd stood next to Nana as a child, trimming beautiful long-stemmed roses and placing them in glass vases—was incredible. I had to pinch myself. This was really happening.

It was happening!

My mind should be completely focused on my new business venture. I had so much to do, order, prepare, decorate, hire. I'd sunk a ton of my blood, sweat, and tears into it already. Years of saving, scrimping, scratching, taking extra accounting jobs, trying to make ends meet while living in a tiny apartment, just so I could make my dream a reality.

But instead of being laser-focused on the task ahead, I'd allowed myself to become completely Obsessed with Marco Cruz. Again. The urgent words he'd uttered before tugging me into the closet tonight were front and center in my cerebral cortex, like a blinking billboard in Times Square. Those words weren't going away any time soon.

It was actually *our* closet.

The man was my business partner. He'd pulled me into *our*

closet. The one we co-owned. Or co-leased. But it was still *ours* together.

Then he'd kissed me like a knight in a medieval tale of unrequited love, sweeping me back over one arm and going in for the kill. Except this love was very much requited. I'd loved him nonstop for seven and a half years, so it was quite possibly *hyper-requited.* I'd clawed at his hair like an alley cat and lapped at his tongue like a dehydrated pony.

I'd been a goner for the man from the first time I'd laid eyes on him at the student bookstore where we'd both worked those first few months of college until right this very second.

Now my Obsession was billboard-bright.

How did I get rid of something seared into my brain by a hot, scorching kiss? A kiss I'd been waiting for my entire life.

I had no idea.

"So, um, earth to Eve. You had quite a night. Want to talk about it?" Poppy helped me stack up some extra platters I'd brought. "Annabel's getting the car, but I can have her leave without me." Poppy's sister, Annabel, had recently decided to move to Seattle. It was going to be so much fun having her around. They were polar opposites in everything except personality.

There, they shined like two pithy queens of witty comebacks.

"Yeah, the party was great," I agreed, trying to recenter myself so I could start becoming an active participant in this currently one-sided conversation. "I think people had a really good time."

Poppy crossed her arms, her patience draining out of her body. The look she shot me was part Scarlett O'Hara, part Rocky Balboa. You couldn't get past Poppy when she was on the scent of a juicy tidbit. "Eve, that's not what I'm talking about. Of course people had a good time!" She flung her arms wide. "You throw amazing parties. You always have. What I'm trying to get at is what happened in that closet midway through the festivities." She gestured toward the back of the store. "You were in there with a tall, dark, and *supremely* handsome man from your past. Who, I shouldn't have to add, is now your business partner and who has a *fiancée.* That woman was literally storming the place looking for him." Poppy dropped her arms and some of the drama, her expression easing back into that of the sympathetic pal who loved me. "What gives? This is not like you. You've always been in control—bordering on methodical—in your past relationships. I need some answers. Summer told us you had a thing for this guy freshman year, but you literally haven't mentioned him to anyone since. Things aren't adding up, and you're an accountant, for cripes' sake."

Was an accountant. Currently working toward flower maven.

"I need it to make sense," Poppy went on. "If I don't know the full story, I can't help you, and I want to help you."

I glanced at the door, thinking about making a break for it. But it wouldn't do me any good. Poppy would hunt me down, and she'd drag Summer and Jenny with her. It would be a full-on intervention. I might as well get it out now.

"Fine. I'll tell you." I blew out a breath, resigned to spilling my guts as I sat back down on the stool, arms limp, head bowed toward the floor, which was a very pleasant light hardwood that was going to look great refinished. I loved all the dings and stains in it.

"Take your time," Poppy offered, coming to stand next to me, placing a hand on my shoulder, rubbing lightly. She was trying her best to make this easy on me. I appreciated that.

I took a fortifying inhale.

It was hard not to feel ashamed that I'd kept one of my biggest love life tidbits a secret for all this time. But I hadn't felt like I'd had much choice, so a secret it'd stayed. "I met Marco Cruz the second day on campus freshman year when I reported for my job study at the bookstore." I remembered that day vividly. The bright sunshine, the deep green of the Pacific Northwest, how the air had smelled vaguely floral with a hint of salt. I was so happy to finally be away at college. I'd grown up in Connecticut, and I was a long way from home. It'd already been a banner day and had only gotten better from there. "He was assigned to the same store. The exact moment I laid eyes on him, I pretty much fell completely, blindingly in love." I massaged my forehead with my fingertips. "He hit all my buttons just right. He was adorable, sweet, smart, funny. He was the fairy-tale prince from my childhood come to life. We hung out here and there in the beginning. I tried to get him to notice me in a romantic way, but failed miserably. After a month or two, he switched bookstores. I tried to make peace with the fact we weren't meant to be. It was either that or become a crazed stalker. And thankfully, the empathetic humanitarian in me wouldn't allow me to cross that line, even though my devious OCD side thought it was a spectacular idea. Wondering what he was up to all the time killed me." I closed my eyes. "I really thought the feelings I'd manufactured would go away over time. I mean, I hardly knew the guy. We never hooked up. He never showed any interest in me. But they never did." I'd honestly felt at some point I would forget about him—I had to. But I wasn't lying when I said I never did. "He continues to occupy my dreams, all my fantasies, and a good chunk of my day-to-day thoughts." It was exhausting at times. "It's why Brandon, Tate, and Lucas didn't work long-term. I was into them in the beginning, excited at the prospect of something new. I had high hopes they would slide right into Marco's spot. But in the end, they couldn't match my idolization of a guy who didn't even know I was alive." It was hard not to feel a little miserable. Poppy kept rubbing my shoulders. That was nice. "They were great guys who treated me like royalty, but they never made me *feel* like I did when I was around Marco."

"Aw, honey." Poppy hugged me against her side, jostling one of my arms up and down. "Why didn't you tell us all of this before?"

"Because I felt weak," I confessed. I hated feeling less than. I'd been raised by a strong, confident single mother to be a strong, confident woman. My obvious hang-up on Marco, something I'd been unable to shake after all this time, made me second-guess myself all the time. I hated it. "I've basically been Obsessing for years over a guy who had no interest in me. Even so, I made him my *actual* pedestal—he didn't need to be up on one, he was the entire thing." I made circular motions with my hands to convey the bigness of Marco's impact on my life. "And because of that, every man I've dated hasn't stood a chance. It's dumb and pathetic and lame and just…sad." I rubbed my palms over the cute green pants I'd worn for the celebratory christening of our store. My restless energy needed an outlet. "By the time the four of us got together and became friends, I was already mourning a love that would never be. There was no reason to bring him up. We banded together to help Summer out of her heartbreak with Mitch, and since I'd never dated this guy, my own heartbreak seemed to pale in comparison. So I left it to fester on its own."

"You had legitimate heartbreak." Poppy rocked me back and forth. "Unrequited love counts as heartbreak. It's one of the worst kinds. Had you told us, we would've fed you treats, too. We would've tried to make you feel better. We would've showered loved on you straight out of our friendship garden hose."

"I know. And I adore you for it." I laid my hand on her forearm and rested my head against her side. "But you would've told me that there were other fish in the sea. That he wasn't worthy of my love fetish, or whatever it was I'd manufactured. That I'd get over him eventually. You would've tried to set me up with other guys. I would've felt pressure to forget him and move on. I didn't want that. The man… He…" I struggled for the right words, since Marco was an all-encompassing emotion for me instead of actual words "He excites every single cell in my body. He always has. I feel like a massive ball of uncontrolled energy around him, and it's literally the *only* time I like to feel that way. Being out of control is not my thing. And," I added with a sniff, "not only is he handsome, but he's completely amazing, funny, intelligent, devoted to his family, gives to charity, kind, caring… I could go on and on. I didn't want to forget about him. He's what I want in a long-term partner." I knuckled away a tear. "Now he's telling me things I've waited what feels like an eternity to hear, and I can't have him." I let go of Poppy and mopped my hands over my face, trying to dam the tide I could feel coming from behind my eyes. "He proposed to his live-in girlfriend recently. He's taken. I have no idea what happened here tonight or why he decided now was the time to drag me into a closet for an epic kiss. I'm trying to figure it out, which is why it seems like I'm out of my mind. And maybe I am. It's been…a lot to handle."

"Well, damn." Poppy sighed, her arm still around me. "That was a big secret to hold on to all these years, but I understand what you're saying. We would've definitely tried to change things, distract you, set you up with a new guy. Anything to help ease the pain."

I nodded. "The only thing that made the heartbreak bearable was that he was *my* secret. My fantasy. My private Obsession. I liked him taking up space in my brain. It was comforting." I sniffed, wiping a corner of my eye with a finger. My tear ducts weren't listening to me. "Up until now, that is."

"Have you kept in touch with him all this time?"

"No." Not that I hadn't tried. "I kept tabs on him through acquaintances at the bookstore during college. He dated a few girls here and there, but I lost track of him until just over a year ago. He's not on social media. We actually ran into each other at the bank, if you can believe it, and it was like day one for me at the bookstore all over again. I've honestly never been so turned on by a man before or since. I almost self-destructed in the teller line. My nipples jutted to attention like two pointer puppies waiting for a treat. I acted like a complete space case, incapable of basic human communication."

"There is no way that happened," Poppy scolded, pressing her lips to the top of my head while smoothing my hair. She was going to be an excellent mother someday. "I'm sure he regretted every single day he let pass by without having you in his life. You're a feast on the eyes, Eve. Don't forget that."

I giggle-sniffed. "He was definitely not feasting. But we did end up talking for a while outside the bank. In the end, he invited me to dinner, which was a surprise. I gladly accepted, and we met a few nights later. It was wonderful to catch up. We laughed and told stories. It was perfect. Until he told me he about his live-in girlfriend." I wiped away a few more tears. Poppy made the appropriate *aww* sounds. "I pretended it was fine and that I was happy for him. That's all I could do. I told him about the floral business I was planning, and he seemed interested. He'd gotten a job at a hedge fund out of college and has done really well for himself. So, after that, we kept in touch occasionally via email. When I was ready to set the business plan in motion a month ago, I pinged him. To my surprise, he asked to meet to discuss it." I shrugged. "I figured if I couldn't have him in my life romantically, being partners in business would be good enough. It turned out to be a huge mistake." I shook my head, thinking about how hard I'd stumbled. "Summer warned me that night at the Driftwood when we were celebrating the business collaboration. She said we looked really into each other, but I didn't believe her. Or didn't want to. I assured—insert *fooled*—myself that everything would stay businesslike. That we were two mature adults who could handle it."

"I take it that's not what happened," Poppy murmured.

"Not at all. Sparks flew between us like a candle tossed onto an old Christmas tree. Even though my mind knew it was wrong, my body wanted it so much." That was the hardest part. "So, when he pulled me into the closet tonight, I went willingly. I allowed myself to be tugged along by his raw, animal magnetism. I was a salivating lion prancing after a nice, juicy antelope. Honestly, these last few weeks have been hell." I massaged my temples. "We've been getting closer and closer, spending more and more time together, getting along amazingly, almost in perfect harmony. And it all came to a head tonight. If we hadn't acted on these feelings, we were both in danger of popping."

"Popping is not advisable." She smoothed my hair. It was keeping me grounded. "So how was the kiss, then? Worth it?"

My eyes slid closed. "Oh my, yes. It was like biting into the ripest, sweetest peach. Full and wet and soft and luscious. His lips were freaking magical." The memory of feeling them for the first time against mine shot through my brain, causing my entire body to break out in gooseflesh. I shivered. "Far better than I ever could've imagined. We were lost in it for a while. He was slow and methodical, and I was giddy, devouring everything he gave me like a starved owlet. But as soon as it was over, I was instantly regretful." I wiped my eyes. Poppy's hand settled on my shoulder. "He has a fiancée. He hasn't tried to hide it, and he hasn't indicated he wants to break it off with her. I'm pretty sure that kiss is all we'll ever have." I glanced around my new storefront, feeling a little bewildered. "I've been brainstorming my next step. This is it for me. I hit my lowest of lows when I walked out of that closet. I'm determined to find a way to get over him, once and for all. That's where my mind has been these last few hours. This Obsession is finally coming to a close. If the Watering Can is successful, I can buy him out within a year, two at the most. Then he'll physically be out of my life forever. I'll work toward moving on emotionally after that. Until then, I'm going to avoid him. I'm creating an iron-clad schedule that we'll both agree to abide by. There'll be set times when he's at the shop and set times I'm there so our paths won't cross. I'm not a homewrecker." The last word came out in a sob. I rubbed my shirtsleeve under my nose, uncaring about manners at this point. "Even though he's my deepest fantasy"—I sniffed—"I will not be responsible for breaking up his relationship with Yasmine. I don't want to hurt her."

"Come on, stand up. Give me a hug," Poppy ordered as she stepped back and opened her arms.

I stood and embraced her, my head dipping comfortably onto her shoulder. I was almost a foot taller, but we made it work. I always forgot how tiny she was.

"It's going to be okay. I promise it is," she cooed softly. "We'll find a way to deal with this together, like we always do. I'm not going to promise it's going to be easy, but I know you can get over him if you set your mind to it. You're one of the strongest people I know. Of course you're not a homewrecker. Nobody thinks that."

The front door whooshed open, and Annabel burst in, taking in the scene. "Okay, um, what's happening? Did somebody die?"

"I'm giving my friend some comfort," Poppy said, shushing Annabel as I raised my head. "Give us a minute."

Annabel gestured toward the street. "I totally would, but there's an aggressive dude who wants my parking space. He's resorted to hand gestures that aren't very nice. And, you know"—she brought her phone up to flash the time—"I've given you, like, a thousand minutes already. I've been waiting out there for, like, an hour."

"Fine, fine. We're ready," Poppy announced, detaching from our hug.

I tried to fix my hair, knowing I probably looked like hell, while brushing away any liquid stuck to my cheeks, paying close attention to the finger swipes under my eyes to get rid of any runny makeup.

"I'm sending you on an errand first," Poppy said to Annabel. "We need a large pepperoni pizza—extra cheese, extra pepperoni—and a pint of double chocolate ice cream, stat. A fancy brand, not one of those cheapy tub ones." She waggled her finger. "We'll meet you at Eve's place once you have the goods."

"You don't have to do that, Annabel," I told her, ashamed that she was being ordered to take care of me. "Your sister's just trying to be nice. I don't want you to run errands."

Annabel snorted. The sound was equal—to the note—to her sister's. Dainty, precise, and to the point. "Nice try, but you're not escaping an emotional intervention with that tyrant in charge." She gestured at Poppy, who huffed, then giggled. "I'm happy to do the running. It's no hassle. And, I mean, it's clear you need a pick-me-up. I'll see you both at your place in thirty."

I lived a few blocks from Poppy in Capitol Hill. Annabel already knew her way around the city. "I'm assuming the pizza has to come from Giovanni's?"

"No—" I started.

"Of course it has to be from Giovanni's," Poppy snapped. "Have I taught you nothing?"

"Fine, but I'm charging that guy for my parking space. He owes me."

About the Author

Ivy Daniels lives in Minneapolis with her husband. She enjoys traveling, sunny beaches, and playing scrabble. She loves writing romantic comedy with a heave dose of humor. If you're interested in reading more, check out her website. She loves to hear from fans. Happy reading!

www.authorivydaniels.com

Stay tuned for more hilarous romantic comedy novels!

Sign-up for Ivy Daniel's Book Alert newsletter

so you don't miss a thing!

www.authorivydaniels.com

Nothing is completed without a great team.

My many thanks to:

Awesome Cover design: Estella Vukovic
Copyedits/proofs: Joyce Lamb
Final proof: Marlene Roberts